WITCH'S BANE

URBAN FANTASY ROMANCE

ANN GIMPEL

Edited by

ANGELA KELLY

Illustrated by

Sly Fox Cover
Designs

CONTENTS

WITCH'S BANE

DEMON ASSASSINS, BOOK TWO

Urban Fantasy Romance With a Heaping Side of Hexes, Spells, and Magick
By
Ann Gimpel

COPYRIGHT PAGE

BOOK DESCRIPTION: WITCH'S BANE

*L*ast of the demon assassin witches, Roz, Jenna, and Colleen have escaped disaster so far, but their luck is running low. Demons strike in the midst of Colleen's wedding, and Roz launches desperate measures. As she shape-shifts to keep one step ahead of evil, at least it takes her mind off her other problems. Personal ones. She burned through a couple of marriages and hooked up with a string of loser men before, after, and in between. Though she wants to be happy for Colleen, the jealousy bug bit deep and hasn't let go.

In Roz's secret heart, she's attracted to Ronin, one of the Daoine Sidhe. He's so profanely beautiful she can barely breathe around him, but he's also headstrong and arrogant. Not good partner material—unless she wants to end up dusting her heart off one more time.

Ronin set his sights on Roz the day he met her, and he can't get her out of his mind. Unfortunately, she's so prickly getting close to her requires scheming. He casts an enchantment to lure her at Colleen's wedding, but she senses the spell and calls him on it. Demons swarm out of the ether before he can come up with another strategy. Killing them trumps everything.

Roz is used to calling the shots. So is Ronin. Sparks fly. Tempers run hot, right along with an attraction too heady to ignore.

CHAPTER 1

*R*oxanne Lantry—Roz to everyone who knew her— paced up and down the sodden lawn outside the huge old Victorian that housed the Witches' Northwest Coven headquarters in Seattle. Rain pelted her from beneath a gunmetal sky, but it was better out here than inside. She fought an unfamiliar thickening at the back of her throat and balled her hands into fists.

"I will not cry," she muttered to an inquisitive ground squirrel that ran across her boot tops, but telling herself and controlling her emotions were two different things.

One of her two best friends, Colleen Kelly, would be getting married in less than half an hour. Roz had been inside, in the midst of all the bride-craziness, but seeing Colleen swathed in cream-colored lace sent her into a tailspin. She'd headed for the nearest door intent on finding breathing room. Solitude to sort her thoughts.

What the fuck is wrong with me?

She kicked at a hummock of grass and yelped when it didn't move, but the pain from her stubbed toes helped her focus. If she was honest, not an easy task when men were involved, she knew exactly what was bothering her.

"Yeah," she mumbled, lecturing herself. "Two failed marriages and a whole bunch of loser dudes before, after, and in between. I'm jealous and I need a good, swift boot in the backside. Just because Colleen finally stumbled across Mr. Right doesn't lower my odds of ever finding someone who's gorgeous and magical and worships me."

Now if I could only believe that...

Roz was happy for Colleen and Duncan, the Daoine Sidhe she was marrying. They made a great couple, but surely there was enough connubial bliss in the universe to sprinkle a little her way too. Her last go-round with a strikingly handsome Oklahoman she'd met online had ended in fireworks when he'd admitted all he really wanted was to tap into her magical ability. When the rubber met the road, he didn't even like women. Her stomach churned. She hated being made a fool of. She'd turned the guy in to his Coven for false advertising and laying a trap to delude a fellow magic wielder, but she doubted they'd done much to censure him.

Water dripped off her nose. She stuck out her lower lip and blew upward, but the rain kept on dripping. Roz shook her fist at the low-hanging clouds, recognizing it for displacement activity. What she really wanted to do was pound her fist through the Oklahoman's nice, straight nose.

Enough of this. Give it a rest. That happened months ago.

For Christ's sake, I need to get moving, go inside, and trade my jeans and serape for fancy duds.

Roz took a few deep breaths to settle her angst. She couldn't show her tear-stained face to the world. She'd never live it down. When she closed her eyes, the Oklahoma asshole formed behind her lids, taunting her. Roz clenched her jaw and summoned a calming spell. It seemed like cheating, but time was short. As the wispy edges of magic caught her up, they soothed her frazzled nerves. She turned hard right and headed for the house at a brisk trot.

She, Colleen, and Jenna Neil were the last of a long line of demon assassins. Witches with specialized powers, they lured Irichna demons, immobilized them, and sent them packing to the netherworld. When things worked right, she and her sister witches—along with Colleen's familiar—shanghaied the demons and locked them behind the gate guarding the Ninth Circle of Hell.

The demons didn't go without a fight, though, which was what had killed off the other demon assassin witches. It didn't help that demons as a group had been gathering power these last fifty years or so. Witches lived a long time, but they were far from immortal, and demon assassination ability was genetic. She, Jenna, or Colleen would have to produce children or that strain of magic would die out. None of them had a shred of domesticity, so no one had signed up for motherhood. At least not yet.

I can't put two weeks together without a major demon battle these days. How the hell could I take time off to raise a kid?

Rain ran down her neck and Roz shivered. Thinking about demons chilled her to her bones. Realizing she'd stopped walking, she plodded toward the house again and forced her thoughts to the magicians' supply store she owned with Colleen and Jenna in Fairbanks, Alaska.

The other two witches had moved there months ahead of her. She hated the idea of all that snow and cold and winter nights that lasted twenty hours, but she'd boxed herself into a dicey situation and hadn't had much choice. Her temper, never very controllable on a good day, had gotten the better of her, and she made short work of her cheating husband and his two—yup, count 'em—girl-friends. After that, she'd packed up and headed her aging Subaru north. Next stop, Fairbanks...

That had happened a few years ago. So many, it was almost

time to move on before anyone noticed she and the other witches didn't seem to grow any older.

Roz shook her head, not wanting to go there, either. She forced her mind back to the special skill she shared with Colleen and Jenna. She hated to admit it, but demons held the high cards these days, and she had no idea how to even the odds.

Aren't I just the queen of cheerful?

She gave herself a mental shake with instructions to snap out of her funk.

Roz made it to the huge house and tugged on one of the ground level doors. When it didn't open, she hit it with a jolt of magic, and the deadbolt snicked aside. She stopped long enough to shake water off herself and then loped down a long corridor with a concrete floor toward one of the old mansion's many stairwells. Fluorescent lights, recessed into the ceiling, gave off a sickly yellow gleam that matched her sour mood.

She'd just begun climbing upward when a rush of footsteps sounded from the hallway below.

"There you are," Bubba, Colleen's familiar, cried out and leapt up the stairs after her.

Roz glanced over a shoulder and saw he was in his normal form: a three-foot-tall changeling with oversized feet, long arms, and a bow-legged gait. His shaggy, black hair had been brushed until it shone, and his dark eyes glittered mischievously. Colleen had a hell of a time keeping him dressed, but today he sported black pants and a black jacket over a white shirt.

"Yes," Roz countered, still feeling out of sorts. "Here I am. The question is why aren't you upstairs with everyone else?"

"Colleen got worried. She sent me to hunt you down." Bubba crossed his arms over his chest, looking pleased with himself.

Roz rolled her eyes. "Bubba, look—"

"Uh-uh." He uncrossed his arms and waggled a finger at her. "Niall. Remember, you all promised to use my real name from now on."

"So we did. Crap! I don't have time for this." She unkinked her neck and trudged upward.

"No kidding," he agreed. "Everyone's here, and you're not even dressed yet."

Rather than focus on her shortcomings, Roz changed the subject. "You're looking pretty spiffy, bud."

"Do you like it?"

"What I saw of it. It's sort of like a black tuxedo, but with Velcro instead of buttons."

"I hate buttons."

Roz grinned in spite of herself. "I know you do, sweetie."

She came to the third floor landing and pushed the stairwell door open, holding it for the changeling. "Run and tell Colleen I'll be there in about fifteen minutes."

Without waiting for an answer, she walked briskly halfway down the long hall and let herself into her bedroom. Locking the door behind her, she unlaced her wet boots and toed them off. Next, she shucked her sodden clothes, ducked into the bathroom, and gathered strands of coal black hair, pulling it into a ponytail with both hands. Once she had her hair together, she wrapped her head in a towel. She didn't believe in hair dryers, so once she'd soaked as much water as she could into the towel, she grabbed her comb, made several sections, and plaited her knee-length, straight-as-a-stick hair, weaving it into a pseudo-French braid.

Before she left the bathroom, she inspected her face in the mirror. She never wore makeup because it made her look like a clown. Her bronzed skin and stark bone structure declared her Native American blood more clearly than words could have. She smoothed her eyebrows with a few drops of water and considered which of two outfits to wear. Colleen had said it didn't matter to her, so long as Roz didn't show up in her usual tattered blue jeans and combat boots.

With a snort of amusement, she padded back into the bedroom and pulled a long, beaded black buckskin skirt off a hanger. She stepped into it and laced the side fastening. Next came a turquoise deerskin top, also beaded, that clung to her like a second skin. In addition to not bothering with makeup, she also didn't care for underthings, so the outline of her breasts was clearly visible through the soft leather. She slipped a heavy silver and turquoise necklace over her head, arranging her braid on top of it, and grabbed a matching ring off the dresser.

The only thing left was her moccasins. Roz wriggled her feet into them, enjoying the way the deerskin warmed and hugged her feet. Jenna always wore high heels, but Roz had never understood how she could tolerate them. They'd had a few heated discussions years ago before Roz finally gave up.

"To each her own," she told the mirror.

Satisfied she looked presentable, she focused the threads of her calming spell, strengthened it a bit to make certain she'd last through the ceremony without breaking down and bawling like an idiot, and let herself into the hallway.

The buzz of a crowd reached her from the main floor. She glanced toward the stairs and then the other way, wondering if Colleen was still up here. Figuring it couldn't hurt to find out, she walked two doors down and knocked. The door flew open almost immediately and she looked into an accusing set of pale blue eyes.

"It's about fucking time," Colleen exclaimed. Auburn hair with lily of the valley woven into it swirled around her, falling to waist level. At six feet, Colleen was normally a good four inches shorter than Roz, but today she wore heels and they were of a height.

"Huh?" Roz murmured, confused. "I almost went downstairs. I had no idea you were waiting for me."

"We'd planned to all go down together." Colleen sounded sullen. "You know, like a proper wedding party."

"If we were all that proper," Roz said, "Jenna and I would be wearing matching—"

Jenna made chopping motions with both hands and unfolded her well-rounded frame from off the bed. Blonde hair, hacked off at shoulder level, framed a gamine's face with shrewd, hazel eyes. Rather than her standard, thrift store couture, today she wore a short beige silk skirt, a lacy blouse, and her trademark high-heeled boots. Huge, golden hoops graced her ears.

She walked to Roz's side and looped an arm through hers. "Don't think anything of it. The bride—" she waved an airy hand Colleen's way "—has been antsy as a scalded cat all day."

Colleen closed her teeth together with an audible clack. "Maybe I'm making a mistake."

Roz and Jenna turned to stare at her. "What?" Jenna asked, incredulous.

"Hey, if you don't want him—" Roz began.

"No shit," Jenna interrupted. "Tall, blond, drop dead gorgeous. Those green eyes are to die for and those shoulders... " She made panting noises. "The couple of times I saw him without a shirt, I almost came just watching his muscles rustle beneath his skin when he walked."

Colleen rolled her eyes. "You two are impossible. Can't a bride have a case of jitters without her two closest friends turning into vultures?"

"No." Roz looked down her nose at Colleen. "Considering how long and hard I've hunted for decent partner material..." She let her words trail off before the extent of her jealousy leaked out.

The door blew inward and Bubba marched in, hands on his hips. "Come on. Everyone's ready." He lowered his voice, but not by much. "I think Duncan's worried that you—" he pointed at Colleen "—got cold feet."

"She nearly did," Jenna muttered.

"Aw, crap. Guess I need to go tell everyone the wedding's off." Bubba did an about face, but before he could sprint through the open door, Colleen snatched him up.

"You'll do no such thing." She swallowed audibly. "I'm ready. I guess."

"Let go of me." Bubba writhed in her grasp.

"Not before you promise to keep your mouth shut."

Roz smirked. Circumspection was not exactly the changeling's long suit. She walked to Bubba's other side. "I'll take him." She held out her arms.

"I can walk," the changeling said with a great deal of dignity, "as soon as Colleen lets go of me."

"You haven't promised," Colleen said. "Please, sweetie. It's important to me. A girl needs to have some things stay private."

He blew out an annoyed sounding breath. "All right. I promise." Colleen relaxed her grip. Shaking himself like a dog might have, the gnome-like changeling chuckled. "Too bad. Something like that's a prime piece of gossip."

Colleen broke into a broad grin. "Right up your alley, eh?"

Roz made shooing motions. "Let's get going. You don't want all that food the Sidhe catered to get cold do you?"

"I don't care about food," Colleen mumbled. "I'm so nervous I probably won't be able to eat a thing."

"Well I do," Jenna said. "I'm with Roz. Let's get this show on the road."

"Have a couple belts of whiskey," Roz suggested. "It'll do wonders for your nerves."

Rather than answering, Colleen shot her an annoyed look, tinged with pleading.

Roz stepped to her side and hugged her. "It'll be all right," she murmured.

Colleen hugged her back before disentangling herself. "I sure as hell hope so. Something's felt off to me all morning, but I can't put my finger on exactly what—"

The hallway air brightened and shimmered. When it cleared, Titania, Queen of Faerie, shook floor-length silvery hair out of her ice blue eyes and pushed it over her shoulders. A diaphanous gown, more jewels than fabric, floated around her tall, thin frame. "Is there some problem?" she inquired with asperity, her gaze zeroing in on Colleen.

Colleen half curtseyed.

Roz considered it, but didn't because Titania wasn't her queen.

"No problem at all." Colleen inclined her head. "We were just on our way."

The Queen of Faerie's severe expression softened. "Thank the goddess. For a minute there, I was afraid you were going to break Duncan's heart." She strode forward and thumped Colleen's chest with a bony forefinger. "If you ever hurt that boy, I'll hunt you down and make you very sorry."

"That *boy*—" Colleen held the queen's gaze "—is a thousand-year-old man."

Titania furled her perfect silver brows. "Details. Besides, it's rude to contradict me. Privilege of age and rank and all that. Let's go. I haven't performed a marriage in centuries. I'm quite looking forward to it."

Colleen's eyes widened. "I thought Naomi, the leader of this Coven, was going to join Duncan and me."

"We both have roles to play." Titania's mouth twitched. "Surely you didn't think I'd let one of my own be bound in marriage without my magic involved."

"I have no idea what I thought," Colleen managed, but she looked ready to throttle the queen.

Before things got any tenser and Colleen started in about it being *her* wedding, Roz herded them out the door and down the hallway. Colleen stopped for a moment at the head of the stairway, tension rolling off her in waves.

Roz wrapped an arm around her. "Keep your eye on the ball," she whispered. "In this case, it's your dishy new husband-to-be waiting at the altar." After a quick squeeze, she let go.

"Thanks for the reminder." Colleen's nostrils flared as she inhaled sharply. After one more breath, she smiled brightly and swept down the long, curved staircase, looking regal.

Roz, Jenna, and Titania jostled one another as they made their way down the twenty-five steps. Bubba made an end run around them and fell in behind Colleen, where he picked up her lace train.

They marched through the dining area, where caterers and witches bustled about laying out a spread of food that smelled delicious, into a large, luxurious room that took up much of the bottom floor of the old Victorian. At one point, they'd talked about having the ceremony outside, but the weather put the kibosh on that idea. Roz wondered why they'd wasted their breath even considering an out-of-doors event. It was the winter solstice in Seattle. She bet there'd never been one when it wasn't raining like crazy—or else snowing.

Chairs lined the wood-paneled great room, and a fire burned merrily in a huge stone fireplace that took up one end of the sumptuous space. Old-fashioned chandeliers were festooned with hundreds of blazing candles. Witches sat on one side of a center aisle, Daoine Sidhe on the other. Roz guessed between three and four hundred people were in attendance—more Sidhe than witches. Everyone turned in their seats to stare at Colleen, and a collective *aaaaah* surged through the room.

Roz clamped down on a grin. Colleen really did make a lovely bride, with her Irish complexion and red tresses. The creamy lace dress was perfect. White would have made her look washed out. Titania strode around all of them and took her place at the head of the room. Roz noted with amusement that Naomi held her ground when Titania tried to push her to one side.

Before she and Jenna left Colleen to find their seats, her gaze landed on Duncan—Lord Regis—and her heart nearly stopped. All Sidhe had an ethereal beauty, but Duncan practically glowed. Dressed in a black tuxedo with a crimson cummerbund and diamond studs, he cut an impressive figure with his high forehead, sculpted cheekbones, and strong jaw. Longish blond hair had been braided in tight rows, but the severe style suited him and make him look like an ancient warrior.

Roz averted her gaze, afraid he'd catch her staring, but he only had eyes for his bride. She said a quick prayer asking the goddess's blessing on their union and turned toward the witches' side of the room.

Because Ronin came up from her other side, she didn't notice the Sidhe leader until he wove an arm around her shoulders and murmured, "I saved you a chair next to me."

Her heart slammed into double-time rhythm. She'd met Ronin two weeks before at his castle in northern England, and they'd shared several spirited conversations over meals. Something magical and electric had sparked between them, but she'd chalked it up to everyone's emotions running full tilt. She'd just escaped demons by the skin of her teeth, and he was dealing with shame or guilt—or whatever he felt—about forcing witches into being demon assassins two centuries before. While his attentiveness had been welcome—and more than a little flattering—she'd been more focused on her relief at being alive than anything else.

Besides, after the Oklahoman, she'd sworn off men—forever.

Ronin smiled, not looking anything but glad to see her, and her heart did a funny little flip-flop, in addition to beating much too fast. Dark hair hung loose to his shoulders, and his blue eyes twinkled warmly. Every bit as handsome as Duncan, he was dressed in formal clothing. Black jacket and trousers, an ivory frilled shirt with a blue cummerbund, and what might have been ruby studs.

"I can't join you," she whispered. "I'm supposed to sit over there." She gestured in the general direction of the witches' side of the room.

"No one will notice," he assured her and hooked his hand beneath her arm.

Roz didn't fully understand why she let him guide her to a padded straight-backed chair near the front of the room and help her into it, but there was something irresistible about his energy. Too late, she recognized a mild compulsion spell. Anger spiked, but now wasn't the place to give in to it. With every shred of self-discipline at her disposal, she forced her attention to Duncan and Colleen reciting their vows, and to Naomi, who'd muscled her way in before Titania could get rolling.

When Ronin draped an arm around her shoulders, she shot him a harsh look that made him move it damned fast. *Good,* she thought. *It's about time the Sidhe realize their days of pushing witches around are over.*

Yes, he was gorgeous, and he seemed interested in her, but the last thing she needed was some overbearing mage mucking things up. She still wasn't quite certain how Colleen's marriage to Duncan would impact her and Jenna. They'd always been kind of like The Three Musketeers, witch style. The permanent addition of a Sidhe was bound to have some effect. Exactly what was hard to gauge.

Who am I kidding? We didn't just get Duncan. We're stuck with his kinfolk now too. All of them.

She bit back a sigh. If the series of meetings a couple of weeks before in the U.K. were any indication, she, Jenna, and Colleen would have to fight to be recognized as anything remotely close to equal.

Roz snuck a glance at Ronin. He sat straight in his seat, his profile heartbreakingly beautiful. His long-fingered hands were clasped together in his lap. She couldn't stop herself from wondering what they'd feel like stroking her body. Warm. Electric. Compelling.

Maybe I should give him a chance, a tiny, inner voice piped up.

Bosh.

Roz tried for a stern note, but the other part of her brain wouldn't shut up.

CHAPTER 2

*R*onin Redstone unwound his arm from Roz and gripped his hands together in his lap to lessen the temptation to touch her again. Where he figured most of the guests were anxious to see the bride, he'd been waiting for Roz. Feeling like a prime idiot, but unable to stop himself, he'd bounced to his feet the moment she entered the room. Not sure how she'd take his interest, he'd spun the mildest of spells to coerce her to sit near him.

He pressed his lips into a flat line as he wrestled with his thoughts. Ever since he'd met the tall, imposing witch at his home in northern England, he'd been able to think of little else. She even entered his dreams with her silky black hair, pronounced cheekbones, and hawk-like nose. In those dreams, she was naked, her bronze skin glimmering in moonlight.

Her heady scent, pine forests and jasmine, tickled his nostrils and made him wonder what she'd feel like in his arms. Once he kicked the door open to that slippery slope, his cock sprang to life, clearly eager to find out. He tried to clip his libido before things whirled out of control and she noticed his arousal, but his cock wasn't in the mood for negotiation—or retreat. He wove the tiniest *don't look here* spell and draped his lower body with it.

In years past, he'd simply have created a love charm, imbued it with compulsion, and bedded her. That probably wasn't a good idea, though. Roz would sense his magic, be outraged he tried to coerce her, and that would be the last he ever saw of the striking witch. Never mind, she had good reason to not want much to do with him since he was one of the key players who'd foisted demon assassination onto the witches two hundred years ago.

He tightened his jaw muscles. Who could have guessed his little machination to get his kin out from under a highly unpleasant task would nearly be the death of the few witches who'd inherited the power through a magical version of gene splicing? Of course, he'd also been the one to send Duncan to fetch one of the witches to quell a demon uprising in the U.K. last month. That was how they'd discovered only three of the special witches remained...

No wonder she's not overly fond of me.

Ronin grimaced, not liking the truth in his thoughts. An inner voice huffed, reminding him it wasn't his fault the witches in question hadn't produced more offspring, but he shushed it.

Surely I can at least charm Roz out of that sour expression on her face.

He forced his breathing into a regular pattern and glanced toward Duncan and Colleen at the front of the room. The resident witch had completed her part of the ceremony, and Titania was speaking in Gaelic so old he had trouble following it. The Sidhe binding ceremony lasted at least half an hour, so he let his thoughts drift. Anywhere but to his cock, which still throbbed uncomfortably.

As de facto leader for the Sidhe, a post he held more because no one else wanted it than because of any special skills on his part, he sensed they stood at the brink of a cataclysmic event. Abbadon and his henchmen, the Irichna demons, had grown appallingly strong. Capturing them one at a time and shepherding them to the Ninth Circle of Hell where they were trapped for all eternity wasn't a workable solution anymore. There were too many of them, and maybe not enough space in the bottom of Hell.

Because he was afraid of a firm answer regarding Hell's demon storage capacity, he hadn't asked Titania, though surely she'd know. If they couldn't dump Irichna behind the Ninth Circle's gate, he had no idea what they'd do with them. And if Abbadon consolidated his full power, Earth would be laid to waste. Ronin clamped his jaws together. Apocalypse didn't come close to describing what would happen if Abbadon was freed from protecting his demons and could concentrate on taking over Earth.

In addition to not inquiring too closely about the Irichna, I also haven't asked about Oberon.

Ronin grimaced again. If the King of Faerie were truly so tired of immortality he'd let himself fade into the *Dreaming,* Ronin didn't want to know about that, either.

When did I turn into such a craven that I avoid unpleasant answers?

Even though he wasn't expecting one, a response popped up anyway. He'd loved a human woman once, but she'd died bearing their son, who'd perished right along with her. The major vessel serving her heart had ruptured, and no amount of Sidhe magic could heal her or breathe life into their dead child. Ronin withdrew from the other Sidhe after that, mostly because he didn't want to hear their lectures about the whole debacle being his own fault. They weren't supposed to mate outside their blood. He had, and it hadn't ended well. No one to blame but himself.

When he finally picked up the reins of command a couple of centuries later—or maybe it had been three—he held himself aloof and avoided confrontations with anyone, about anything.

He ground his jaws harder. His internal inventory was damned depressing. It forced him to take a harsh look at himself, and he didn't like what he saw. He glanced at Titania. She clasped

Duncan's and Colleen's hands between her own, and his eyes widened. Had he truly spent the entire ceremony sunk in memories and self-pity?

It would appear so, he thought dryly.

In moments, Titania would utter the final words, Duncan would kiss Colleen, and the ritual would be done. He barely had time to wonder why Titania hadn't kicked up more of a fuss about Duncan marrying a mortal, when the bridal pair kissed.

The tiniest sigh escaped Roz, and he glanced sidelong at her. Her full lips were parted in half a smile, and she looked captivated by the traditional ceremony that had unfolded, mostly without him paying one whit of attention to it.

She leaned toward him, her earlier ire apparently forgotten. "They make such a lovely couple," she whispered.

Ronin narrowed his eyes and looked hard at Duncan and Colleen, wrapped in one another's arms and kissing enthusiastically. He didn't know about the *lovely couple* part, because he didn't view the world that way.

"They do look happy," he whispered back because he thought he ought to say something.

Bubba, who'd been standing off to one side, made a grab for a bag Ronin hadn't noticed before. The changeling reached inside, and Ronin's internal alarm went off. The changeling was about to throw something at the couple. Had the creature been co-opted by demons? It wasn't unheard of since their race contained a smattering of demon blood. Afraid if he hesitated he'd be too late, Ronin pulled strong magic and rose to his feet.

Before he could loose it, Roz fastened a hand around his lower arm. "It's just rice," she said, her voice still low. "He's going to throw rice at them. Stand down."

Ronin met her dark, luminous gaze. "What sort of custom is that?" he demanded. Magic thrummed around him, making the air shimmer in iridescent hues. The changeling indeed tossed rice high in the air, showering everyone within a ten-foot radius of him, laughed uproariously, and then did it again.

"An old one." Roz tugged on his arm and he sat reluctantly. "Bubba adores Colleen. He's laid his life on the line for her a bazillion times. He'd never hurt her."

"Better safe than sorry," Ronin muttered, feeling like an ass. "How was I to know?"

"It's okay." She let go of his arm and patted one of his hands.

As long as he was in an apologizing mood—they were rare for him—Ronin exhaled sharply and said, "I'm sorry I, um, suggested you sit next to me."

She cocked her head to one side and quirked a brow. "If you'd only *suggested*, it would've been fine, but you did a tad more than that."

Flutes and guitars began to play Mendelssohn's "Wedding March." Colleen and Duncan turned and floated up the center aisle with Bubba right behind, still throwing rice. Even Ronin had to admit they looked radiant. He'd known Duncan his entire life, and he'd never seen his fellow Sidhe look so carefree and besotted with joy. In one wild, unrestrained moment, before he glossed his emotions over with rationality, he wanted the same for himself.

Ronin felt Roz's gaze still on him and knew he couldn't ignore her comment. "You're right," he said stiffly. "I did do more than that."

She repositioned herself so he had to look at her. "Why?"

Because I've wanted to strip you naked and worship your body from the day I met you.

He cloaked his mind, hoping he'd been fast enough and she hadn't read his thoughts. "I'm not quite sure." He stumbled over the words, because they weren't the truth.

Her dark gaze never left him as she weighed his statement. Finally, she nodded, almost to herself. "When you figure it out," she said and winked broadly, "be sure to let me know."

Heat rose from his neck and swooshed over the top of his head. Damn! He was a Sidhe and a warrior. It was unseemly to blush like a love-struck maid. He opened his mouth to stammer some sort of reply, but she got up, along with the rest of the guests.

"Come on," she said. "I'm starving."

He'd been afraid the second the ceremony was over, she'd race away from him as far and as fast as she could, but she'd just invited him to eat with her, at least he thought she had. He bit back a smile until just the edges of his mouth twitched. Maybe she didn't abhor him as much as it seemed when she'd shot him that poisonous look once she sensed his magic.

I learned something. I have to ask her, not simply push her to do what I want.

Ronin hurried after her swishing skirt, not wanting to lose her in the crowd. He could always locate her, but the less magic he used until she got to know him, the better.

ROZ CAUGHT up to Jenna just inside the dining area and hugged her. "Wasn't it just perfect?" she gushed, still caught up in the mystical pull of dual wedding ceremonies.

Jenna hugged her back and nodded. She disentangled herself and eyed her friend. "What the hell, Roz? It isn't like you to fall all over yourself."

Roz settled her face into its usual, stern planes. "There. Is that better?"

Jenna grinned. "Yup. There's the grumpy old witch I know and love. What happened to you anyway? I looked back and you were trailing after that hunky Sidhe."

"He snared me in a spell."

"Ooooh." Jenna clapped her hands together. "He must be interested." She leaned close. "What did he do during the ceremony?"

Roz felt her face redden. "Nothing. I got mad at him once I realized he'd bamboozled me. Hush. Here he comes."

"Awesome." Jenna practically vibrated with enthusiasm. "He can eat with us."

"I already invited him."

A knowing look crossed Jenna's face and she opened her mouth, but Roz hissed, "Can it, sister," just before turning to Ronin and asking, "Where would you like to sit?"

He half-bowed—a courtly, old world gesture that drove home just how old he really was—lifted Jenna's hand to his lips, and said, "Nice to see you again, Miss Jenna. Anywhere the two of you wish to settle is fine with me."

"Maybe we should get our food first," Jenna suggested brightly, "since the tables will fill fast."

"Good idea," Roz snapped, feeling unaccountably jealous. Ronin hadn't kissed her hand, but he'd been quick enough to snatch Jenna's.

"If you don't want him..." Jenna spoke in their telepathic speech.

"I thought you were interested in Tristan." Roz led the way to a buffet table and picked up a plate.

Jenna smirked. *"I am, but he's not here."*

"Any slut in a storm." Roz shot a meaningful look Jenna's way.

Jenna laughed, grabbed a plate, and agreed far too cheerfully. "Guilty as charged."

"Guilty of what?" Ronin glanced up from the buffet table.

"Ask Roz," Jenna countered still grinning like a mischievous cat.

Since she wanted to cut this conversation off at the knees, Roz turned her back on both of them. She dished up an interesting looking salad, brimming with shrimp and crab, and followed it with a few slices of rare beef and a roll. They found a table beneath a leaded glass window and laid their plates down.

"I'll get us something to drink." Ronin smiled. "Preferences?"

"What are you getting?" Roz asked, avoiding Jenna's gaze.

"Mead," he answered. "It's what I prefer."

"I'll take Irish whiskey," Jenna trilled and settled into her seat.

"Just bring me a glass of one or the other," Roz muttered. "I'm not picky." As soon as Ronin was out of earshot, or close enough, she glared at Jenna. "Leave him alone."

"But you're not even sure you're interested in him," Jenna protested.

"And how would you know that?" Roz stuffed a forkful of salad into her mouth, chewed with a vengeance, and swallowed.

The other witch dropped her gaze, looking sheepish. "I, um, peeked."

Roz slammed a fist on the table hard enough the dishes rattled. "You looked inside my head without asking?"

"'Fraid so. Sorry." Jenna started eating with a studied nonchalance.

Roz exhaled and then did it again. Both of them were lonely—had been for years. Getting angry with her longtime friend wouldn't serve any purpose other than creating bad water under the bridge that they'd have to clear at some point.

"Jenna." Roz touched the other witch's arm. "It's the wedding ceremonies. Both of them, witch and Sidhe. The ancient magic in the bindings makes us want what Colleen and Duncan have."

"I suppose you're right." Jenna's hazel gaze met hers and she looked repentant, her brows drawn together. "I'm sorry."

"Me too." Roz smiled crookedly. "Let's not fight. Not today."

Ronin plunked two bottles on the table. Glasses were already there, along with silverware. "Here you go." He folded his tall frame into a chair and reached for the mead. "Did you decide which you want?" he asked Roz.

"I'll try mead." She held her glass toward him, and he filled it with amber liquid that smelled heavenly. She took a sip and rolled it around her tongue before swallowing. "Interesting. I've never had honey wine before."

"I'm glad you like it." Ronin filled his own glass. "It's a traditional libation for my people."

Jenna tipped the Irish whiskey into her glass and drank. "So…" She skewered Ronin with her hazel gaze. "Where's Tristan? I thought he was coming to the wedding."

Ronin pressed his lips together, looking uncomfortable. "Deciding who had to remain in the Old Country was quite a task." He rolled his deep blue eyes. "Everyone wanted to come to the wedding, but we had to leave a sufficient number of us in Britain."

"Why?" Roz asked, and then she knew the answer and mumbled, "Never mind."

Demons were running amok through the northern English countryside. It was why Duncan had sought out Colleen in the first place. And why the three witches planned to return to England just as soon after the wedding as they could manage.

"Exactly." Ronin set his glass down and laid a hand over hers. "Better not to speak of evil out loud. It tempts fate—and not in good ways."

"Is Tristan one of the men holding down the fort?" Jenna pressed.

Ronin nodded. "I'm certain he'd rather be here with you."

Jenna ducked her head, but Roz saw a flush spread upward from her neck. "That's a nice thing for you to say," Jenna murmured, "but he and I barely know one another—"

"Ronin." Two male Sidhe that Roz didn't know converged on their table. Ronin raised a questioning brow, and she caught the magic of telepathic speech, though she had no idea what they said to one another.

"If you ladies will excuse me." Ronin flowed to his feet in a supple motion and walked briskly from the room with the other Sidhe.

"Wonder what that was about?" Jenna gazed after them. "Those other two were pretty damned gorgeous too."

Roz smirked. "All Sidhe are stunning, or did you miss that little detail?"

"Whatever. I'd take any of them in my bed at this point."

Roz would too, but the one she wanted was Ronin. Though she didn't have much of an idea regarding Sidhe mores, she was pretty sure it would muck up her chances with Ronin if she had a roll in the hay with whoever asked her first. She went to work on the rest of her meal, feeling thoughtful.

Bubba trotted over, grabbed the whiskey bottle, and drank deeply. He wiped his mouth with the back of one hand. "I'm having a great time," the changeling announced.

"You're getting drunk," Jenna observed.

"You should know." He glared meaningfully at her from beneath his thick eyebrows.

"Sometimes I do drink too much," she agreed and belted back half her glass of whiskey.

"I'm happy for Colleen and Duncan." Bubba danced a small jig and took another swallow from the bottle still clutched in his hand.

"We are too, sweetie," Roz said. Her head snapped up. "Shit!"

"What?" Jenna glanced around, clearly searching for what had alarmed Roz.

Nostrils twitching, Roz surged to her feet and raked the corners of the room for what she was sure she'd smelled. She didn't see anything, but the smell didn't go away.

"Demons!" Bubba barked and craned his neck from side to side. "Where are they?"

Jenna bolted up from the table and joined Roz. "It makes sense," she said through clenched jaws. "All three of us are here."

Bubba took off for the dais at the head of the room. "Gotta warn Colleen," he cried over one shoulder.

"Yes," Roz growled. "We need to warn everyone."

"Do you suppose that was why those Sidhe came for Ronin?" Jenna asked.

"Does it matter?" Roz shot back.

Jenna shook her head. "Let's get Colleen. If we have to fight, we're stronger together."

Roz couldn't agree more, so she pulled her skirts aside and sprinted after the changeling.

Ronin followed Jon and Terrence out a side door into driving rain. The Sidhe who'd rousted him were brothers. Both of them had bright red hair and silver eyes and were dressed in traditional black ceremonial robes, sashed with deep green.

"What's this about?" Ronin asked, thinking it better be good since they'd pulled him away from what promised to be an enjoyable meal with Roz and her friend.

Jon shook his head and summoned magic to muffle their conversation. Once his brother's spell settled around them, Terrence said, "Demons are massing."

Astonishment rocked Ronin, but he masked it. Good leaders didn't show emotion. "How do you know? I didn't feel anything out of the ordinary."

"They're concealing their energy, but I've been sensing bits and pieces of it since the middle of the ceremony," Jon cut in.

"We need to get Titania out of here," Terrence said, "but I didn't want to do anything until I told you what we were up to."

"Do you have any idea how many demons?" Ronin asked, running a mental tally of the Sidhe who were inside enjoying their meals. Of the group, maybe half would be useful in a fight, and he had no idea if any of the witches beyond Roz, Jenna, and Colleen would be much help.

"Lots," Jon said succinctly. "And not just Irichna."

"We need to get moving," Terrence prodded.

"Agreed." Jon neutralized his spell and the shrouding dissipated.

"Good you two were on top of this. I'll marshal a defense." Ronin clamped his teeth together and strode back inside, hoping Titania didn't give Jon and Terrence a hard time. The Queen of Faerie loved battle, but she was so frail, allowing her to fight, let alone lead troops like she'd want to do, wasn't a good idea. He scanned the room. Jenna and Roz were huddled with Colleen and Duncan, their faces set into harsh lines.

It appears they already know. Good.

He loped toward them, ignoring Sidhe who made a grab for him as he passed. Quizzical expressions marred their perfect, ageless faces. Naomi closed from the other side about the same time he reached the group. Her long dark hair was piled atop her head, and she wore a heavily embroidered gold silk tunic that stopped just north of her knees.

"Demons! Goddammit! It's got to be that goddess-forsaken gateway," Naomi grunted. "The one Mathilde opened for them."

Ronin knew the story. The previous leader of the Witches' Northwest Coven made a pact with the Irichna in exchange for limitless power and opened a gateway from one of their hell-spawned enclaves. The portal linked to a third-floor room in this building. He kicked himself for not bothering to check if the gateway was still a danger. He'd arrived the previous night and certainly had the time.

"I thought we closed the wretched thing," Duncan muttered. "After we killed Mathilde."

"So did I," Colleen said, "but apparently we didn't do a very good job. Crap!" She got to her feet and kicked off her high heels.

"Look at me." She smoothed her hands down her cream-colored lace dress and made a low, hissing sound. "Not very good for fighting, assuming I don't ruin it shape-shifting."

"Your dress is least of our problems," Roz snapped, sounding surly. "I suppose getting your wedding day off from demon attacks was too much to hope for."

"I didn't ask for a respite." Colleen snorted derisively. "Who the hell grants things like that? But I assumed Duncan and I would at least have a few hours of peace."

"I'm fighting with you." Bubba hopped onto a chair, and Colleen lifted him so he stood on the table.

"Of course you are," she said. "No one gets a bye on this fight."

"Stay inside our wards." Roz glared at the changeling.

"Yes, and do what we tell you," Jenna added.

"We're wasting time," Ronin said, certain the changeling had heard exhortations to behave before. The creatures were strong-willed, and he suspected no amount of advice would alter Bubba's proclivity to do exactly as he thought best. Regardless of whether it put him smack in harm's way or pissed off Colleen, who was bonded to him.

Duncan met Ronin's gaze, grim-faced, all business now that their backs were against the wall. "How do you want to do this?" he asked.

Colleen shifted her gaze to him, incredulous. "It's not a choice," she said. "You'll do whatever you have to and support Jenna, Roz, and me."

Duncan elbowed Ronin. "Remember that magic I sketched out? The spell that annihilates demons?"

"The one from the ancient source we've all avoided like the plague?" Ronin nodded gloomily. "How could I forget?"

"Did you practice summoning it after I described the process?"

Ronin considered lying, but that wouldn't be fair. "No. I'll be going in cold. You'll have to show me and the rest of us."

Sidhe and witches had picked up on the disquiet emanating

from the bridal pair. Everyone in the room was on their feet moving toward them. As if the demons knew they'd been discovered, their putrid stench, reminiscent of road kill rotting in the sun, intensified.

"Goddamn it all to hell," Roz growled. "They'll be here soon." She turned to Naomi. "Gather the twelve most powerful of you to stand with us. Have some of the others get that ironclad room ready and a bunch of handcuffs and leg irons. Binding the bastards will be our first fallback tactic."

"Assuming we can capture any of them," Jenna blurted sourly.

"Done." Naomi sprinted away from the dais, calling out names.

Ronin glanced after her and realized she was barefoot. Then he remembered her saying something about contact with the earth being critical to the marriage ceremony.

He shook his head. Weddings weren't important. Not now. He raised his voice, no reason for telepathy since the demons would break through any moment. "To me. Battle formations. We follow Duncan's lead."

Duncan uttered a muted expletive. "Thanks. Of all the times I didn't want to be in command…"

Ronin closed a hand around his arm. "You want a chance to bed your bride, don't you? We need to fight to make certain the witches make it through the rest of today. You're the only one who's actually channeled that power source, so you have to lead. No choice, old friend."

A stricken look crossed the other Sidhe's face, and Ronin wished he could take back his words about Colleen maybe not surviving the coming battle.

Duncan jerked away from his grasp. "Form power circles," he told the Sidhe. "Twelve to a circle."

"Do it now," Ronin thundered when they didn't move fast enough to suit him. From the corner of his eye, bright light flashed, and Titania shimmered into being right in front of him. He blinked to clear the spots dancing through his visual field and realized the queen had teleported from wherever Jon and Terrence tried to drag her.

She pounded a fist into Ronin's chest. "You will not banish me like some worthless piece of baggage."

Arguments flitted through his mind. She was their queen and last remaining royalty. No one knew what had happened to Oberon. Ronin gazed into Titania's pale blue eyes. She bristled with outrage. Her jaw was set in a tense line, and her perfectly sculpted brows lowered until they nearly touched over the bridge of her nose.

"Stop pounding my chest." He kept his voice mild. "We were just trying to protect you. If you want action, jump in. You can help us funnel power from that eldritch source Duncan discovered last time he fought demons."

A feral smile etched into Titania's face, and she looked like an avenging fiend straight out of Hell. Ronin stepped back a pace. In that moment, he questioned if he knew his queen at all.

"Wise of you," she said and strode to Duncan's side, joining his circle.

Ronin gazed after her for a long moment, wondering what she'd been prepared to do. The queen's magic was strong, powered by Faerie's roots. Had she truly been poised to strike him down and march over his inert form if he stood in her way?

A racket behind him drew his attention back to the witches. A dozen hard-faced women, with Naomi in the lead, converged behind Colleen, Jenna, and Roz.

"Tell us how to help," the head witch of the Coven demanded.

"Yes. We want those abominations out of here for good," another witch cried.

"Indeed," a third chimed in. "And the gateway sealed permanently."

Colleen smiled bitterly. "We all want those things. The question is whether we'll get them."

Roz shook her head and made a hacking motion with one

hand. "No pessimism. We need a can-do attitude here." She turned to Naomi and the witches. "When we chant, add your magic to ours." Before she could get any more words out, the air broke into fire-tinged gateways, and Irichna stepped through. Tall and wraithlike, with red-rimmed, glowing charcoal eyes, they sported claw-like hands tipped with sharp, crimson talons. Gray-black robes fluttered around them.

Ronin counted ten demons before other creatures followed in their wake. Though not much rattled him, his heart sped up and his mouth went dry. Bats spewed from the fiery portals, along with goblins and incubi. He narrowed his eyes and summoned magic. It had been centuries since he'd faced incubi or succubi. Not certain he remembered quite how to get rid of them, Ronin shot power their way and grunted in satisfaction when a couple of them vaporized in a red mist. The undead were a scourge. Since they were already dead, killing them was out of the question. They kept on fighting—or fucking—until someone blew them back to Hell with magic.

"The goblins look a lot like me," Bubba screeched. "Don't hurt me by mistake."

"Shift," Colleen screeched right back, and the changeling's form shimmered. Because his race had some demon blood, Bubba could borrow demon energy to shift. Absent that, Colleen had to help him.

Ronin watched with grudging admiration as Bubba grew scales. In moments, he looked like a smallish dragon. When he opened his mouth, fire spewed. The table he was still perched on cracked under his weight, and the changeling spread his wings.

Bubba ignored Colleen's frantic shouts and took to the air, breathing gouts of fire at everything in front of him. Bats shrieked and fell, leaving small, smoking pyres. An unlucky goblin burst into flames. One of the Irichna stormed to Bubba, floated a few feet into the air, and reached with hungry fingers. The changeling blew fire right into his face, but the demon just laughed.

"I was formed in fire, little changeling." the demon purred. "Go ahead. Give me more. It feeds me." Bubba hit him with another blast of flame. The demon made a grab for him, but the changeling was nimble.

Before the exchange grew more heated, Colleen stomped over, leapt into the air, and made a grab for her changeling. "Don't bait them," she snarled. "It's not wise."

The dragon shimmered back into his usual form. "You do it," he protested.

"That's different. Take your snake form. It's easier for me to keep track of you when you don't have wings."

The demon whooshed closer since they didn't exactly walk. "Not so fast, witch."

Colleen shoved Bubba behind her and raised her hands to call power. "Or what?" She curled her lips back from her teeth and directed a huge jolt of magic that sent the Irichna sprawling sideways. Before it could recover, Jenna clipped handcuffs around one wrist. Roz grabbed its other hand and forced it toward the dangling cuff. Colleen lobbed magic at it again, giving Roz and Jenna what they needed to fasten the handcuffs together.

Ronin winced. The proximity to iron made him feel ill. He imagined it had the same effect on the Irichna—and all the other Sidhe.

"Have someone collect this one," Roz yelled toward Naomi. "Slap a set of leg irons on it and stash it in that upstairs room."

Ronin glanced at the other Irichna engaged in one-on-one combat with Sidhe and witches. He'd underestimated their numbers, since at least fifteen remained, along with over twenty goblins. Counting bats was impossible. The same was true of the undead since they faded in and out. The portals that had disgorged them were still open.

Who knew how many more planned to join the battle?

He shifted his attention to the Sidhe power circles. "Now would be a good time," he yelled at Duncan.

"Get the hell over here." Blond hair had escaped Duncan's braids, and the lines of his face were set in stark concentration. Ronin hurtled to his side. "Draw earth power, as much as you can," Duncan instructed. "Once you can't hold any more, go even deeper and add water and air."

"And then?"

"If you did it right, you'll hit the mother lode. The spell picks up fire on its own. Let it flow through you. It'll feel like you're channeling lightning, but don't let it get away from you."

"While you boys are doing that," Titania chortled, "I'll close off their gateways. No point in leaving a conduit so more can show up." Her lips thinned. "Not much I can do about the upstairs gateway, which is probably how they're getting inside this house to start with, but at least they'll have a harder time moving from there to here."

"Excellent," Duncan gritted out. "Just stay out of the way once we tap into that pool of arcane magic and the juice starts flowing."

The queen rolled her eyes. "What? You think I've never been in battle before?" She raised her hands to summon power and flexed her long fingers. "I'm having a grand time. I feel more alive than I have in centuries. We need to do this more often."

Ronin stared incredulously after Titania's retreating form. How could he not have realized how bloodthirsty she was? Once she blew the first demon portal to kingdom come, barely breaking a sweat, Ronin stepped to the next circle, relayed Duncan's instructions, and sent another Sidhe to tell the rest. The air grew thick, heavy with the smell of ozone and the crackly feel of Sidhe magic.

Ronin tossed his inner wards aside, the ones that protected him from a surfeit of unexpected power, and dug deep. Deeper than he'd gone in centuries, but there wasn't a choice. Capturing the demons individually and jailing them in an ironclad room wasn't practical since each of them would require a personal escort to the Ninth Circle of Hell. Either the witches had to take them, or they'd need to call on the Celtic gods.

Bottomless magic slammed into him and left him reeling. Barely containable power ignited every nerve ending. It took everything he had to move out of the circle and focus his sights on one of the Irichna. As soon as he was certain he wouldn't hit any Sidhe or witches, he let the magic flow. It spun the Irichna in rings before the fell creature, shrieking imprecations, folded in on itself, and disappeared. Ronin didn't waste time worrying about where it had gone.

If Duncan's information was correct, the demon was permanently eradicated, but Ronin had his doubts about that. Particularly since that piece of intel had come from a dark fae who'd helped Duncan during an earlier demon battle. Ronin targeted another demon and let the wild magic use him as a lightning rod. The sensation stole his breath, but it held a heady aspect that drove him onward.

A succubus came from behind. She wrapped shadowy arms about him and blew cold, dead air into his ear. "Pretty Sidhe," she murmured. "I could show you a time like you've never had before. How would you like a climax that lasted hours?"

He tried to shake her off, but spectral hands covered his cock, and he realized to his horror it was hard. Well past aroused, every cell in his body was suddenly primed for sex. When Ronin pulled his attention from the magical source he drew power from and came back into himself, he was hotter than he'd ever been. So filled with lust, it was all he could do not to…

"Stop!" He batted at the thing's hands, but she didn't let go. Another joined her dead sister, draped her arms around him, and sought his mouth with hers. Ronin knew better. If one of the undead kissed him, they could suck his soul out through his mouth and hold him captive. His cock throbbed, his balls ached. When he caught himself thrusting his hips against the dead thing plastered against him, fury heated his blood along with desire.

"No!" He grasped the succubus pressing her breasts against his chest and threw her as far as he could. The second one took up the same position her sister had just vacated. Dark, intoxicating magic flowed from her. It held him on the ragged edge of losing control. Every Sidhe close enough to help was caught up with the magical source he'd been lost in, but Irichna were disappearing. Ronin couldn't see the whole room, but it looked like only five or six remained.

Colleen, Jenna, and Roz, along with a Gila monster lookalike, presumably Bubba, were in the center of the room chivvying a demon toward Naomi and a group of witches holding iron chains. Two more succubi slithered to him, their hands cupping his cock, stroking, teasing. Lust became a living thing, tearing at him. Suggestion, graphic and lethal, filled his mind with sexual imagery. Even with his eyes open, he visualized a ghoul taking him in her mouth while another plumbed his anus. Yet a third sucked and tweaked his nipples. Bouncing breasts and slick pussies filled his mind along with the musky scent of aroused females.

It's illusion, he shouted to himself, but a much bigger part of him didn't give a good goddamn. All he could think about was the heat of a woman closing around his shaft and semen jetting out of him.

They're not warm. They'll suck the life out of me.

Ronin repeated the words like a mantra. He kicked one succubus, thrust another away, and channeled magic. Not from the deep place, but from his usual source. Once he had it in hand, he focused it and watched with satisfaction as all three succubi exploded into nothingness. He sucked air like a farrier's bellow and shoved his cock, still achingly hard, into a more comfortable position in his formal trousers. Alarmed by how close he'd come to giving in, Ronin resurrected the wards he'd taken down to tap into the arcane magic.

He twirled in a circle, surveying the room, and sprinted for the witches. While they'd taken down one demon, the remaining half dozen had circled around them, pinning them in. "Duncan," he shouted. "Look over there."

Gasping as if he'd just run a marathon, Duncan screeched, "Get the witches out of the center. We'll kill them if we funnel power at the demons since it travels right through them."

"Right." Ronin ran scenarios through his head with the speed of a card shark shuffling hands. The goddess-blasted demons had stumbled onto a formation where they were safe, at least for the moment. Or maybe they were smarter than Ronin gave them credit for.

Titania glided to his side with long rents in her jeweled gown and the same wicked smile on her face. She put her hands on her hips, looked pointedly at the belled-out front of his trousers, and said, "That was interesting."

Ronin balled his hands into fists so hard his nails sliced into his palms. "You just stood there and watched while those things crawled all over me?" he ground out through gritted teeth.

"It's always best when you rescue yourself," she pointed out and then added, "Save your anger for our enemy."

It was good advice. He took a deep breath, coughed when he inhaled demon stench, and jerked his chin in the direction of the Irichna. They'd drawn a magical barricade around the witches and the changeling and were adding to it. The air smoked and sizzled with their fell power. Ronin's lungs felt dirty, and the iron manacles and cuffs the witches slung around weren't helping.

"Listen up," Titania said into his mind. *"This is what we shall do."*

CHAPTER 4

Roz was so furious she could've spit nails. They knew better than to let themselves fall into an Irichna trap, yet here they were anyway. While she and Colleen had battled a demon, with Jenna diving into the fray with handcuffs, the other Irichna had taken advantage of their inattention to create an impenetrable barrier. It protected them from Sidhe magic, at least the potent variety that came from goddess only knew where, and isolated the witches from anyone outside the demon-forged ring. Fortunately, it sealed the goblins, bats, and assorted incubi on the far side of the circle.

At least we don't have them to contend with, she thought, astonished she'd reached a point where only having Irichna to deal with was a good thing.

The undead had left her, Jenna, and Colleen alone, but they'd suckered at least a few of the Witches' Northwest crew into their sex games. Roz bit down hard on her lower lip. She'd dragged four incubi off witches with stern instructions to ward themselves, but she couldn't be everywhere at once. Kisses from the undead could steal souls. For some unknown reason, the succubi had ignored the male witches. She pounded a fist into her open palm. What a fucked-up mess this had turned into.

Don't worry about that. She made her mind voice stern. *We have to survive, all of us, to fight another day. If we don't, Earth is doomed...*

Distant screams and the sound of battle rang from every sector of the large room. She felt the Irichnas' power, dank and deadly, in the pit of her stomach and it chilled her. The demons were tightening the magical netting around them. How long before one of them summoned a portal and whisked her, Jenna, Colleen, and Bubba to their doom?

The demon nearest her developed an odd hue, the air around it glistened wetly, and it morphed into a large, scaly reptile. Breath whistled from Roz's lungs, and the sound of ripping fabric filled her ears as she summoned the same shape. It was the only way to fight the damned things. Too bad about her clothes, but they could be replaced. Her life couldn't.

She stole a quick glance at Colleen and Jenna. Both witches were turning into creatures to match the demons, except there were six demons and only three of them—four if she counted Bubba—which meant they'd be at a huge disadvantage, unless the Sidhe came up with something damned fast. Colleen was shifting into a wolf, Jenna into a lion. Roz took a good hard look to make sure which animals were her friends and which were the demons.

She whirled on her heavy hind legs, flexed her talons, and tried to map out a battle plan. Bubba was in his snake form, the one with four arm-like appendages sprouting from the upper part of his body. An Irichna made a grab for her, but Roz pivoted out of its way. The bastard was probably trying to bite her. Maybe it didn't realize she was immune to its poison.

"We need a plan." Colleen's mind voice sounded desperate.

"No shit." Jenna sidestepped an Irichna and whirled so her long, thick, leonine tail thwacked it.

"Teleport," Roz shrieked. *"We can teleport out of this fucking circle."*

"Do it," Colleen cried. *"Before they open a goddamned portal and pull us through. I'll take Bubba."*

"Roz?" Jenna's frantic voice was high and thin. Teleporting wasn't in her magical repertoire.

"I'll take you. Christ! Hope we didn't wait too long. I'm not sure we can break through whatever they wrapped around us."

Power raced through her like molten fury. Her animal forms brought it closer to the surface and made it easier to access. She sidestepped two Irichna to position herself next to Jenna. An unholy screech battered her hearing, and the Irichnas she'd just skittered past burst into flames. They stank of sulfur and rank vegetation, formed enormous conical pyres, and disappeared amid a barrage of ear-splitting howls.

What the fuck?

Had the Sidhe launched some sort of attack? She craned her neck, but it didn't have the range she did in her normal body and she couldn't see much. Another Irichna exploded, showering her with stinking black blood and bits of bone and sinew before it caught fire.

Roz reached for her human form about the same time Jenna and Colleen shifted. If she didn't have to grapple with a shape-shifting demon—and the last three Irichna had withdrawn into a tight knot off to one side—there was no reason to remain in her current clumsy body. The air was thick and smoky and reeked of charnel pits when her bare feet connected with the floor. She joined hands with Jenna and Colleen. Still in snake form, Bubba slithered in front of them and they converged on the demons.

"Stay back," someone shouted. "And get down."

Roz gripped the other witches' hands hard. All of them hit the floor. She kept her head tilted so she could see what happened next.

A blast of magic so potent it made her hair stand on end whistled past, but the demons disappeared before it could connect.

With nothing to absorb it, the magic blasted a wall outward, pulverizing it to the accompaniment of breaking glass and shattered timber. Dust drifted down from the ceiling. One of the candle chandeliers fell with a clatter, and a group of witches congregated to douse it with pitchers of water.

Roz's heart hammered against her chest, and her vision blurred. She forced herself back to her feet along with Jenna, Colleen, and Bubba. Before panic could take over and she started screaming, she inventoried the trashed room. Piles of dead bats and goblins littered the floor. No undead, but that wasn't surprising. They never stuck around when things got dicey. She shivered as cold air whooshed through the fractured wall and realized she was naked.

"Christ on a fucking crutch. They're gone, but that was too goddamned close," she sputtered.

"Took the words right out of my mouth, sister." Jenna aimed for a jaunty tone, but her normally bright complexion had turned sallow.

"Colleen." Duncan hurried to her side, slipped his jacket off, and draped it around her shoulders. She let go of everyone's hands and let him fold her into his arms, but she only remained there for a few seconds.

"Bubba," she hunkered next to the changeling. "You need to shift."

"Doesn't he need demons here for that?" Duncan looked worried.

"We'll help him if he needs us to," Colleen answered.

"Once he's himself again, I'm teleporting all of us back to the U.K." A fierce possessiveness ran beneath Duncan's words.

Jealousy speared Roz. Why the hell couldn't she have someone like Duncan? Someone who'd love her and protect her and take care of her? She looked at the floor, hoping no one had chosen that moment to help themselves to her thoughts.

"We can't leave," Colleen said firmly. "Jenna, Roz, and I have to stay together."

Duncan blew out a tense breath. Muscles rippled in his jaw and neck. "At least I can escort you and Bubba upstairs to our rooms. Once you're comfortable, I'm going to make good goddamned certain that gateway to Irichna-land has been destroyed."

Colleen smiled softly. "Sure. I'd like to get away from the mess in here." She shook her head sadly. "Hell of a wedding day, huh?"

Duncan tossed her a grim smile. "Something to tell our children about. I'm just grateful Naomi and Titania got through the ceremony before things went to hell."

Roz stopped listening to what was becoming a more personal conversation. She watched the changeling morph back into his gnome form, with an assist from Colleen, and glanced at Jenna. "Let's go upstairs and get some clothes on."

"Grand idea." Jenna kept hold of her hand, and the two of them picked their way through carnage on their way toward the main staircase. Before they even left the room, Ronin caught up to them.

"Are the two of you all right?" he asked.

"What does it look like?" Roz snapped and kept walking.

"Be nice," Jenna murmured. "Whatever rabbit they pulled out of their hats saved our bacon."

Curiosity about what that *something* actually was got the better of her. Roz came to a halt and turned to stare at Ronin. She crossed her arms beneath her breasts. "What exactly did you do?"

He stared back before turning crimson and averting his eyes. "I'd be glad to tell you, but first, maybe…"

Roz snorted. "I get the picture. We were heading upstairs to find some clothes."

"You could follow us and wait in another room or something," Jenna suggested helpfully. In response to a baleful look from Roz, she added. "I'm not horning in on your territory. I want answers too."

"Find me near the stairs when you've set yourselves to rights," Ronin replied and turned toward a group of Sidhe who were beckoning to him.

Roz moved closer to the long, winding staircase. If she caught up with Ronin, fine. If not, Duncan would tell Colleen, and she and Jenna could find out that way.

Jenna hurried after her. "I didn't mean anything—"

Roz felt her face heat. "He's not *my territory*." She quickened her pace once they reached the carpeted stairs, and she didn't have to wend her way through the disgusting bits of debris littering the floor.

"Don't be so touchy. We've all had a hell of a time here." Jenna sounded sullen.

Roz rounded on her at the top of the stairs. "Why can't you learn to keep your fucking mouth shut?"

"What's wrong with you?" Jenna countered. "Jesus! We escaped by the skin of our teeth, and you want to read me the riot act for trying to find out how they saved us."

Chagrin twisted her already unsteady stomach into a painful knot. Jenna hadn't done anything wrong, not really. "Sorry. I'm sorry."

Roz charged down the hall, barreled into her room, and shut the door. She raked her hands through her hair, but all she managed was to tangle them in what was left of her French braid. Her next stop was the bathroom where she turned the cold tap on full in the sink, sank her hands into its icy flow, and sluiced cold water on her face. It didn't help. To her horror and consternation, a sob shot up from her chest, followed by another. She couldn't remember the last time—before today—that she'd given in to tears. A strangled sensation clawed the back of her throat, and her eyes burned.

"I am not pathetic," she told the stormy-eyed stranger staring back at her from the mirror.

The hell I'm not. I'm crying like a ninny.

Nothing she told herself had any effect. Roz clung to the sides of the basin and sobbed until she didn't have any tears left. Weak, wrung out, and deeply ashamed, she sank to the tiled floor and wrapped her arms around her knees, rocking back and forth. Colleen was with Duncan, which meant she wouldn't come hunting for her. About the only blessing right now was that Jenna hadn't tried to chase her down.

Why would she? I treated her like shit.

Feeling perfectly wretched—and guilty on top of everything else—Roz sent a jolt of magic to heal a headache that throbbed dully at the base of her skull. She trudged into the bedroom. Her discarded jeans and serape from earlier hung over a chair. They were still damp, but she slipped into them and a black turtleneck before scooping her boots and socks off the floor. Because she felt too wiped out to balance from foot to foot to get them on, she sank into the room's only chair, let her head fall against its back-rest, and prayed she'd have enough time to pull herself together before anyone needed her.

RONIN WAITED at the bottom of the stairs. Time passed, maybe half an hour, but neither Jenna nor Roz appeared. Sidhe ebbed and flowed around him, stopping for instructions. The first order of business was converging on the upstairs room that had held the demon's pathway into the house. Titania led a group of a dozen, including Duncan, to finish it off. Ronin offered to accompany them, but Titania left him in command of the remaining Sidhe, who were purifying the house of demon taint and helping the witches haul bat and goblin remains outside to salt and burn what was left.

Someone clapped a hand on his shoulder and Ronin jumped. "Calm down," Duncan said. "It's just me." Lines carved deep into his face, and his green eyes were pinched with exhaustion.

"Damned shame about your wedding."

"I feel worse for Colleen than myself." Duncan's nostrils flared. "I wanted to whisk her and Bubba, err Niall, off to my manor house in the U.K., but she wouldn't hear of it." He walked around Ronin and placed a hand on the balustrade. "Maybe she's come to her senses."

Before Duncan had taken half a dozen steps, Ronin caught up to him. "Hold on. She's right."

"Huh?" Duncan stopped moving upward and turned to stare at Ronin. He dragged the heels of his hands down his face, distorting his even features, and shook his head. "Sorry. I'm tired and probably not thinking very straight."

"Colleen has a point. The witches need to remain together, at least the three demon assassin ones, until we can get a few of us back into the game."

"Did we ever home in on volunteers to take back demon assassin duty?"

"I have a list of about twenty of us. It's a start." Ronin pressed his lips together, ashamed his kinsmen had deceived the witches and tricked them into taking over as Irichna hunters two hundred years before. At the time, it had seemed like a brilliant solution, but he hadn't foreseen the consequences.

Duncan quirked a brow, turned, and started back up the stairs. "Fine. So we'll move all three of them—and the changeling—to the U.K."

"What if they don't want to go?" Ronin countered. "Last I checked, they had homes, and a business, in Fairbanks, Alaska."

Duncan exhaled sharply. "I know. I was there. Do you have any idea how little daylight they have during the winter? Three hours. It's dark until past eleven in the morning. And again at two or three in the afternoon."

Ronin turned his hands palms upward. "Your point?"

Duncan smirked. "Sometimes you sound more modern than me. I'm not sure I had a point. I'm going to go talk with Colleen. Maybe we can all go out to dinner somewhere—or order something in. That way we can each weigh in on what happens next."

"I'll talk with Roz. I was going to do that anyway." They reached the top of the stairs and headed up the hallway. "Do you know which room is hers?"

Duncan nodded. "Follow along, mate. I'll point it out, though you could find it easily enough by deploying magic. What about Jenna?"

Well, what about her?

"Maybe Colleen and Roz can talk with her once we've had a chance to…" Ronin caught himself. He'd been about to suggest they simply coerce the witches into compliance, but that was how they'd gotten into the current mess. If they hadn't driven a few witches into becoming demon assassins, that particular bloodline wouldn't be all but wiped out.

Duncan shot him a knowing look and pointed at one of the hallway's many closed doors. He murmured, "She's in there," before continuing toward his suite at the end of the hall.

Ronin stood in front of the door for long moments after Duncan disappeared through his. What would he say? Roz had seemed pretty put-out, and it hadn't been chivalrous of him to stare at her unclothed form, but she had an amazing body. Long, lean, lithe, with full breasts and slender hips. Picturing her acres of shapely legs made his cock, which had finally subsided from the succubi onslaught, twitch with need.

The door jerked open. A blotchy-faced Roz stood before him, glaring balefully. "What?"

"How did you know I was here?"

She rolled her eyes. "Oh, please. I may be out of sorts, but your magic is so strong, I'd have to be dead not to feel it."

The corners of his mouth twitched. It had been a stupid question. She was a witch, not a mortal. "May I come in?"

"I suppose so." She turned away from the door, but at least she didn't slam it in his face.

He glanced around a room similar to his one floor down. A double bed with an intricately carved headboard sat beneath a dormer window. Bedside tables graced both sides of it, and a matching dresser butted against one wall. The room's only chair had a brass floor lamp next to it. She hadn't exactly invited him to sit, so he kept his gaze on her and waited.

"You may as well take the chair," she said at length. "I'll sit on the bed."

"Do you mind if I close the door?"

Her full mouth turned down in half a frown. "Is there a reason I should worry?"

He blew out an amused breath, shut the door, and sat in the chair. "Somehow, Miss Roxanne Lantry, I have a feeling you can take care of yourself." He summoned magic to weave a privacy spell.

"What are you doing?" She perched on the edge of the bed, but looked ready to bolt at any moment.

"I want to talk with you and I don't want anyone to overhear us." He kept his voice low, soothing. "You need to tell someone what's bothering you, and it may as well be me." He settled deeper into the chair and folded his hands in his lap. "I think you'll find I'm a decent listener, plus I give you my word nothing you say will ever leave this room."

"If I needed a therapist, I'd—" Her lower lip quivered and she clapped a hand over her mouth.

"I don't want to be your therapist, but I'd like to be your friend." It took self-discipline, but Ronin made himself stay put. He wanted go to her, gather her close, and tell her everything would be all right. It wouldn't, though. Not until the Irichna were all either captured or dead. To say otherwise was an insult to her intelligence.

Her dark gaze bored into him. "I read minds even better than Colleen."

"Fine." He threw his wide open. "I mean you no harm, and I have nothing to hide. Go ahead. See for yourself."

CHAPTER 5

*R*oz hesitated. It seemed wrong to just dive into his offer, yet it held an irresistible aspect. He was old. Sidhe lived for thousands of years, balanced against a witch's few hundred. What would she find inside his head?

All he suggested was for me to check his intentions, not riffle through his life...

Suddenly shy, she rested her feet on the bedframe and wrapped her arms around her legs. Peeking into his thoughts when she thought she could slip by unnoticed was one thing, an open invitation quite another.

She cleared her throat to mask her discomfiture. "Even though I was just doing it, it feels like cheating to help myself to what's in your head. Why are you being kind to me?"

She forced herself to meet his gaze with stern internal warnings not to get lost in his eyes. A deep, mesmerizing blue, they drew her in anyway. Silvery flecks danced around his pupils in an intricate pattern.

"Do you think I'm not in the habit of being kind to everyone?" His words broke into her fascination with his eyes.

Roz narrowed her own eyes to slits. "You've been the Sidhe

leader for a long time. Leaders are lots of things. They're pragmatic, used to calling the shots and making hard decisions. I'm not sure *kind* makes the hit parade. At least not very often."

"You'd be right. My fall from grace can be our secret." Understated humor crackled beneath his words, and Ronin cocked his head to one side. "I'll keep your confidences, whatever you choose to tell me. In exchange, perhaps you won't tell anyone about my, um, softer side."

It was an attractive offer, but she hesitated. Other than Jenna and Colleen, she wasn't in the habit of talking to anyone, and there were many things she'd never even told the other witches.

Ronin leaned forward. "You've stood against demons, probably hundreds of times. What was it about today that unhinged you?"

Crap! He's got my number.

"I've been sitting here asking myself the same question," she muttered.

"What'd you come up with?"

She'd never stopped looking into his eyes. Something in their depths encouraged her, offered her a lifeline, suggested maybe this wasn't as big a risk as she feared. Roz swallowed hard around her dry throat. "It's not easy to talk about."

"Which is exactly why you should." Ronin crossed the space between them and sat next to her. "If you want me to retreat to the chair, just say so."

She swallowed again and shook her head. Thoughts tumbled through her mind. She ought to send him away. Needing anyone was a weakness. She'd always managed before... When he draped an arm around her shoulders and pulled her against him, she tugged away and said, "We shouldn't."

"Shouldn't what?" His voice buzzed near her ear. "You look as if you need comforting." He rubbed her shoulder. "Just let the words flow, Roz. I won't judge you. Goddess knows I've done many things over my long life I'm not particularly proud of."

She leaned into him, craving his warmth and the solid presence of his side pressed against hers. "I—I was so scared when the Irichna made that circle around us. And then I felt like a dolt once I understood we could just teleport ourselves to safety. Or we might've been able to—if we'd acted fast enough." She bit hard on her lower lip.

"It might have worked," he said encouragingly.

Roz pushed back and twisted sideways so she could look at him. Even though she hated to cut herself off from his touch, it muddied things, so she ducked from beneath his arm and pushed it toward his lap. "What exactly did you Sidhe do to get rid of those three Irichna?"

"Ah yes, I was supposed to tell you that." Ronin leveled his gaze at her. "The problem was hurting one of you with the ancient magic Duncan tapped into, so we split forces. Some of us called the magic, while others of us gathered it once it was harvested and mixed it with our own." A muscle in his jaw twitched. "Once we had mastery of the ancient magic, but we haven't used it in millennia because it has quite a bite if it gets away from you. In any event, Titania remembered how to force it to work for us, rather than us being its slave."

"So you somehow targeted the demons and made the magic stop before it went through them and hit us?"

He nodded. "Close enough. I'll have to admit I was anxious with the first one, but once I saw how well it worked, the other two went smoothly." He grimaced. "Damned shame we couldn't knock off the last three, but the yellow-livered bastards ran like cravens."

"Thanks. It appears I owe you—and some of the other Sidhe—for my life." Roz tried to keep a tremor out of her voice and almost managed.

"You're welcome." He tilted his chin upward. "Your turn."

"For what?"

"You were off to a good start, telling me you were scared. Irichna scare the crap out of me too. I want to hear more."

She snorted. "More about what a ninny I feel like?"

"No, more about what upset you."

She put another inch or two between them and squared her shoulders. "All the years I've done this, I've told myself I'd be fine, that they'd never get Jenna or Colleen or me. Today changed all that. For the first time, I took a realistic look at how vulnerable we are—and that there are only three of us left. When we were twenty or so, it was easier to delude myself we might win."

He looked solemn. "And now?"

"It feels like there's no way. When I was standing there inhaling demon stench and trying not to puke, I knew it was only a matter of time before we were history. The demons will bolt from Hell, overrun Earth, and—" she swiped her hands against each other "—that will be that."

He didn't look away, and she was relieved not to pick up disgust after her revelation. "That's not all," he said softly.

Because this wasn't as tough as she'd feared, Roz forged ahead. "No, it's not. I've always been the strong one. Jenna and Colleen count on me, but when I heard Colleen's mind voice just a few degrees south of full hysteria screaming we needed a plan..." Roz's voice ran down. The next part stuck in her craw and choked her.

"It's all right," he prodded. "I won't judge you."

She turned her hands palms up, feeling as if she was balancing the rest of her life between them, and dropped her gaze because it was too hard to run up against the compassion in his eyes.

"When Colleen did that, I felt like a colossal failure. Like I should have taken the lead. Hell, like I shouldn't have let us get trapped in the first place. If anything had happened to any of us, it would've been all my fault." Her throat thickened with grief and guilt. "I'm not sure I could've lived with that."

"Others of your kind have died at Irichna hands. Why was this different?" He reached across the gap between them and tipped her chin so she had to look at him.

"Colleen, Jenna, and I are a team. We're all about the same age. We came into our powers within a year of each other, and we practiced magic together, learning how to stand against the Irichna." She sucked in a ragged breath. "In a way, we're a lot like sisters. And then we adopted Bubba, or Colleen did, and the rest of us welcomed him into our family. Hard to fathom that was over forty years ago."

Ronin moved the finger he had beneath her chin to her lips and brushed it gently over them. "See. That wasn't so bad."

"You weren't the one telling it. I can't believe what a fool I've been. It's not that I've underestimated the Irichna so much as I overestimated how strong the three of us were. Four if you count Bubba. He's a lot of help, actually. Especially when we ferry demons to Hell." Her eyes widened, and she slapped a palm against her forehead. "Crap! There are at least two of them upstairs."

"They're not going anywhere. We'll help you escort them, or maybe Titania has already taken care of it."

"How?"

"By asking the Celtic gods for assistance."

He was still running a gentle finger over her face, stroking her chin, cheeks, and lips. It felt good. Too good. Without thinking about it, she leaned into his touch. "They've never helped us. Not that we'd have the first clue how to ask for their aid."

"No. They wouldn't help, even if you asked. Frequently they don't help us, either, but we're a bit higher up the food chain."

"Where does that put us?" She tried to modulate the bitterness in her tone but failed. "Never mind." She pushed his hand away. "I'm used to being at the lowliest rung of magicdom."

"But you're not." He reached for her again, but she shook her head.

"What do you mean?"

"Don't you read your own history?"

"Apparently not." She gritted her teeth, annoyed with herself.

I'm either so pissed I see red, or I'm sobbing my eyes out. Damn, but I need to find some middle ground.

He quirked a brow, and she recoiled. "Awk, were you just in my head?"

He nodded. "Sorry, but I'm trying to understand you. Magic is so second nature, I don't think about using it, I just do."

Scrabbling for neutral territory, she asked, "What were you going to tell me about witches' history?"

"You're as strong as we are. Ceridwen made you that way. She angered the other Celts but held her ground."

"Nah, you're just saying that. It's all part of being kind."

"No, I'm not. Does this Coven have a library?" At her nod, he went on. "I'm sure they have a *Witches' History Primer*. We could find it, and I could show you. Or you could look inside my mind and see for yourself."

"If we're so strong," she countered, "why are almost all of us dead?"

"Because the Irichna are stronger." Worry stitched his brows into a straight line. "None of us expected them to become so aggressive."

"Why not?"

He reached for her hand and she let him take it. His fingers were warm, and they felt comforting when they first enclosed hers and then laced between them. "We look at history as the best predictor of the future. For millennia, the Irichna were pests. They'd sashay out of their hidey-holes, take down a few unsuspecting victims, and disappear for fifty or a hundred years."

Roz squeezed his hand. "What's different now?"

"Abbadon has grown much stronger. None of us know quite why, and if the Celts do, they're keeping it to themselves." He pulled gently on her hand. "Come here."

"I am here."

In answer, he scooted closer to her and threaded his free arm around her, while still clasping her hand. His intense blue gaze caught hers and held it. Up close like that, the flecks of silver around his pupils seemed to expand. Ronin snugged her against him and kissed her forehead. Roz thought she should pull away, but she was drawn in by the tenderness in his touch.

His scent—sandalwood and amber—eddied about her,. The ironclad control she'd clapped over her emotions after her earlier crying jag slipped just a little. He trailed his mouth down the side of her face until his lips hovered over hers. "I won't hurt you," he murmured.

Why not? Everyone else has.

If he'd heard her thoughts, he didn't give any indication. He settled his mouth over hers in the softest of kisses, as if he were giving her a choice. She flicked her tongue out, tasting him. He kissed a little harder and teased her tongue with his. His arm tightened around her back, and he rubbed small circles atop her shoulder blade. The iron band of tension running up and down her back started to melt.

She opened her mouth to his tongue, and his kiss became harder, more insistent. Her nipples came alive, forming peaks where they rubbed against her turtleneck, and her crotch flooded. Almost ashamed by her instantaneous response, she broke their kiss, but he ran the tip of his tongue over her lips, inviting, teasing, and she sparred with it, loving the taste and feel of his mouth.

Ronin let go of her hand, wrapped his other arm around her, and pulled her close. He crushed his mouth over hers and slipped his tongue back inside her mouth. She sucked hungrily, wondering what his cock would taste like, and closed her arms around him. Hard muscles flexed beneath her touch. She wanted to see his body, run her mouth over every inch of it. Roz had never been shy about sex, but that was when her emotions had been wrapped up in a tidy box and buried deep. Today, she felt raw and vulnerable. She'd let the man holding her past inner walls she'd never taken down before.

He rubbed his chest against hers, and it sent spikes of lust from her nipples to her pussy. The sense of dread that had dogged her from the moment she realized she, Jenna, and Colleen were surrounded by demons faded into the deeply shuttered place where she'd always corralled her fears. Ronin tumbled them sideways onto the bed. She kicked a leg over one of his and ground her pelvis against him. Her breathing quickened, and she felt his cock press against her.

Ronin moved his mouth away from hers and smoothed hair from her face. "You're so beautiful," he said, his voice catching with lust.

"No." She smiled softly and positioned a hand to cup the side of his face. "You're the beautiful one. All you Sidhe—"

He placed a finger over her mouth. "Beauty is so much more than outward appearance. You have a beautiful soul." He closed his eyes for a moment as if he were considering something. When he opened them, he said, "I only let myself fall in love once before. She was a mortal and she died birthing our child. My son died too. There wasn't enough Sidhe magic in the universe to save her. I know, I summoned every trick at my disposal."

Compassion flooded her. "I'm sorry. Was it very long ago?"

"Almost six hundred years, but there's hardly a day I don't think about them."

"Why did you tell me?"

A crooked smile formed on his face. "Because for the first time since I lost Lorelei, I've met a woman who sings to my soul like she did. I wasn't just trolling for your secrets earlier. I want you to know mine too."

Pleasure warmed her heart. He was uncloaking his own vulnerabilities and showing them to her. "Thanks for trusting me." She ran a finger down his face and traced the lines of his cheeks and jaw.

He turned his head, captured her finger, and drew it into his mouth. When he sucked on it, she felt an answering twitch deep in her core and dug the fingers of her other hand into his back.

He let go of her finger and said, "If I can't trust you, we shouldn't be lovers."

"We haven't been, not quite yet anyway." Roz heard husky yearning in her voice and knew the *not yet* part was just a formality at this point.

"No," he agreed, "but I'd say we're headed in that direction." He rocked his pelvis against her, and she felt his cock jerk against her belly. "I've wanted to hold you like this ever since I first laid eyes on you at my home in the U.K."

"More like your castle, you mean."

"I'd like to take you back there." He must have seen protest form in her mind because he hurried on. "All of us would go. Jenna, Colleen, and Bubba. I understand you need to be together."

"Maybe we can talk about it later." Roz wriggled against his body, hungry for the touch of him naked against her. She moved her arm from behind him, pressed it between them, and found his cock. When she closed her fingers around him, he groaned.

Desire clotted in her throat. She wanted to see—no, make that had to see—him. His shaft felt incredible against her palm. Its heat seared her through the fabric of his trousers, and she couldn't close her hand all the way around his girth. She glanced at the studs holding his dress shirt—with its rows of rills and tucks—closed, decided they'd take too long to unfasten, and repositioned herself to tackle the buttons on his pants.

He grappled with the zipper on her jeans. "My boots," she panted. "Got to get them off first."

"That means I have to let go of you—" his voice deepened with need "—and I don't want to."

Roz felt the same way. She longed to stay in Ronin's arms forever, but she wanted to be naked too, to explore the hardness of his body with her fingers and mouth. "Can't be helped." She pulled away and bent to the laces of one boot.

A sharp rap vibrated against the door. Roz's head snapped up.

"Who in the hell?" she panted, so caught up in her desire for Ronin, it was all she could do to shift her focus.

"Damn!" Ronin bolted from the bed, rearranged his mussed clothing, and dragged the door open.

Duncan and Colleen stepped into the room. A knowing leer coated Duncan's face. "Och, if I'd realized…"

"Don't listen to him," Colleen said. "We could smell sex wafting down the hall."

"I was attempting to be a gentleman," Duncan chided her, which earned him a sharp look from his brand new wife.

Roz unfolded herself from the bed, grateful she was still dressed. "Okay." She strode to Colleen. "You knew we were, um, busy, but you knocked anyway. What's up?"

"Naomi and Titania have called a meeting. It starts in five minutes downstairs." Duncan looked pointedly at them.

The changeling bounded into the room and stopped. A shocked look bloomed on his face and he stared at Roz. "I smell sex." He shifted his beady gaze to Ronin and half-bowed. "Congratulations. The virgin warrior here is usually so caught up in—"

"Shut up!" Roz rounded on him.

"What'd I say?" Bubba exuded a charming insouciance that almost made her forget he was three times her age and canny as hell.

"Is the downstairs fit to meet in?" Ronin inserted smoothly, and Roz silently blessed him for changing the topic.

"More or less," Duncan said. "They patched that one wall with magic. It'll hold until they can mortar it."

Jenna shoved into the room, exchanged a reproachful glance with Roz, and muttered, "I could've used someone to comfort me."

Maybe because it was her go-to position, Roz's temper marched to the fore. "There's a houseful of Sidhe and witches. Nothing was stopping you from picking a likely candidate."

Jenna made a sour face and said, "Never mind. Let's get moving."

*R*onin followed Roz out the door. They were last to leave, and he pulled the door closed behind them. His groin tingled with unfulfilled need, but his heart soared. They may not have made love, but something better had happened. Roz had dropped her barriers and let him into her private world. He'd done the same. It was a good beginning for them, and he vowed to do his damnedest to build on it. Titania would probably read him the riot act for taking a brief break from his command post, or maybe she wouldn't. The Queen of Faerie was enjoying the holy hell out of being back in the center of things. If she censured him for anything, it would be his attraction to Roz.

The nauseating miasma of demon reek intensified as he moved down the long, curved staircase. He wrinkled his nose in distaste. It took a long time to rid a place of the Irichnas' particularly putrid emanations, but maybe that was a good thing because it would remind them to keep their guard up. Roz descended in front of him. With her shoulders squared, she had a regal bearing that would have done a queen proud. The curve of her slender backside tantalized him. How he wished they could have had another half hour together. Just enough to…

He shook his head. This wasn't the time to fantasize about the enticing woman in front of him, with her high cheekbones, strong chin, and mysterious, dark eyes. Serious business lay ahead. If they couldn't make a dent in the Irichnas' offense, they may as well pack up and move to one of the borderworlds. Even as he thought it, he knew that wouldn't work, either. Abbadon wouldn't rest until he controlled everything.

No. They had to launch an effective counterattack. One that would at least slow Hell's minions down, even if it wasn't quite enough to annihilate them.

They reached the bottom of the stairs. He moved to Roz's side and hooked a hand beneath her arm. He'd hidden his last relationship from the world, even though it hurt Lorelei's feelings. Women had been different then, more subservient and accepting of their lot, so she'd never complained, but he'd seen the wounding in her eyes and felt it in her heart. He was damned if he'd make the same mistake twice. Not that he and Roz exactly had a relationship yet, but he didn't want her to think she wasn't good enough for him to show affection openly before his Sidhe brethren.

He leaned close. "They did an amazing cleanup job."

Roz nodded. "Better than I would've thought, for sure." She stopped dead and pointed through a high, rounded archway that led into the room where they'd battled Irichna. "Who's that?"

Ronin jerked his head up, and his mouth fell open. "Goddess's tits," he muttered. "It's Oberon. I haven't seen him in two or three hundred years."

Roz grinned. "It looks as if Titania hasn't, either. I'm not sure if she looks deliriously happy or totally ticked off."

Ronin snorted and strangled a gout of laughter because neither regent would appreciate it. He tightened his hold on Roz's arm. "You nailed it. Titania's probably caught somewhere between wanting to kill him and vowing to never let him out of her sight again."

Ronin hurried toward the far side of the great room. "Maybe you should leave me with Colleen and Jenna," Roz whispered.

"Let me introduce you," he said into her mind. *"After that, we'll see."*

Ronin took in his liege. Oberon looked much the same. Where Titania's hair was silver and so long it swept the ground, Oberon's was golden and done in his usual Celtic warrior braiding pattern. His shrewd, amber eyes zeroed in on Ronin, and he motioned him forward.

"Thank you, my lord." Ronin let go of Roz and bowed until his forehead practically swept the floor before straightening. "By the goddess, it's good to see you again, my liege, my king."

Like all the Faerie-folk, Oberon looked like a Greek god with sculpted facial lines, well-defined cheeks, and a strong, square jaw. His ageless face creased into a smile. "Don't spread it around—" he pitched his voice low "—but I was getting bored in the *Dreaming*. So when Titania told me I was needed, leaving there wasn't a difficult decision." He shrugged and smoothed his hands down black silk robes sashed with crimson. A slender, golden circlet, symbol of his office, circled his sleekly braided head just above eyebrow level.

"I'd like you to meet one of the demon assassin witches." Ronin drew Roz forward, grateful when she at least inclined her head.

Titania made a hooting sound. "Now you bow?" she inquired acerbically. "Before the wedding, when it was just me, you considered bending your neck but discarded it out of hand."

Roz's bronze skin developed a rosy hint, and her low, melodic voice vibrated with surprise. "You were in my mind."

"I'm in everyone's mind, dear." Titania waggled an index finger at the air between them. "You'd do well not to forget that, particularly since it appears I'm about to lose another subject to a non-Sidhe union." She focused her unearthly pale blue eyes on Ronin. "You've had almost six hundred years to get over the last one, why in Danu's name couldn't you—"

Oberon grabbed her arm. "Stop. The gods, Danu being one, determine whom we're attracted to. Leave him be."

"Oh, very well," Titania huffed.

"Thank you." Ronin bowed again. "We have more important matters before us."

"Indeed we do," Oberon concurred.

Ronin glanced about the room and then remembered the imprisoned demons. Before he could get the words out to ask after their fate, Titania said, "I called in a few favors, and two of the Celts came and got them."

"Excellent," Ronin replied and breathed a sigh of relief. Hell was a hideous place, and with good reason. He hadn't been looking forward to journeying there, although he'd have gone willingly to spare Roz the task.

One less thing to worry about.

"It was very nice to meet you both," Roz said. "I'm going to join up with the witches." She winked at Titania. "You know, my rightful place and all."

To Ronin's immense relief, because Titania did not have a sense of humor, the Queen of Faerie winked back just before Roz turned and wended her way through the crowd.

He switched to telepathic speech, including both regents. *"Do you have a plan?"*

"It's under development," Oberon said, sounding cautious.

Naomi, flanked by half a dozen witches, walked toward them and asked, "Are you ready to begin?"

"We've come to a few decisions," Titania said. "We'd be glad to share them with you."

Naomi shook her head. Somewhere along the way, her long dark hair had come out of the elaborate up-do she'd assumed for the wedding. It hung to her knees in drooping curls, but her blue eyes flashed. "Either we're full partners in this, or you can teleport out of here right now."

Titania drew herself up. "You can't talk to me like that."

"I just did." Naomi pursed her full lips together and folded her hands over one of many rips marring the front of her embroidered silken tunic. "Look. Thank you for getting rid of the Irichna and for closing off the gateway, hopefully once and for all. The thing you don't get is Earth is our home too. If the demons escape from Hell and there's no one to stop them, none of us will be able to remain here. You've got other worlds you can run to. We don't."

"We may have access to the borderworlds," Ronin said, "but they're no guarantee of safety. Irichna can travel there as easily as here."

Naomi shifted her gaze from Titania to Oberon. "Full partners or nothing. I warn you, it's a mistake not to avail yourselves of every single possible ally. If we can't work together, never mind we haven't in the past, we're going to lose this war."

Oberon turned to his queen. "I agree with her."

Titania arched a silvery brow. "You deserted us. You wouldn't even be here if I hadn't called you back—"

"I made a mistake. Two of them won't cancel each other out." Oberon turned his attention to Naomi. "Get everyone together. Standing, seated, it doesn't matter. Let's see if anyone has a better idea than what we came up with."

Roz caught up to Jenna beneath a window on the far side of the room. "Are you still tweaked out?"

The other witch shook her head. "I'm not sure I ever was. I was just feeling sorry for myself."

"I meant what I said. There are a lot of men here. Oodles of willing bed material."

Jenna leveled her hazel gaze at Roz. "I don't just want to get laid. I want someone who'll look at me the way Duncan looks at Colleen." She hesitated a beat. "And the way Ronin looks at you."

Roz rolled her eyes. "Don't be ridiculous. We barely know one another."

Jenna shook her head. "That may be true, but I recognize when a man is besotted. Christ! I'm a witch. I can smell things like that. Look me in the eye and tell me you don't like him."

Roz trained her gaze on the floor. "I'm not sure how I feel. It's too new to talk about."

A warm glow began in the pit of her stomach, though, when she thought about Ronin. About how he'd drawn her out, been patient with her, and understanding. She hadn't mistaken the compassion flaring in the depths of his eyes when she admitted how scared she'd been and how responsible she felt. And then there'd been his mouth and his hands and the lean muscles of his body—and that amazing cock she'd felt, if only for a few moments. Heat flickered between her legs at the memory.

"Interesting." Jenna's gaze burned into her until Roz finally looked up again. "New, yes, but look at the possibilities."

"You were in my mind." Roz stared at her friend, feeling betrayed.

"How else can I find things out?" Jenna didn't even have the grace to look ashamed. "I'm happy for you. Really I am."

Roz made a disgusted sound. Her sense of violation swelled, and she made a grab for her temper before she said something she'd regret. "You might hold those congratulations. Good God, Jenna! I've spent all of an hour alone with him."

"Yes, but it's not the first time you've been together. Look at all those hours when we were in the U.K."

"That was business—" Roz began.

"Hey, you two." Colleen trotted up with Bubba in tow. She looked tired. Dark smudged spots sat beneath her eyes. Like Roz and Jenna, she was back in blue jeans, a sweater, and boots. Her fancy hair from earlier had been deconstructed and swept into a ponytail.

"Where's Duncan?" Jenna asked.

"Up there with Ronin and them." Bubba gestured.

Roz looked from Jenna to Colleen to Bubba. "I owe all of you an apology."

"For what?" Colleen asked.

"Yeah, I was just teasing about Ronin," Bubba cut in. "I'm glad you found someone you like."

"Not that." Roz swallowed hard. "I didn't act fast enough, and I let us get trapped earlier." She dragged her mouth into a hard line and pounded a fist into her other hand. "I promise to pay better attention."

"Aw, sweetie." Colleen hugged her. "It was all our faults."

Jenna moved in from one side and Bubba from the other so everyone got in on the group hug. "I love you guys," Bubba announced and planted a wet kiss on the back of Roz's hand.

"I love you all too," Roz said, surprised the words didn't stick in the back of her throat. As emotion-avoidant as she was, words like that didn't come easy.

"This appreciation fest is grand," Colleen said, "but what the fuck are we going to do? They damn near had us today."

"I've been thinking about that," Jenna said slowly. "My prediction is the Sidhe are going to want to drag all of us back to the U.K."

"You guessed right," Colleen said. She made an indignant face. "If Duncan had his way, Bubba and I would already be there."

Jenna smiled grimly. "While it's tempting to let them take care of us, we need something to make the demons overconfident, something to draw them out." She switched to mind speech. *"I came up with this. See what you think..."*

They were still huddled together talking when Naomi walked close enough to shake Colleen's shoulder. "It's time," she said. "We need everyone front and center."

"Be right there," Roz said, distracted because she was still rolling Jenna's plan around in her mind. It had holes. Big ones, but it held a certain elegance too. It was sure to lure the demons, but she wasn't certain the three of them could hold off another onslaught like today's.

"Well?" Naomi placed her hands on her hips.

"We have one more thing to work out," Colleen said, smiling too brightly, "and then we'll join the group."

"Two minutes." Naomi clumped away. The set of her shoulders displayed deep weariness, and Roz's heart went out to her. She'd only been leader of Witches' Northwest for a couple of weeks. The previous leader, Mathilde, had been killed in a huge fight. Even though there was a touch of poetic justice—she'd been killed by the Irichna she'd parlayed with—still any witch's death was a loss. Mathilde had been a valuable ally until she became maddened by a thirst for power.

"I tell you," Jenna persisted, once Naomi left, "it's the only way. If we let the Sidhe call the shots, they'll get us into a war that'll last a hundred years."

"Hell, a thousand," Colleen muttered.

"Your plan is rough," Roz said. "It needs refinement."

"I get that it's not perfect." Jenna made circling motions in the air with her hands. "Are you in?"

Roz exhaled raggedly. "I suppose so. If it works, we'll be out of the woods."

"Maybe forever," Colleen agreed.

"I like it," Bubba spoke up. "It'll be just like the old days with us against the Irichna."

Colleen bent close to him. "You will keep your mouth shut and just listen. Okay?"

"Why?"

"Because the Sidhe will try to argue us out of this. They're used to getting their way. Come on. Let's get moving."

The four of them trooped to where witches had massed on one side of the room. It didn't surprise Roz that there was zip in the way of intermingling. Sidhe were on the right, witches on the left.

Naomi stood tall in the front of the room, next to Oberon and Titania.

"I think we should hear them out," Roz hissed, "before we float our idea."

"I'm good with that," Jenna said.

Bubba opened his mouth, but Colleen shook her head. "Keep silent, or I'll turn you into a cat for a while."

The changeling's wide mouth twisted into a frown. "You treat me like a child."

"Yes, well, the Sidhe stripped your Scottish cousins of their powers," Colleen whispered. "Compared with them, I'm Mother Teresa."

"Who's she?" Bubba brightened.

"Tell you later. Ssht."

Titania clapped her hands together and waited until the last conversations died away. "It's been a difficult day and we're tired," she said, "so it's in all our interests if we keep this meeting short. We need rest and sustenance in case the Irichna are ill-advised enough to launch a second attack on the heels of their first."

Roz gritted her teeth together. She'd been afraid the demons might try something like that, knowing their opponents were depleted, but with the gateway shut they'd lost the element of surprise.

Oberon stared at the segregated assemblage. "We don't look like we want to work together," he pointed out.

"Old habits die hard," Naomi said. "It will take time for us to trust one another."

Titania looked shocked the witch had spoken independently, but she didn't say anything, just elbowed Oberon.

He exchanged glances with her and nodded. "All right." He took a step forward. "I'll lead out. The basic plan is this. The Sidhe will return to their homes scattered throughout the U.K. We will bring the three demon assassin witches, and their familiar, with us. The volunteers among us who are willing to take back demon assassination responsibilities will be injected with the witches' blood."

He stopped to clear his throat. "We anticipate the gene splicing will move forward rapidly, with a bit of a magical assist if needed. Within a week or so, maybe less, we should have an enhanced cadre of magic wielders capable of doing battle with Irichna, and escorting them to the Ninth Circle."

"What happens then?" Colleen asked.

Oberon drew his brows together. "We wait. What else? They'll show up eventually, and we can resume our battle to defeat them."

"What if we'd rather return to Alaska?" Jenna asked. "You're welcome to draw some of our blood and take it back to the U.K."

Titania shook her head. "That's not a good idea, dear. You'll be much safer where we can keep an eye on you."

"Not that we're not grateful for the offer, but we don't want your protection." Roz stepped forward, her heart hammering. Very soon, the die would be cast. Part of her, a shockingly large part, wanted to stay with Ronin. If that meant crossing the Atlantic, so be it, but she, Jenna, and Colleen were a team. They'd made a decision and she wouldn't play turncoat.

Duncan pushed away from the wall he'd been leaning against and trotted to Colleen's side. "What's this all about?" he asked. "You and I talked about going home."

"We didn't clarify which home." She tilted her chin up and looked at him. "I have one too."

"We'd be safer where there are more Sidhe." His clear, green eyes clouded with worry.

Jenna, who hadn't bothered to find a chair, took a few steps and planted herself in front of Titania, Oberon, and Naomi. "We have our own plan," she began. "We've been living your plan—"

"It's not mine," Naomi cut in, her voice sharp.

"Whatever," Jenna retorted equally sharply. "Sitting around waiting to see where the bastards show up next isn't working very well. We're always on the defensive. Roz, Colleen, and I are going to be proactive. We'll lure them, and once they show up, we'll be ready."

"You could do that in the U.K." Duncan said in a strangled sounding voice.

"It wouldn't work nearly as well," Roz said. "You believe the Irichna are stupid. Well, they aren't. If we go home to Alaska, and it looks like business as usual, we think they'll come to us."

"You're not going without me," Duncan told Colleen.

Ronin hurried to Roz's side. "You're not going without me, either."

Joy so poignant it nearly choked her whooshed from her toes to the top of her head. She arrowed her gaze straight at Ronin. "You don't have to."

"I know that." A muscle twitched in his jaw. "You couldn't stop me if you tried."

The crowd burst into a hundred conversations. "Quiet," Titania cried. "Quiet, everyone." It wasn't until she sent a jagged bolt of magic crashing against the far wall that both witches and Sidhe complied. Ronin blanketed his amusement with a neutral expression. The queen was used to being obeyed. She must be seething.

"Get up here." Titania stabbed a finger at Roz, Jenna, and Colleen.

"Do you want me too?" Bubba spoke up brightly and started toward her. Titania glared at him. The changeling smiled guilelessly, but Ronin wasn't fooled. Bubba was still furious the Sidhe had stripped his Scottish kin of most of their power because they'd argued some point no one probably even remembered. If there was a subtle way the creature could take Titania down a notch, he'd do it.

"Hold up." Colleen made a grab for Bubba's shoulder and held on.

"But she said—"

"I heard her loud and clear," Colleen cut in. Still hanging onto the changeling, she straightened and faced Titania across fifty feet of suddenly empty floor space where Sidhe and witches had cleared a path. "If you want something from us," she said in a clear, ringing voice, "you can ask nicely, and then we'll decide if we want to do it."

"Colleen, please," Duncan murmured as he hurried to her side.

She shook him off. "I married you, but that doesn't mean I have to obey you, either."

"This is what comes of marrying outside our bloodlines—" Titania started, but Oberon made a chopping motion with one hand.

"I don't care where you stand," the King of Faerie said to Colleen. "I can hear you fine. I would like to know more about your actual plan once you return to Alaska."

"And if we don't want to tell you?" Jenna drew herself up to her full height, which was about six feet seven with her three-inch heels.

Oberon met her gaze, his amber eyes sparking against her hazel ones. "That's your choice, but not a very wise one. We must work together, regardless of where we are physically located."

Roz made her way to Jenna's side. "It's fairly simple, really. We'll go home, back to running our magicians' supply store. We'll retrieve our second car if it's still at the ferry dock in Haines, and we'll spend a lot of time talking about how scared we are and about how our days are numbered."

"Irichna are tuned in to us." Jenna jumped into the conversation. "They've always known when we're vulnerable." She spread her hands in front of her. "They'll figure we're ripe for the plucking and show up for what they assume will be a final showdown. Hopefully, lots of them will want in on the action."

"Of course they will." Roz took over. "We've been a bone in their craw for two hundred years. Not us, exactly, but other demon assassin witches." She took a measured breath and whispered something to Jenna. The other witch shook her head emphatically, but Roz just said, "Too bad."

She crossed her arms under her breasts and said, "There's one other thing."

"Keep talking," Oberon urged. "We need to hear everything."

"We're not the only ones with magic. When Duncan helped us with Irichna who invaded our home, he called on the dark fae for help."

"You did what?" Titania screeched, staring right at Duncan.

"I didn't summon them directly," he protested. "I put out a distress call, and they were who showed up. Damned helpful, I might add."

"That's just it." Roz dove back in before Titania could say anything else.

Ronin was proud of her tenacity, but scared shitless the witches' harebrained plan would be the death of them. Fear for the woman he was falling hard for rocked him to his core.

"We're all in this together," Roz went on. "And I say we solicit help from everyone with magic, not just witches and Sidhe. Colleen told me the dark fae made a point of saying this was everyone's battle, which was why they were willing to help a Sidhe."

"Duncan almost told them to get lost." Colleen glared at her husband. "We were standing outside my house in Fairbanks trying to decide whether to let them help us. Then Roz and Jenna started screaming. I bolted for the house, and I guess Duncan rethought things."

"In my defense," Duncan spoke up, "at that point I was willing to take help from any quarter offering it."

Ronin strode briskly to where Jenna and Roz stood, faced Titania, and said, "I knew about the dark fae. Damn good thing they showed up since they apparently hold power that allows them to rid Earth of Irichna poison."

"They were decent healers too," Bubba spoke up. "The man saved me."

"How do you propose to gather the divergent races that wield magic?" Oberon asked, studiously avoiding mentioning the dark fae by name.

"We were hoping you'd help with that," Roz said. "You seem to have a pipeline to the Celtic gods. If what Ronin told me a little bit ago is true, Ceridwen created all the magical races, so maybe she'd know how to locate their leaders."

"Och." Oberon shook his head and made a sour face. "That one has a nasty temper."

Roz snorted. "So do I. Unfortunately, it doesn't stop people from bothering me."

The corners of Titania's mouth twitched and she chortled, but got hold of herself fast. "At least you're not under any illusions about yourself," she muttered.

Ronin squelched the desire to tell Titania to shut up. Protectiveness surged and he wrapped an arm around Roz. She glanced at him and raised a quizzical brow, but he shook his head and said, "Assuming we can find some volunteers from the Unseelie Court to help, and druids and mages—"

"Don't forget us." Bubba surged forward. Either he'd escaped Colleen's iron grip, or she'd decided she didn't need to hold onto him anymore. "Changelings have strong Earth magic—now that you deigned to return it to us."

Ronin smiled. "And changelings." He shifted his attention back to Roz. "How do the different races play into your plan?"

"Simple," Roz said. "Since we've always worked alone, or we did until very recently, the Irichna won't expect us to troll for support. If things go well, we'd hoped for a small army of allies ready to attack once the demons show themselves."

"You'd have that with the Sidhe, if you'd just behave and trot along to the U.K. like good witches," Titania said. "Then we wouldn't need to go to all the trouble of tracking down the Unseelie." Her voice cracked on that last word, and a visible shudder traveled down her tall, thin frame.

"I didn't trust them, either," Duncan said, "but they proved their worth." He wove an arm around Colleen and drew her close.

"Maybe then," Titania countered, "but they're notoriously fickle."

"Look." Colleen ducked from beneath Duncan's arm. "We can't control all the variables, but we can set a trap. I've hunted Irichna for the past half-century and then some. I know how they think. They'll show up." A feral smile split her face. "When they do, we'll nail them."

"If we follow along to the U.K. like *good little witches*—" Roz mimicked Titania's inflection so well Ronin bit his lip to keep from grinning "—it wouldn't be nearly as effective. The Irichna won't want to face a Sidhe army, so they'll revert to their stealth tactics where they pop in, wreak destruction, and disappear."

"Ronin and Duncan." Titania crooked a finger. "We must discuss this."

Ronin bent and whispered into Roz's ear. "Wish I could tell her to bugger off, but she's my queen and it would be poor form." With a final squeeze of her shoulder, he strode to the front of the room with Duncan a few paces behind.

Titania summoned magic and shrouded the four of them. "Why can't you just talk sense into your wife?" she asked Duncan. "If one of them agrees—"

"I already tried," Duncan cut her off. "I actually thought we had a plan, but then she got with the others and things changed."

"It's a decent plan," Oberon observed, his tone warily neutral.

"If it works," Titania retorted acidly.

"Why wouldn't it?" Ronin asked. "Duncan and I will be there to help it along."

"With a phalanx of others you have no history of working with," Titania said.

"This type of discussion was one of the reasons I left," Oberon muttered. He turned to face Titania and placed his hands on her shoulders. "I argued the Sidhe had become much too insular and that we'd cut ourselves off from virtually everyone, humans and other magic-wielders alike." He took a considered breath. "You disagreed rather vehemently as I recall."

"After that you left." She tightened her jaw. "I assumed you'd be back so we could continue the conversation, but you never returned. Maybe now you'll tell me why."

Ronin felt he was trespassing on a very private exchange. He coughed and said, "Perhaps Duncan and I should leave you two alone."

"No. Stay," Titania said. "Too much trouble to open the wards around us and redraw them." She tilted her chin up defiantly and met Oberon's gaze.

"I left because I saw no hope for our people," the king said sadly. "We were already damned near insufferable. We needed contact with others outside our blood. Since most of us sided with your worldview, it seemed easier to withdraw than to engage in constant philosophical battles where our subjects sent pitying glances my way."

"I wish you would have said that before you left." Titania narrowed her eyes in thought.

"Would it have made any difference?"

"Probably not."

He smiled dejectedly. "My assessment exactly. Fortunately, it's a new day with different players. I like the witches. They're a breath of fresh, very welcome, air." He met Duncan's gaze. "Congratulations on marrying one."

"So you're willing to endorse their half-baked idea?" Titania moved from beneath Oberon's hold on her and put her hands on her hips.

"Yes. Not only endorse it, we need to give them all the help we can. I was thinking of sending at least half a dozen Sidhe along with Duncan and Ronin."

"They'd have to keep their energy well masked," Ronin said. "Like Roz pointed out, the Irichna are fairly sharp."

Duncan pursed his lips together. "How about this? Let's see what sort of luck we have raising the Unseelie Court. Bubba, er Niall, can see if he can come up with a changeling or two to help."

Ronin picked up on Duncan's line of thought. "More than fifteen or sixteen of us would become unwieldy. As I think about it, ten's an even better number. So, three witches, two of us, two Unseelie, and three changelings might do it."

"What if there are sixteen demons like there were today, plus all their hideous minions?" Titania asked.

Duncan smiled grimly. "Then we'd be a tad undermanned."

Ronin snapped his fingers. "I've got it. We could have first string and second string, like the Americans in their sports games. So an additional ten or so ready to jump in if called."

Oberon nodded. "It could work."

Ronin bowed before Titania. "My queen. May I tell the witches they have our unconditional support?"

She frowned, but then her features cleared. "Goddess knows I do not like to lose, but maybe this has been a good lesson. I actually like your wife." She eyed Duncan. "I was prepared not to, but she's everything I was when I was young. Bright, gutsy, determined, not afraid to speak her mind."

"I think you'll find Roz has those same traits," Ronin said then held his breath, waiting for a barrage of criticism from the queen.

"She's much more abrasive," Titania said, "but it's understandable because she holds more magic than the other two balled up together. It pains me to admit it, but she might be a good match for you."

Ronin bowed again. "Thank you. I think."

"May we take our leave?" Duncan asked.

"Of course," Oberon said. "I'd actually like a little time alone with my wife." He held out his arms.

"I was wondering when you'd get around to that." Titania stretched her body against his and turned her mouth upward. Oberon slashed his down over hers and clasped her close.

Ronin averted his gaze so as not to trespass on an intimate exchange that was becoming more heated by the moment. He cleared his throat and said, "My liege, if you could alter your magic to let us out…"

Without breaking their kiss, Titania—or maybe it was Oberon—did something. A portion of the magic surrounding them shimmered, and Ronin stepped through with Duncan on his heels.

"Whew!" Duncan grinned. "For a minute there, I figured we'd be witnesses to the royal bed."

Ronin turned to him. "That makes two of us."

Colleen, Jenna, Roz, and Bubba converged on them. "Well?" Roz asked.

"Yeah, you were in there forever," Jenna said.

"They agreed to your plan," Ronin said, "with a few additions from us."

"Now you just wait a red-hot minute," Jenna snapped.

"Don't worry," Duncan broke in. "We just tacked numbers onto who will actually fight on our side, assuming they're willing."

"We wanted to see if you could scare up a couple more changelings," Ronin told Bubba.

Bubba jumped up and down. "Yes!" He fist-pumped the air. "Finally, someone appreciates us."

"Holy shit!" Colleen looked from Ronin to Duncan. "I adore Bubba, but—"

"Niall, my name is Niall," he corrected her.

She blew out an exasperated-sounding breath. "Yes, all right, but you don't follow directions very well. I can't imagine what it will be like trying to corral three of you."

"Well—" the changeling drew himself up "—you're about to find out."

Roz grinned. "So we are."

"I don't know about the rest of you," Jenna said, "but I'm beat. I'm going to take a bath and sleep until someone tells me I have to wake up." She kissed Colleen's cheek and then Roz's. "Come on."

She gestured to Bubba. "You could use a bath too. I'll draw you one." The changeling trotted after her, still chattering about how excited he was.

Duncan threaded an arm around Colleen's waist. "Bath and bed for us too, eh?" She leaned into him, and the two of them walked slowly away.

"Guess that leaves you and me," Roz said.

Ronin nodded. "Are you hungry?"

"Maybe a little. We could cruise through the kitchen. I'm fairly certain the demons didn't pollute it."

"Do you know where it is?"

Roz shot him a crooked smile. "You bet. Food's pretty important to me. The kitchen is usually the first place I scope out."

He took her hand and laced his fingers with hers, pleased when she not only let him, but also squeezed his hand. They made their way through the dining area to a pair of double swinging doors. He shouldered one open and motioned her through. A few witches milled about, grazing on food that sat out on stone countertops.

"I'll make us a couple of plates," Roz said. "We can take them upstairs. What would you like?"

"I'm not picky. Just select double of whatever you're having."

He glanced around the large room with its shiny stainless steel appliances. Bottles of liquor lined one ledge. He let go of her hand and wandered over to peruse the labels. Hoping mead would be all right, he took a full bottle and a couple of paper cups. When he caught up to Roz, she held an overflowing plate in each hand and was gazing at an uncut wedding cake. Multiple levels, each smaller than the one below, were covered with sugary, colored flowers.

"It looks wonderful," Roz said, "but I'm sure Colleen won't want to come back down here to cut it. We have enough to worry about without tempting fate by violating any customs."

"We can have it for breakfast." Ronin picked forks and knives out of a pile near the sink. "Ready?"

He held the door for her and they walked toward the main staircase. "Is your room bigger than mine?" she asked.

"No, but mine has a table with two chairs, so it might make eating easier if we didn't have to perch on the bed."

"Sounds good. I'll follow you."

He stepped off on the second floor landing and proceeded down the long hallway. His heart pounded just a little too fast, and excitement ignited his nerves. To hell with the food. He wanted Roz back in his arms, pressed against his body. He wanted to peel the layers of clothing off her so he could actually see her wonderful breasts, not just their outline through her clothes. He wanted to touch her and kiss her and sink himself into the heat of her body…

She giggled.

"What's so funny?" He pushed his door open, took one of the plates from her, and laid it on the small table, alongside the bottle of mead and the paper cups.

"Remember. I read minds."

He took her plate and placed it on the table across from his before closing the door. "I hadn't actually forgotten, but it wasn't front and center, either." He smiled broadly. "If you saw what's in my head and you followed me into my lair anyway…" He let his words trail off, hoping she'd say something encouraging.

Roz didn't disappoint him. She ran the tip of her tongue over her very kissable lips and held out her arms. "It means exactly what you think it does. The food can wait."

CHAPTER 8

Roz closed her arms around Ronin, and he hugged her back. They stood like that for long moments, bodies pressed together, breathing each other in. He was the same height she was, which made it easy to lose herself in his amazing eyes. They flickered warmly, but something hot and untamed flared in their depths. He moved an arm from behind her and laid his hand against her cheek.

"I wonder if you truly know how lovely you are," he murmured, with a catch in his voice.

Pleasure from the compliment warmed her, but truth intruded. "Thanks, but I'm too tall and too thin, and my face is stark and arresting, not lovely. Colleen's lovely."

He rubbed his thumb over her lips. "She's not my type."

"Maybe I'm not, either." Roz could have kicked herself, but her old habit of holding men at arm's length was impossible to break free of. "Sorry," she mumbled. "I—"

"Ssht." He wrapped his other hand around the back of her neck and kneaded tense muscles. Roz relaxed into his touch, not understanding how tightly wound she was—until he dug his fingers in.

"I like that," she said. "Don't stop."

He moved his hand higher, burying it in her braided hair. "You'll like this too," he said just before he slanted his mouth over hers and kissed her.

Roz tightened her arms around him and opened her mouth to his questing tongue. Because they'd kissed earlier, it felt safe, familiar, and hotter than hell.

Don't delude yourself, sweetie. He's anything but safe.

As if he'd been in her mind, he upped the ante on his kiss. His lips became firmer and more demanding, his tongue more aggressive. Her nipples pebbled against his chest, and breath caught in her throat. With a small, moaning sigh, she gave herself up to the hot tide roaring through her. He moved the hand that had been against her cheek around her body. When he reached her backside, he cupped it and pulled her against him. His erection jutted into the juncture between her stomach and thigh. Her throat tightened, and her heartbeat revved into double time.

With no warning, he moved his mouth away from hers. She pressed forward, wanting more kisses, but he said, "Turn around."

"Why?"

"I'm going to take your hair down. It's beautiful. Shiny and dark like raven's feathers." As he spoke, he placed his hands on her shoulders and turned her. His knowing fingers pulled pins and elastic bands from her hair. Once he had everything out, he undid her braids and ran his fingers through each section as soon as it was free.

"Are you sure you didn't have a hidden life as a hairdresser?" she asked a bit breathlessly. What he was doing to her head and locks felt amazing.

"Quite sure. You have the most wonderful hair. Dear goddess, I had no idea it would reach past your knees." Ronin swept her hair to one side and planted a kiss on the nape of her neck. He ran his tongue around the side of her neck and she twisted in his arms, wanting to kiss him back. He let her press her lips against his, but pulled away. "We'll have lots of kissing," he said with a husky yearning undernote to his voice. "Let me undress you. I've imagined what you look like ever since I met you at my home across the Atlantic."

"You already saw me naked downstairs," she countered.

He winked lewdly. "That didn't count since I was trying to be a gentleman and not look."

Roz choked back a laugh. "Fair enough. What about me undressing you?" She reached for his jacket, but he batted her hand away.

"That can come later." He unclipped her serape and unwound it from her body. Goose bumps rose along her arms in anticipation. Next, he took hold of the bottom of her black turtleneck and lifted it over her head, taking care not to catch her unbound hair.

A deep, satisfied male sound emerged as he gazed at her breasts. He filled his hands with them and rubbed her erect nipples before bending his head to take one in his mouth. He suckled her, the heat from his mouth almost unbearably sensuous as his tongue swirled her nipple into an even stiffer peak. Roz reached between them and closed a hand over his erection. His cock jerked against her hand, and he groaned low in his throat. She loved that noise. It was full of wanting and barely leashed desire.

He fumbled at the waistband of her jeans and undid the buttons. She helped him push her pants down her legs and then remembered her boots. A giggle escaped her. Ronin stopped licking her breasts and looked at her. "What?"

"Nothing. This is where we got to last time. My boots. Half of me is expecting Duncan and Colleen to come blasting in here."

"They won't."

"How can you know that?"

He furled his well-arched brows. "Because I set wards around this room. Strong ones." He snorted. "No interruptions this time. I plan to make love to you, and neither of us is leaving until we're sated." He made a little shrugging gesture. "Who knows? We may be in here for days."

A slow, lazy smile spread from her heart to her face. "I think I'd like that."

He glanced at her feet and her half-removed jeans. "I see the problem. Let me help." He knelt before her, loosened her boots, and steadied her while she stepped out of them. "My, my, a red serape and red socks. Never would've figured you for the flamboyant type."

Roz giggled again. "Red is a power color for Native people."

"Does that mean you have powerful feet?"

She mock-slugged his shoulder and slid out of the rest of her pants. "Get back up here."

"Why? I'm quite enjoying the view from this level." He cupped a hand over the tight, black curls between her legs. Warmth from his hand shot sensation through every pore of her body, and she rubbed her vulva against him.

"You still have your clothes on." She shoved at his jacket, and he let it slide off his shoulders.

"We'll worry about the rest of them later." He moved his hand and placed his mouth over her center. His tongue flicked out and caught her sensitive nub, circling it. Roz opened her legs to give him easier access. Heat poured through her, kindling each tiny nerve ending. Desire slicked her crotch. He reached around and held the globes of her ass. His questing fingers dropped lower. He moved them between her legs and pressed inside her while he continued to nuzzle and suck her clit. Her hips bucked against his face, but he just held on tighter. She could almost feel him willing her to come. He moved farther inside her, catching her most sensitive places with his fingertips.

Her belly tightened almost painfully. An orgasm spooled, liquid heat just waiting to be ignited. She buried her hands in his hair and thrust against his mouth. Spasms racked her as she came, and just kept on coming. Maybe he'd spun some arcane magic, but she'd never been so high, and he pushed her higher still.

Squeals and shrieks filled the air. Shock filled her when she realized they'd come from her, the original silent lover. Roz lost count of how many peaks he created for her, leading her skillfully from the apex of one to another, even stronger, climax.

Finally, panting and weak-kneed, she said, "No more."

He lifted his mouth from her streaming pussy. "You taste so sweet. I'm enjoying myself."

"Bed." She pointed. "I don't want to stand anymore."

"Whatever my lady desires."

He got to his feet, folded her into his arms, and closed his mouth over hers. He tasted of her and it made her hot all over again. Their kiss developed its own life, with his mouth covering hers and him breathing desire into her. Time stuttered and then stopped while they stood clasped together.

The jut of his cock against her belly brought her back into herself. She reached between them and undid the fastenings of his trousers. He helped her push them down his hips, followed by his underwear. She broke their kiss and stepped back a little. "I want to look at you," she said, her voice thick with desire. "All of you." She traced the line of his cock with an unsteady hand. He was perfectly formed, perfectly huge, perfectly beautiful. His skin held a dusky, golden hue, and he had a sprinkling of fine dark hair on his lower abdomen that led to a thick mat of black curls between his legs.

He toed off his loafers and stepped out of his dress slacks. She wanted to keep hold of his cock forever, but she moved her fingers to the studs that held his formal shirt closed. Once he was undressed, she could go back to his penis. He shook his head and went to work on his shirt. "Let me. They're tricky. I forget from time to time how they go."

"No formal afternoon teas at your castle?" she teased.

"Not often," he murmured, adding, "I thought you wanted to lie down."

"I do, after you're naked and I get a good look at you."

"Hussy."

She glared down her nose at him. "You've gotten quite an eyeful. I want the same."

He laid a handful of ruby studs on the table between their untouched plates and slid his shirt off his shoulders. Roz gasped. Her eyes widened. The man standing before her was flawless. Broad shoulders, bunching with muscle, led to a long, flat abdomen. His nipples were dark copper with the same sprinkling of hair around them that he had on his stomach. His arms and legs would have done Adonis proud. Even his feet were beautiful, with high arches and long, shapely toes.

He smiled softly. "I hope that little sigh means you like what you see."

"A woman would have to be dead not to appreciate you."

"I could say the same for you, substituting man for woman, of course." His gaze traveled appreciatively up her body and settled on her face. "Are we going to stand here admiring one another, or will you come to bed with me?"

"I could look at you until the end of days."

Roz had to remind herself to breathe. She ran her hands from his shoulders down his arms to the ends of his fingers and then moved to his torso. Touching him sent little shocks through her fingertips and up her arms until they settled deep in her stomach. She was hungry for more of him, which surprised her. She'd had more orgasms in the last half hour than she'd had in the whole last year, but they hadn't muted her desire at all.

He wrapped an arm around her waist and tugged gently. "Your bed idea was wonderful. Come on."

She walked beside him, their hips thumping against each other, until they covered the few feet to the double bed. He twitched the coverlet aside, sat on the edge, and drew her down beside him. She lay back, thinking he'd join her, but he just gazed at her and then tenderly smoothed a few stray hairs away from her face and shoulders. "You look like an exotic princess with your hair spread around you. Dark, mysterious, beautiful."

Heat rose to her face at the unexpected compliment. Although far from a virgin, Roz had never been with a man who wasn't interested in getting to sex as quickly as he could.

Ronin must have been inside her mind because he said, "I care about you, Roz. I'm not certain why these things happen, but you've been part of my thoughts constantly since the day we met. I want to make love with you, but I want to get to know you too."

He seemed to be waiting for her to say something, but she'd always played her emotional cards close to the vest.

No matter how I orchestrated things, I still got hurt.

"I—" She swallowed and tried again. "It would be a lie if I said I hadn't thought about you."

A crooked smile lit his face. "Even though I had to drag it out of you, I'll take it." He lay next to her and took her into his arms. First, he kissed her forehead, and then both eyelids, before moving his mouth over hers. She wrapped her arms around him and kissed him with a fervor she wouldn't have believed herself capable of. He deepened their kiss, burying his tongue inside her mouth.

Suddenly she couldn't wait. Her pussy muscles clenched in anticipation of his cock. She wanted him to plumb her, stretch her, take her and make her his. Part of her mind recoiled in surprise. Feminism had always been high on her list. So high, it spelled the death of more than one of her relationships when the man in question stomped out telling her she was a high-handed bitch.

What was going on that she wanted Ronin to take her, brand her, set his mark on her for the world to see?

He pushed her onto her back and knelt over her, his cock jutting in front of him. Color heightened the gold of his skin, and his nipples were tight little buds. She took hold of his ridged flesh, stroking it, and rubbing small droplets oozing from his glans to slick the rounded head.

"I need to be inside you," he said hoarsely. "I can't wait any longer."

She raised her legs and locked them around his waist, her gaze never leaving the classic lines of his face and his mesmerizing eyes. The passion in their depths burned hotter now. Roz was thrilled to know it burned for her. She settled her hands on his hips.

He nodded, wrapped a hand around himself and seated his cockhead against the opening to her body. "You created this," he said. "It's all for you, but we'll take our time."

He rotated himself around her opening, setting fire to her nerve endings. Gradually, he sank into her, but so slowly it drove her half-mad. She writhed beneath him, desperate to capture more of his girth inside her. When he hit bottom, he quieted, and his cock jerked with small muscle movements, teasing her. She tightened her hold on his hips and pulled hard.

He withdrew just as slowly and then plumbed her again. The look of ecstasy on his face warmed her. She wanted to bring him pleasure as intense as what he'd brought her. After a dozen long, slow strokes, their control fled like chaff in a stiff breeze. He drove into her and she met him stroke for stroke. Her next climax rocked her to her core, and her pussy dissolved in molten heat. Maybe her contractions brought him over the edge because he juddered hard inside her and cried out in Gaelic.

Still deep inside her body and breathing hard, he lowered himself until he lay atop her and then turned them on their sides. She tossed her leg over his to keep him firmly within her, and he kissed her gently.

Roz's eyes flew open and she drew back. "Awk! Damn it! We should've used something. Not that I can't take care of pregnancies, but…"

He tilted her chin so her gaze met his. "I control who I impregnate, and Sidhe are immune from human disease. I imagine witches are too, at least to a certain extent. Someday, we'll talk about children."

"Oh no, we won't." She wriggled in his grasp, but he held onto her.

"Why not?"

Confusion sparred with delight because he even wanted to have a conversation like that. "Um, maybe because I've never seriously considered having children. Besides, we barely know one another."

He kissed her cheek. "We're attending to that little problem quite nicely, don't you think?"

"Yes." She nuzzled his neck. "We certainly are."

"Back to the topic of children that sent you scurrying for higher ground."

She chuckled. "I did not *scurry*. No children discussions until the demons are dead, or vanquished, or however we get rid of them."

He smiled. "So feisty. It's one of the things I admire about you. Maybe no more children talk until I can court you properly and lay my heart at your feet. Was it good for you, darling? Not over too soon?"

She captured his hand in hers. "Making love with you just now was so unbelievable I don't have words for it."

His grin broadened, and a dimple formed in one cheek. "Men like to hear things like that, and they're even better when they're true."

"You have to stay out of my head."

"Why? It's a skill we share. You're welcome inside mine."

Roz considered it. "It feels like I'm trespassing. Maybe when we get to know one another better."

"Yes." He tilted his head and brushed his lips over hers. "We will get to know one another much better, Miss Roxanne. After what we just shared, the world's not a big enough place for you to hide from me."

"What about whoever you have stashed back in England?"

A surprised look washed over his face. "You mean a woman?"

She nodded, feeling nosy and forward, but she had to know if she had competition. "Or a man."

"Darling, look at me." She did and he drew her in with the sincerity in his gaze. "There's no one. Hasn't been since I lost Lorelei."

For a moment, she couldn't speak. "But that was hundreds of years ago."

"I swore I'd never fall in love again. It hurt too much."

"Why'd you change your mind? Or did you?"

He drew his brows together. "I'm not sure I have an answer—for either question. All I know is the moment you walked into that meeting at my home, I fell under your spell. It felt so right I welcomed it."

"I didn't cast one."

He grinned, and for a moment he looked young and carefree. "I know. There's another mysterious part too. Even though you have the best of reasons to resent me because of the mess with the Irichna and so many of your kin being killed by them, I planted myself square in your path anyway. I don't generally court rejection." He twitched his cock deep inside her, and she tightened herself around him.

Roz tilted her head and covered his mouth with hers. As they melted together in another searing kiss that tingled her nerves and warmed her heart, he started moving inside her again. A distant part of her mind wondered how long they could make love before they fell on their faces exhausted. Heat flared between her legs, and she figured they had a long way to go. If she got sore, she could always summon a spot of magic to smooth things over.

CHAPTER 9

*R*onin woke to daylight streaming through the window. Roz nestled against him, asleep in his arms. Taking care not to waken her, he let his gaze roam over her face. Strands of silky dark hair had fallen across her cheeks and forehead, and the tiny worry lines between her eyebrows had relaxed. She looked young, though he knew she wasn't, and vulnerable, though he knew she wasn't that, either.

They'd made love for hours, drowsing and then waking to pleasure each other again. She was an exquisite lover, ardent and forthright. Lorelei had been more passive, though he understood it wasn't a fair comparison since women had changed a lot in the intervening centuries. He closed his eyes and recalled an image of Roz kneeling before him, her dark hair falling around her and her mouth locked around his shaft. She'd worked him with her hands and mouth, bringing him to heights that filled him with unmanageable desire. He'd tangled his hands in her hair and driven himself hard into her mouth. He hadn't expected her to tease his anus with her skilled fingers. The added sensation shot him into a frenzy, and the world had dissolved around him.

Without quite realizing what he was doing, he pushed a brand new hard on gently into her belly. A soft smile parted her lips, and her eyes fluttered open. "Again?" she murmured sleepily and shifted a leg over his hip to open herself.

"Ronin!" Titania's strident mind voice startled him and he frowned.

"What?" Roz drew her brows together.

He shook his head and placed a hand over her mouth. *"I have wards up,"* he told the Queen of Faerie.

"Yes." Her voice held a dry note. *"Like a Do Not Disturb sign, but we need you. You've had hours to bed the witch. And you'll have hours more. Right now, we're holding a meeting to finalize our plans."*

"Let me guess." Roz snorted and batted his hand away from her face. "Our time's up."

"For now." Ronin cradled her close for another long moment. "Do you want to bathe before we go downstairs?"

"I probably should. This whole room reeks of sex, so I suppose we do too." She laid her cheek next to his and then pushed to a seated position and dropped her feet onto the floor. "Want to join me?" She twisted to look at him and winked lewdly.

"As much as the vision of you spread-eagled against the shower wall makes my cock quiver, I'll pass. If I join you, we'll never get out of here."

"Sissy." She stood and strode into the bathroom, giving him a luscious view of her acres of legs, slender ass, and strong shoulders. He heard the rush of water as she flipped the taps. To divert himself, he wandered over to the food still sitting on the table and munched a carrot stick, a piece of celery, and a buttered slice of dried-out bread.

Much sooner than he expected, the water quieted and Roz stepped from the bathroom swathed in towels. He smiled. "That was fast."

She shrugged and eyed the food. "Good idea. I'm famished. Maybe wedding cake for breakfast wasn't as far-fetched as it seemed when you said it last night."

He resisted an impulse to hug her because Titania had sounded quite miffed by his absence, and settled for blowing her a kiss as he went into the steamy bathroom. It smelled like Roz, and he inhaled hungrily. Ronin stepped into the tub and started the shower. As he soaped and rinsed, he thought about the Sidhe and how spoiled Titania had gotten because he was always at her beck and call. Hell, he'd always been there, even when she took long breaks from everything on one borderworld or another. He made it to drying himself before he decided things needed to change. The queen—and king—would just have to appoint a second-in-command because he was done being the go-to guy twenty-four seven.

Ronin snugged a towel around his hips and caught a glimpse of himself in the steamy mirror. A smile broke the grim determination stamped onto his face. It had never occurred to him to carve out a life for himself after Lorelei and his son died. He'd been grateful to be so busy he didn't have to think—about anything. He caught himself whistling and understood he was deeply relieved those days were over. He'd thought they'd never end, and it was invigorating to finally have something to look forward to.

"You're sounding much too happy." Roz stood in the bathroom doorway.

He turned to look at her. "You're smiling yourself," he observed. "Too bad you put your clothes on. It's a shame to cover such beauty."

She rolled her eyes. "I bet you say that to all the girls."

With a practiced flip of his hand, Ronin loosened his towel. It puddled around his feet and revealed his cock, fully erect. He wrapped a hand around his shaft. "For you." He repeated the words he'd said last night. "Look what effect you have on me. I can't remember how many times I came last night, and if Titania hadn't intruded, we'd still be in bed."

Roz crooked a finger and opened her arms. He walked into

them and bent his damp head to kiss her. She opened her mouth to his tongue and threaded her arms around him, pushing her body as close as she could.

Breath caught in his throat and he pulled away. "Hold that thought," he said. "I'm certain we'll find a private alcove later."

"There's always my house in Fairbanks." She was as breathless as he was, and her bronze skin held a rosy tint.

"I'm quite looking forward to it." He kissed her forehead, stepped out of her arms, and went to find clean clothing.

The patter of her footsteps followed him. "Be warned," she said, with a tension that hadn't been in her voice earlier, "my place isn't grand like yours."

He pulled on shorts and trousers, and then yanked a pale blue lamb's wool sweater over his head. Ronin shook water from his hair and finger combed it before turning to face her. "You could live in a hovel, and I wouldn't care because you were there."

One corner of her mouth turned down. "You say that now. I don't have servants."

He reached for her hand. "Instead of thinking what might go wrong, try thinking of all the things that are going right. Ready to leave?"

Roz looked at the floor. "You just uncovered one of my short-comings. I'm the original pessimist."

"I was too—" he tilted his chin "—until I met you. Come on." He opened the door, and she followed him into the hallway. They made their way downstairs and found everyone in the kitchen feasting on wedding cake, coffee, and tea.

"Have a piece," Colleen said around a mouthful. "No point in it going to waste." She quirked a brow at Roz. "My you're looking, well-fuck—, er relaxed."

"I've just got to find me one of those Sidhe studs." Jenna laughed warmly.

After a long moment, Roz joined in. "No secrets ever, huh?"

"Nope." Bubba moved from the other side of the table with a plateful of cake. "This is good, Colleen. Can I eat whatever's left?"

"No! You'll be throwing up all the way back to Alaska."

Ronin cut a slice of cake and handed it to Roz before cutting another for himself. She gave him a cup of coffee. "Do you want anything in it?" she asked. "Or maybe you'd prefer tea."

"This is fine. Maybe a little honey or sugar, but I'll chase something down in a bit." He strode to where Titania and Oberon sat with Duncan at a round oak table on the other side of the huge kitchen. Ronin inclined his head.

Titania peered at him for so long he grew impatient. "What?" he asked. "Have I grown two heads?"

"Sorry. Your energy is different. I was simply figuring it out."

Since he didn't want to touch *that* conversational gambit with a ten-foot pole, he asked, "What did you work out?"

Duncan got to his feet. "We made quite a few decisions. I suppose we might alter some of them if you have other ideas."

"Just tell me." Ronin took a sip of coffee. It was hot and bitter, but bracing. He drank again and set the cup down so he could go to work on his cake.

"We'll return to Alaska today," Duncan said. "We being you, me, the witches, and Bubba."

"And we will teleport to the U.K.," Oberon said. "Once there, we'll approach the Unseelie Court."

Naomi slipped into the kitchen, flanked by several witches. She made her way to the group around Oberon and Titania, her spine arrow straight. "We will raise the druids and other mages and solicit volunteers. I will assume a direct role in whatever happens next, as will three of my witches."

Ronin chewed and swallowed. "What about other changelings?"

"I knew I'd forgotten something," Duncan muttered. "Someone will have to escort Bubba, er Niall, back to the U.K."

"I heard my name, the right one." The changeling darted

forward. "I can locate changelings here, maybe not in Alaska, but if I put out a call, they'll find me—I hope."

"Excellent." Ronin played the plan through his mind, looking for flaws and grateful Bubba had a way to find his kin. He was certain Duncan wouldn't have wanted to take Bubba back to the U.K. because it would have meant leaving Colleen's side. For his part, he wasn't anxious to leave Roz, so that would have left Titania and Oberon to escort Bubba, a plan the changeling would probably never have agreed to. He hurriedly finished the cake and considered a second piece since he was still hungry.

"We're hoping the demons will hold off for at least a few days," Duncan said.

"So everyone can take their places," Titania added, "and be ready."

Something about her words caught Ronin's attention. "Where will you be?"

She arched a brow. "Canny of you to ask." She waved an airy hand toward Duncan. "He never did."

That's because he doesn't know you as well as I do.

Ronin smoothed his features and hoped to hell she hadn't been in his mind. "Are you willing to answer, my liege?"

"We'll be close." Oberon draped an arm around Titania's thin shoulders.

"It's better if you don't know exactly where," Titania went on. "That way no one can pluck the knowledge from you."

"You may need our help," Oberon said. "We control the power of Faerie. It could give you an added edge."

Ronin half-bowed. For once, it wasn't for show because he was truly grateful. "Thank you." He picked his coffee back up and took another sip.

Titania's mouth twitched. "Wasn't it you who said we were all in this together?"

"Not exactly," Duncan murmured. "It was one of the Unseelie."

"Are we done here?" Ronin asked before Titania could react.

She hated dark fae. It was nothing shy of monumental she'd offered to lay her feelings aside and solicit their assistance.

Oberon nodded and made shooing motions with the hand that wasn't threaded around Titania. "We'll communicate as we need to."

Duncan inclined his head and walked toward where Colleen, Jenna, and Roz had their heads bent together over cake and coffee. Ronin stopped next to the cake and cut himself another generous slice. He rustled through a couple of canisters on the ledge, found sugar, and added some to his coffee before joining the witches and Duncan. The changeling had settled in a corner with more cake.

"We can leave right after we're through eating," Duncan said once Ronin joined them.

Roz glanced around the group. "How? I mean we'll teleport, but who goes with whom?"

"Good question since we all have small travel packs," Colleen said, her gaze landing on Jenna, who cringed.

"Don't say it," Jenna muttered. "I'm sorry. I can catch a plane or something if it's too much trouble to—"

Roz held up a hand. "Not your fault. We all have magical strengths and weaknesses. Teleporting isn't one of your talents. I'll take you." She met Ronin's gaze. "Could you manage our things and maybe Bubba?"

"Certainly." He cocked his head. "I'll need one of you to tell me exactly where I'm aiming for. Or I can just show up in Fairbanks and Bubba can give me an address."

"What do you want to do about the car that's in Haines?" Colleen asked.

"Crap!" Roz slapped a palm against her forehead. "It's my car, so you'd think I'd remember it. How about this? Jenna and I will teleport there, get the car, and drive home. If we leave now, we shouldn't be too far behind you. It's something like a five or six hour drive."

"Unless there's a blizzard, and then it'll take longer. Lots longer," Jenna said gloomily.

Roz shrugged. "We'll do the best we can." Her dark gaze traveled around the group. "Does that work for everyone?"

Ronin bit his lower lip. It didn't work for him because he didn't want Roz by herself.

She won't be, she'll be with Jenna.

Doesn't matter, she won't be with me.

Roz made her way to his side and hooked an arm through his. "We'll be all right. Truly we will. Jenna and I have faced worse things than winter weather."

"I'm not sure I like it, either," Colleen said, her forehead furrowed in worry.

"Do they have driving services here in the States?" Ronin asked.

"What do you mean?" Roz glanced at him.

"Transport services, where you pay someone to drive a car somewhere for you."

"I'm sure they have them," Roz said, "but maybe not in Alaska in the dead of winter."

"I can call the ferry terminal and ask," Colleen offered. "If we slap enough money on the table, someone will take us up on it. The ferry authorities have the keys. They needed them to transfer the car from one ferry to the next after we dropped it off in Bellingham." She slipped her cell phone out of a pocket, tapped its display, and asked Directory Assistance for the number.

While Colleen took care of that, Ronin set his plate and cup down. He moved to Roz's side and spoke low into her ear. "I think splitting up is a bad idea. I can't articulate exactly why, but we're stronger together."

"Even if you hadn't said that," she whispered back, "Colleen's instincts are rarely wrong." She leaned against him and he wrapped his arms around her, enjoying how her long, lean form felt next to him.

A few minutes later, Colleen put her phone down. "That was easy, maybe too easy, but I found a volunteer. They'll leave later today and drop the car at our shop in Fairbanks."

"How will we pay them?" Jenna asked.

"How else?" Colleen smirked. "PayPal. They gave me their e-mail."

"How much?" Roz asked.

Colleen squinched her pretty face into a grimace. "A thousand bucks."

"What?" Roz shrieked. "Where the hell will we get that? We barely have enough to cover rent, food, and heating oil."

"Don't worry about it," Duncan and Ronin said in a single voice. The men looked at one another and grinned.

"Guess we've got that one covered." Duncan nuzzled Colleen's neck, scooped a dollop of frosting off her plate, and popped it into his mouth.

"If we're back to plan A," Roz said, "I'm going upstairs to get my things together."

"I'll do the same," Jenna said.

"I'll pack Bubba's things and take them with Duncan and me." Colleen got to her feet.

Ronin followed Roz out the kitchen door. Once they'd gotten a bit of distance from the others, she turned to him. "It's one thing for Duncan to help Colleen. They're married. I'm not comfortable with either of you ponying up money for me."

"Noted." Ronin placed an arm around her and rested a hand on her hip as they mounted the stairs.

"What? You're a Star Trek fan?"

"Not exactly, but I liked Captain Picard and Commander Riker. Kathryn Janeway too."

"Seriously—" she began, but he shushed her and walked beside her to the third floor where her room was.

Once they were inside, he turned her in his arms and closed his mouth over hers. He put his heart into the kiss and told her how much she meant to him in a way he hoped would be more powerful than mere words. His cock hardened against her belly, and he considered just lifting her over it, except her pants posed a problem. It would be easier if she wore skirts…

Roz withdrew her tongue from his mouth and moved back an inch or two. "First money, then skirts." She quirked a brow. "What next? Will you insist on selecting my spells for me?"

With a start, he understood she'd been in his mind and was deeply pleased she cared enough to want to know what he was thinking. He kissed the tip of her nose. "Now that you mention it…"

She mock swatted him and gathered her few things into a travel sack with a shoulder strap that slung easily around her body. "It's surprising," she said after a pause, "that I'm not fighting you more. I'm used to being queen of my own ship."

"You'll be my queen," he said. "Maybe over time, you'll find it's better than being alone."

Roz's dark eyes widened. "You can't be asking me to marry you," she sputtered.

"Why not?" His blue gaze met hers in challenge.

"We scarcely know one another."

"Any other reason?"

Though she obviously tried to fight it, her generous mouth broadened into a smile. "None I can think of at the moment, but give me time."

"If the goddess is good to us—" he held out a hand for her packed bag "—we'll have all the time in the world."

She came to him and laid her hands on his shoulders. "I hope to hell you're right about that." Roz glanced at the floor. Her long eyelashes swept the upper curve of her cheekbones. "Come on, let's get your things. Colleen's not the only one who has bad feelings about all this."

He sharpened his gaze, trying to see past the worry in her eyes. "Anything specific?"

She shook her head, and her unbound hair bounced around her. She shoved it aside impatiently. "Nothing I can put my finger on, but it feels like ghosts are having a wake on my grave. Remind me to put my hair up while you get your things together. It'll just get in the way, otherwise. My pins and elastic bands are probably still on the table in your room."

CHAPTER 10

Ronin kept an arm firmly around Roz as he escorted her back through the second floor hallway and down the stairs to meet the others. They hadn't said much while he gathered his few belongings and she braided her hair, but the silence felt intimate—warm and bursting with wonder at having discovered one another. They'd shared a last, lingering kiss before leaving his room, the imprint of her lips still warm against his.

"It will be good to get this ball in the air," Roz muttered as they reached the bottom of the stairs.

He wanted it not only in the air, but firmly dispatched and over with. Voices rose and fell from the vicinity of the generous entry area. "Looks as if everyone is waiting for us," he observed.

Roz picked up her pace. "Let's not make them wait any longer." She fell in next to Jenna once they reached the group.

"We're decided then." Colleen glanced from one to the other of them. "We're aiming for Gibbs Street, one block north of our house."

"Probably better that way," Jenna agreed. "It will give us a chance to make certain no one booby-trapped the house."

Naomi popped into the airy entry hall where they'd congregated. She walked to Colleen and hugged her. "Congratulations on landing a hell of a great guy. Remember, I did your Tarot spread and astrological synastry after Duncan asked me to marry you two, so the marriage will be bulletproof." Colleen hugged her back and Naomi added, "I'll meet you in Fairbanks no later than three days from now."

"We'll look forward to it." Colleen kissed her cheek. "Thanks for everything."

"It was my pleasure, demons and all." Naomi faded back down a long hallway.

"Since we'll be coming out in the open, are you certain it won't be light enough for someone to see us?" Ronin asked and readjusted the straps from his bag, Jenna's, and Roz's so they crisscrossed his chest.

"It's nearly four here," Jenna said, "which means it's three at home, so it'll be pitch dark."

"People don't hang around outside much in the winter in Alaska," Colleen cut in. "It's too cold."

"Come on." Ronin held out his arms and the changeling jumped into them. "*Ooph*." He straightened. "You're heavy. It's all that cake."

Bubba made a face and settled against him. "We'll leave last," Ronin said and watched while the air around Roz and Jenna shimmered and thickened. In moments, the witches vanished. He tipped his head toward Duncan and Colleen, similarly burdened with travel packs.

Colleen smiled at the changeling. "Take good care of Ronin."

Bubba gave a thumbs-up sign, and Colleen and Duncan left. The changeling bounced in his arms. "Come on. Let's get going."

"Anxious to get home?"

Bubba nodded. "We haven't spent much time there lately. Don't tell anyone, but I like being a cat there. The mice are nice and fat, so they don't run very fast."

"I'm sure they were grateful for a break." Ronin smirked, and the changeling smirked right back. "Sit tight and enjoy the ride."

"What is this, an airline?"

"In a manner of speaking." Ronin summoned power, keyed in coordinates, and let his wizardry sweep him and the changeling through the magical ether that blanketed this world and others. The place between the worlds was silent and dark. Ronin hadn't expected a long journey, but the sound of wind ripping through tree branches rose so fast it surprised him.

"Aw shit," Bubba muttered. "It's a mother of a storm."

Must be, if it reached in here.

Ronin adjusted his magic, double checked his coordinates, and brought them out into a snowstorm with tumbling, blowing ice pellets. He peered through the whiteout but couldn't see a thing. His bare hands and head numbed immediately, so he drew warming magic around himself and the changeling.

"Which way?" he asked Bubba.

The creature shut his eyes. "One block dead ahead."

Ronin couldn't see a thing, so he hoped the changeling had a decent sense of direction. Plunging through snow that came past his knees, he decided the first order of business would be coming up with winter clothing. Surely, he could buy what he needed in town. Wind whistled, battering the magical shrouding around them. No matter how hard he tried, Ronin couldn't see houses or cars or anything to indicate they'd even arrived in the correct place.

"Is this weather normal?" he asked.

"Pretty much. It's winter. Back up, and then turn right. We missed it."

Ronin wasn't surprised. "How far back?"

"Maybe six steps, maybe ten. I'll tell you." Ronin backtracked until Bubba said, "Here."

With his shoulders hunched against wind that somehow made it through his shielding and tried to flatten him, Ronin pushed forward.

"Right again," Bubba said. "Watch out, there are steps, but you can't see them because they're buried in snow."

Ronin glanced upward and saw lights flicker through the murk. "There?" He jerked his chin.

"Yes." Bubba wriggled. "Put me down."

"Not until we're inside." Ronin stumbled on something, maybe the ice-coated edge of one of the steps Bubba had mentioned. The lights were actually helpful once he topped a rise and mounted the last set of a dozen steps to a broad wraparound porch he could actually see. The house had at least three stories and was constructed of weathered wood in a nondescript color.

Before he got to the porch, the front door whooshed open and someone shrieked, "Hurry. It's like an icebox in here as it is."

Ronin didn't wait for a second invitation. He sheathed his magic and staggered through the door, grateful when it slammed behind him and the incessant drone of the wind lessened.

Bubba squirmed. "Put me down," he said again.

Ronin set the changeling on a threadbare carpet, and he capered off, dancing in small circles. Roz came to him and bowed. "Welcome to Alaska." She winked. "Weather like this is reserved for the truly special."

"Goddess's tits! Is it always like this in the winter?" He shook snow off his clothing and shoes.

"No," Jenna said from where she was crouched next to a wood-stove. "Sometimes it's worse."

Ronin scanned the room, relieved to see everyone. He'd expected to be the last to arrive since he and Bubba had left last, but it still seemed like a small triumph they'd all made the transit safely. "Has the house been disturbed since you left?"

"I don't think so," Duncan said. "The blizzard complicated things, but Colleen and I did a magical sweep before we walked inside."

"Yeah, they wouldn't let us in until they were done." Roz wrapped her arms around herself and shivered.

Ronin sent his magic spinning outward, questing for clues the others might have missed. He picked up demon stench, but it was old. He dared hope they might get lucky, just this once, and have a respite before they had to fight again. If fortune smiled on them, the Irichna would hold off until they were truly ready for them. He shivered too. "Why is it so cold in here?"

"Because the furnace is acting up," Roz said. "It's old, and the thermostat malfunctions if we're not here to tend it. We'll be lucky if the pipes didn't break. They're wrapped in heat tape, but that only helps as long as the power didn't go out. Won't know till we turn something on if we have a problem."

Ronin sent a grin Duncan's way. "Reminds me of the Middle Ages—except it never gets this cold in the U.K."

Duncan snorted. "Now that you mention it, there is a passing resemblance."

"Don't say I didn't warn you—" Roz began, sounding exasperated.

Ronin moved to her side. "I'm joking, darling."

A blast of magic glittered over by Jenna, and tinder in the woodstove blazed to life. "This'll help some," she said. "Did anyone try to turn the furnace on?"

Colleen muttered curses and then said, "Crap! Let me take care of that." She trotted to the far wall and clicked a thermostatic mechanism. The muted whirr of machinery filled the air. "Thank Christ! It's going to cooperate."

"I'm surprised it gives you so many problems. Do you have any idea why?" Ronin asked. In his experience, modern heating rarely failed.

"Sure," Colleen answered. "If the oil gets too cold, it won't vaporize properly, and the furnace won't light until one of us goes down there and warms things up with magic."

"What does everyone else do?" Ronin asked.

"Who knows?" Roz shrugged. "They probably have newer units than ours."

Bubba danced back into the room and tugged on Colleen. "I'm hungry."

She eyed him. "How about your cat form for a while? It will take time to settle in and get dinner online."

He nodded, after shooting a surreptitious glance Ronin's way. Colleen flicked her fingers, and the changeling shimmered into a large, black cat.

Mewing and purring, he slithered out from the clothing he'd worn, and raced for the far end of the room.

"Never fear, little man, your secret is safe with me," Ronin sent after the scurrying cat, but all he got in return was a tail twitch.

Colleen bent and picked up Bubba's clothes, laying them on a nearby sofa. "I'll take a peek in the pantry and see what we can whip up for supper."

"I'll help as soon as I'm done here," Jenna said from where she fed larger pieces of wood into the stove.

"I need winter clothes." Ronin glanced at Duncan, who nodded agreement.

"Parkas, boots, hats, gloves," Colleen agreed. "We can get everything tomorrow in Fairbanks. If anyone needs me, I'll be in the kitchen."

"Anything I can do, sweetheart?" Duncan asked his bride.

"How about if you come along, and we'll find out." Colleen winked and swished her ass from side to side as she left the room.

"None of that," Jenna called after her. "We want to eat some-time tonight."

Roz locked gazes with Ronin and asked, "May I show you the house?" There was something almost painful in her dark eyes, as if she were afraid he'd find her living space lacking.

Ronin moved to her side and hooked an arm through one of hers. "That would be splendid. Maybe by the time we're done with the grand tour, it will be warm enough I can stop funneling extra magic to my fingers and toes."

"Don't count on it," she muttered and broke out laughing.

~

Roz leaned into Ronin's warmth. She wanted to get this part of things over with, so he wasn't under any illusions about how she lived. "We have a shop in town," she said. "Jenna usually stays in a room above it, but she has a room here too. We'll start with the attic." She traipsed up two full flights of carpeted stairs and then one more three-quarter flight with bare wooden risers. A door at the top opened to a long, low hallway, paneled in knotty pine.

"You probably couldn't see it when you were outside," Roz went on, "but the roofline's complicated. It gives us fits patching it every summer."

Ronin glanced at the various angles butting against one another in the ceiling. "I see what you mean."

"It can be cold up here," Roz said, "because the central heating ducts don't extend this far, but when the rest of the house is warm, and has been for a few hours, heat rises, and it's not too bad when we leave the stairway door open. Colleen's room is there," she pointed, "and Bubba's is across the hall."

"Where's yours?"

She hip butted him. "What a leading question. We're getting to that." She backed down the narrow attic stairs and waited for him to join her on the third floor landing. "Jenna's bedroom is the last one on the left. The other rooms on this floor are for sewing and storage and drying and preparing the things we sell at the shop."

He clasped her hand. "Stop worrying. Everything is fine. I'm not secretly cataloging problems."

"Really?" She risked a glance at him.

He nodded. "Really. Help yourself to my thoughts."

"But it's so different from your castle..."

He turned her so she faced him and placed his hands on her shoulders. "Castles and manor houses are common as goose grass all through the U.K. and the E.U. too. I've lived there for hundreds of years and modernized it along the way. It has leaks and electrical problems and plumbing snafus, just like any house. It's you I want. When I told you I didn't care where you lived, I meant it."

He covered her mouth with his and kissed her. She fell headlong into the kiss until her breath hitched and her nipples ached where they pressed against his chest. When he pulled away, he said, "Where's your room? I asked before, but you didn't tell me."

A corner of her mouth twitched in amusement. She'd been considering just backing him up against a wall, undoing his pants, and sucking him until he shuddered in her mouth.

"We can do that too." He quirked a brow. "But we need privacy. What if someone comes upstairs?"

She waggled a finger. "Tsk, tsk, you were in my thoughts again. If anyone happened on us, they'd have the decency to pretend we weren't there." Roz grabbed his hand. "Come on. Let's go down one more flight. I have two rooms and a bath at the far end of the hall."

She led him to the door that opened to her retreat. At the last moment, she tried to recall how she'd left her quarters, decided it was too late to worry about it, and pushed the door open. Roz glanced at her room and tried to imagine how it might look to him. Her old-fashioned bedframe with its richly carved dark wood head- and footboards sat in front of dormer windows. Thank God it was made—sort of. A matching armoire, two bed stands, and a ten-drawer chest were scattered about. She'd found the furniture at an antique shop and broken every rule in witchdom when she'd used magic to suggest the owner sell the pieces to her at a steep discount.

A thick, patterned Oriental rug covered the floor and hand-painted glass lamps sat on the bedside tables. "The bathroom is through that door, and my study is in here." She crossed the room and pushed open another door to a room paneled in floor-to-ceiling bookshelves. Her huge, messy mahogany desk was pushed beneath a window, and her computer, which she never turned off, hummed merrily. Ronin strolled around her and peeked at some of the shelves.

He turned to face her. "We're quite a pair."

"What do you mean?"

He shrugged. "Just that I do the same thing. Books and scrolls alongside a computer. Grimoires and electrons."

She smiled. "They're not a bad mix."

"Neither are we." He glanced at her desk. "Looks like quite a playground."

Her face heated. Even though it had never happened, she'd imagined being bent over her desk with someone's delicious cock taking her from behind. Had Ronin plucked the image from deep in her mind?

He moved to her side, picked her up as if she weighed nothing, and plunked her on the desk. Once she was there, he bent to unlace her boots. "See?" He looked up and met her gaze, blue eyes twinkling with merriment and lust. "I'm a fast learner. Now if you wore skirts, those boots wouldn't matter."

Breath clotted in her throat, and it thickened with a sudden rush of desire. "No one wears skirts in Alaska in the winter."

"I'll bet the pioneer women did." He dropped her boots on the floor, gripped her waist, and set her back on the carpeted floor. His nimble fingers undid her jeans and slid them down her hips. "Turn around." His voice was rough with yearning. Roz understood perfectly because she wanted him with the same ferocity.

Just like in her fantasy, she leaned over her desk and spread her legs. Moments later, he reached between her legs and cupped her vulva with his hand, inscribing small circles around her clit. She moaned and pressed against him. Electric current traveled from where her nipples were flattened against the desk to her core. He rubbed faster and her hips bucked helplessly.

"Tell me what you want," he said into her mind, the telepathic words seductive, suggestive.

"Your cock. I want you to fuck me." Roz heard raw need in her

mind voice and cringed away from it, but it apparently didn't bother him.

His cockhead pushed against her opening, but he kept on rubbing her clit. *"Was this more like what you wanted?"* He pushed inside her, but only a little bit. She rotated her hips, frantic for more of him. *"No hurry, darling."* He sank a little farther in and stopped.

She gripped him with her muscles and pushed back, but he held her hips with the hand that wasn't teasing her clit, and wouldn't let her move him deeper.

"Come," he suggested silkily. *"Come for me and I'll give you what you want. All of what you want."*

Almost as if he'd used compulsion—who knew? Maybe he had—her belly tightened and her clit swelled and stiffened against his questing fingers. The world canted crazily and she held two perspectives, the one from inside her body, and the one from inside his. Roz had no idea how he'd done it, but the sheer eroticism of sensing the heat of her body around his cock rocketed her over the edge, and she came, shrieking and moaning and rocking her hips into his hand. Before she was done, he sank full length into her, stretching her, spreading her, heating her beyond reason.

"Yes," he breathed into her ear. "Yes. I love to watch you come. Your back is splotchy with passion, and you've got the most amazing ass." He withdrew and pressed back inside, fingers still rubbing her clit.

"Move, goddammit," she said. "Fast, hard. I want to feel you come." And she did. She'd always wanted to know how men experienced orgasm. From her new bifurcated view, she felt her pussy liquefy around him, felt him swell inside her, felt each stroke in his glans and in her vault and in her nub rolling between his fingers. Roz knew when he passed beyond control. She felt his balls tighten, felt semen pool at the base of his cock and shoot outward. Somewhere in the midst of the wonder of his orgasm, she came again, harder than she could have imagined, the spasms so intense the room spun.

He collapsed atop her heaving form, his cock still deep inside her. "How did you do that?" she demanded when she could talk again.

"Do what?" he asked innocently.

"It felt like I was inside your body, and inside mine at the same time."

"Ah, that." He made a deep, contented male sound. "I wasn't certain you'd like it."

"I did. Do it every single time." *Oops! Maybe too forthright.* "Um what I meant was—"

"Don't backpedal. I like my women demanding. I want you to desire me, yearn for me as much as I do for you."

He pulled his cock from her body, wrapped his arms around her, and tugged her upright and against him so her backside nested against his stomach. He cupped her breasts and ran a hand down between her legs. "I'll give you pleasure beyond what you've ever dreamed of, Roxanne Lantry. And then I'll double it."

Somehow, she didn't doubt him in the least. Roz turned in his arms and captured his face between her hands. "You're so beautiful. I'd love to just hole up in here and never come out, but we probably should join the others and help with dinner and making a few plans." She swallowed hard. "In case the demons surprise us, we ought to have something in place."

The planes of his face, which had softened with passion, reformed in solemn lines. "I'd love to stay here too. Hell, what I want to do is drag you back to the other side of the Atlantic and build wards around you so nothing will ever harm you." At the look on her face, he hurried on. "Don't worry. I know that wouldn't work. I don't want to change anything about you. You're perfect just the way you are."

A soft glow began in her belly and spread to her heart. "So are you," she said, and bent to retrieve her jeans.

CHAPTER 11

Two days had passed relatively uneventfully, and they were gathered around the old-fashioned oak table in the kitchen picking at the remains of a pot roast Jenna had cooked. Roz drained her glass of Bordeaux and reached for the bottle. "Damn! It's empty."

"There's another on the counter," Duncan said.

Roz pushed her chair back, wincing at the scraping noise its legs made against the wooden floor. She retrieved the bottle and the corkscrew and set about opening it. When her jaws began to ache, she realized her teeth were clenched together.

"What's wrong, hon?" Colleen's clear, blue gaze sought hers.

Roz shook her head and fell heavily into her chair, bottle in hand. "Not sure. Before we even left Seattle, I had this sense of impending doom. It's ebbed and flowed since then, but it's bad again tonight."

Jenna narrowed her eyes. "Do you sense demons?"

"No, nothing so clear cut." Roz pressed her tongue against her teeth and then blew out an exasperated breath. "I'd feel better if I recognized whatever keeps plucking at the edges of my magic."

"Whatever it is isn't very intrusive," Ronin murmured. "We've been into town a couple of times. Your car even showed up as scheduled."

"Yesss." Roz drew out the hissing part of the word. "Everything's been too easy, as if someone wants us to relax, let our guard down." She shifted her gaze from Ronin to Duncan. "Have either of you heard from the Sid— um, I mean from anyone?"

Duncan shook his head. "I haven't." He raised a quizzical eyebrow Ronin's way, but he shook his head too.

"Naomi should be here by tomorrow," Jenna offered. "Hopefully with a few other witches and the—"

Roz made a chopping motion with one hand and switched to telepathy. *"We shouldn't say too much,"* she cautioned. *"Not out loud, anyway."*

Bubba, who'd been uncharacteristically silent, stopped eating. "I put a call out right after we got back, but so far nada on my end too."

Roz wasn't sure whether to be worried or grateful. One changeling was handful enough, although they were fearless and damned helpful battling Irichna. "Maybe it's nothing," she muttered and refilled her glass. "My nerves must be working overtime."

Ronin clasped her hand. "Your nerves seem intact to me."

Roz nearly spit her wine all over the table. She managed to swallow before shooting him a look. "Those are only *some* of my nerves," she informed him loftily.

"Want to go test all of them out?" He winked broadly and Roz's heart sped up. When they hadn't been shopping and taking care of chores, she and Ronin hadn't missed an opportunity to pleasure one another. So far, they'd made love in the back of her car, up against a wall in the kitchen when everyone else was outside shoveling snow, in the basement when they'd gone down to coax the cantankerous furnace into putting out more heat, and in her bed. He was an inventive lover, and his enthusiasm for her body sparked her blood beyond her wildest imaginings.

Something glimmered at the edges of her vision, gray-blue, then white, then nothing. Roz shook her head, all thoughts of Ronin's hard-muscled body driven from her mind. "There it is again," she said sharply. "The minute I get involved thinking about something else, it moves closer."

"I don't like the sound of that." Ronin drained his wine glass and got to his feet. "I'll just have a bit of a look around. Duncan?"

He rose. "Right behind you."

Once the two men filed out of the room, Roz exchanged worried glances with Colleen and Jenna. Bubba kept right on eating. If danger lurked, it hadn't kicked off his magical senses. "Any ideas?" Colleen asked.

"It's familiar, somehow." Roz squeezed her eyes shut to help herself concentrate.

"Familiar, how?" Jenna asked. "You already said it doesn't feel like Irichna."

Roz bent her head forward and pinched the bridge of her nose between her thumb and forefinger. "Fuck!" she muttered. "I'm missing something obvious. It's like knowing something, having it right on the tip of my tongue, but not being able to find the word." She looked up in time to see Colleen shudder. "What? You too?"

"I'm not sure if I'm picking up on your anxiety vibes, or generating my own. Something felt decidedly wrong a moment ago, though." She glanced at Jenna. "Did you feel it?"

"'Fraid not."

Roz's body stiffened as understanding slammed into her. "It's Naomi."

"Where?" Colleen swiveled her head as she scanned the entire room.

Roz stumbled to her feet. "She's trapped in the void where we teleport. Other witches too, but I don't know how many."

"I'll get the men." Colleen surged upright and bolted for the door, but Duncan and Ronin met her before she left the room.

"We heard everything," Ronin grunted.

"We have to help Naomi and the others." Roz's voice was harsher than she would have liked.

"It won't be easy," Ronin said.

"No, it sure won't. There's a lot of real estate in the magical ether between here and Seattle," Colleen cut in.

Jenna stood too, her features scrunched in worry. Bubba left his chair and trotted to Colleen's side. "Is this the beginning of the bad part?" he asked.

"Maybe." Colleen ground the word out and looked helplessly at Duncan. "Roz and I know how to teleport, but we haven't a fucking clue how to do anything but travel once we enter the ether."

"Have you ever searched it?" Ronin skewered Duncan with an unwavering gaze.

"No." Duncan's green eyes darkened to emerald. "Have you?"

Ronin jerked his head up and down, as if the motion cost him. "We need the dream guardian. He can guide us." A muscle twitched in his jaw. "Once I was in a godawful hurry and skipped that step. Turned out to be a colossal mistake since I nearly ended up in the *Dreaming* for eternity."

"What happened?" Duncan asked.

"When you enter the ether without a firm destination in mind, it turns into a confusing maze. After a very short time, it subverts your ability to think. I barely had the presence of mind to recall anyplace at all." A sheepish expression washed over Ronin's face. "I ended up on an atoll in the Pacific, but at least I escaped."

"Dream guardian… Do you mean the one who watches over the Dreamers' Paths?" Roz asked, half-afraid the answer would be yes. The Dreamers' Paths were a boon to magic wielders, providing both an escape and a way to focus and hone power, but the ancient spirit who controlled them was nasty and intolerant. Only witches with strong precognitive powers ventured into the dream guardian's realm. She'd always avoided it.

"That's exactly who I mean," Ronin confirmed, and the air

around him took on a shimmery hue. He extended a hand toward Roz.

"What?" She stood stock-still.

"You have to come with me. You'll recognize Naomi's energy better than me."

Colleen took a step forward. "I can go. I've been there before."

Duncan made a lunge for her arm. "If you go, I'm coming along."

Ronin made a dismissive motion with one hand. "Too many of us. The dream guardian isn't particularly open-minded." He eyed Roz. "If you don't want to come, I'll do the best I can." The glittery air around him thickened further.

Roz felt annoyed with herself. She covered the few feet between them and wove an arm around Ronin's waist. "I'm in."

He met her gaze and furled his brows. "There's my witch. Hold tight. We're almost gone."

Darkness swirled and the bottom dropped out of her stomach. A shiny, silver path opened before them. Fear gripped her and twisted her gut into a tight knot, but she forced it aside. "What's going on? We're not teleporting."

"We can't. We're walking the Dreamers' Paths. It's the only route to the dream guardian's realm. At least the only one I know. I'm sure the guardian has more direct ways to access his territory. You'll see…things along this pathway. Ignore them." He paused for a beat. "The path will narrow. It's probably better if you walk behind me. Just focus on my back."

Because the track truly wasn't wide enough for two, Roz dropped behind him. Fury at being ordered about almost displaced her discomfort. She'd known witches who became progressively more enthralled with the Dreamers' Paths. Over time, they faded away until the part of them linked to the real world vanished, leaving empty husks. An aunt of Jenna's had fallen prey to the Path's allure. Roz remembered the day they couldn't rouse her. It hadn't been pretty.

Specters crowded in from both sides. Dark, amorphous shapes. Some whined; others moaned. Bony appendages settled on her back and arms. Ice cold, they chilled her worse than an Alaskan blizzard. She glanced to one side, and a writhing mass of horror that looked like an Irichna leered at her.

"What's out there?" she asked, her throat so dry it was hard to talk.

"Your worst nightmares," Ronin said succinctly. "The less attention you pay them, the quicker we'll be off the Path."

"You could have told me that at the beginning," she sniped, feeling put out.

"It's against the rules."

"But you just told me now." Roz set her mouth in a hard line.

"The rule," he clarified, "is no early warnings before a mage sets foot along the Path. Once you're here, limited information is allowed."

"Who the hell would find out?" Annoyance sharpened her tension until it felt like a rodent with sharp teeth was trying to claw its way out of her belly.

"Ssht. We'll talk about this once we've secured help. If we piss the guardian off before we even get there, he'll send us packing."

Roz clamped her jaws shut and kept her gaze on Ronin's broad shoulders. They walked for what felt like hours, except it couldn't have been. Her time sense must be just as skewed as everything else here. Finally, Ronin slowed and the darkness around them grayed at the edges. A few more steps and the Path dissolved in a flurry of silvery motes.

"What now?" she asked.

He didn't answer, just took her hand and led her into a thick grove of ancient- looking trees. Moonlight lit the way, but she had no idea if this was Earth's moon, or another. They came out into a broad opening at the center of the grove. An altar of white stone sat dead center with runic writing carved into it.

Before she could ask anything else, Ronin turned to her and

laid his other hand over her mouth. *"We wait,"* he said into her mind.

She tugged her hand out of his and walked toward a flattish boulder, intent on sitting, but Ronin followed her and latched a hand around her arm. *"Before the altar. Standing,"* he explained.

Roz felt like a fool. Clearly the journey along the Dreamers' Path had rattled her. Of course she wouldn't sit in the presence of a god, or whatever the guardian was. She wished she'd asked more questions before they left, but there hadn't been time. Besides, sometimes she needed to experience something to know which questions to ask. A nasty thought shocked her and she shivered.

"Do you think this is an Irichna trick to separate us?"

"Maybe, but we didn't have much choice once you sensed Naomi." Ronin took her hand again. *"Focus on now. We won't be here long."*

She straightened her back and faced the altar side by side with Ronin. A few steadying breaths and she cleared her mind of everything but locating Naomi. Ronin was right. Even if Irichna were attacking her house in Alaska, there wasn't a damned thing she could do about it from here.

Moonlight brightened, illuminating the white stone of the altar until it glittered. Rustling footsteps approached through the trees, and a tall, broad-shouldered man appeared. He wore brown robes sashed with moonbeams, and his silvery hair was bound by a circlet of moonbeams that sat on his brow.

"Ronin. It's been a long time." The guardian didn't exactly smile, but the harsh planes of his face relaxed a little.

Ronin inclined his head. "Guardian. Yes, too long. Blessings on your house."

"And yours. Who is with you?"

Roz remembered herself and bowed her head. "My name is Roxanne Lantry."

"Ah—" he nodded knowingly "—a witch. What can I do for you, Ronin Redstone and Roxanne Lantry?"

"You're who sensed it. Tell the dream guardian," Ronin urged.

Roz swallowed, but her throat was painfully dry. "I fear some witches are trapped in the traveling ether."

"Why?" The dream guardian leveled his gaze at her. Images floated through his clear blue rises in an ever-changing collage.

Roz blinked, knowing instinctively she could lose herself in those eyes. "I'd been sensing something just out of reach for a while. I finally heard Naomi calling for help. She said she was trapped between teleport destinations."

"Are you certain it was a true sending?"

Roz shook her head. "No. I'm worried it was a ploy on the Irichnas' part to separate us, so they can attack our friends who are still in Alaska."

"Give me a moment. If witches are in the ether, I will sense them." The dream guardian swept his hands to the sides and let them join over his head. His robe fluttered, forming wings, and the moonlight illuminating both him and the altar became almost unbearably bright.

While she waited, Roz realized something. It might not be an either-or situation. Naomi could be well and truly trapped with her witches, and Irichna could be attacking in Fairbanks. The worst of both worlds. She chewed on her lower lip and waited. At least so far, the dream guardian had seemed reasonable.

The moonlight developed a reddish haze, and the guardian dropped his arms. Fury rolled off him in visible waves. "No one uses the ether for malfeasance. Unfortunately, meting out direct punishment to Irichna is beyond my ken."

"If you could help us locate the witches…" Ronin let his words trail off.

"I've already freed them," the guardian said.

"Where are they?" Roz asked, and then thought maybe she should have kept her mouth shut. When the guardian turned his attention her way, his eyes were red-rimmed and fire blazed in their depths. "Sorry." She half bowed. "We'll figure it out."

When she looked up, the altar was empty. She turned to Ronin. "What's the quickest way back?"

"Usually the Dreamers' Paths eject you when your time here is up."

"You didn't answer me."

Ronin draped an arm around her shoulders and hugged her. "No, I guess I didn't. I've never walked the Paths both ways. If we wait, the guardian should send us back. Keep your guard up. We have no idea what we'll find."

"He doesn't seem as daunting as I expected," Roz murmured.

"That's because he wasn't angry with us," Ronin said. "He was furious with the demons for breaking one of the sacred precepts."

"So he controls the Dreamers' Paths and the ether where we teleport?"

"And other pathways as well. All of them actually." Ronin tightened his arm around her. "Get ready. This will happen fast."

Roz spun magic outward to see what Ronin sensed. A subtle humming filled her ears and pressed against her body. Before she had time to assess it, she landed in her basement in Fairbanks with a solid *thunk* that rattled her bones. Ronin flickered into being a few feet away. It took her brain a moment to process the transition. Once it did, screams and the crash of breaking things battered her. Roz surged to her feet. The basement was empty, which made sense since its access was via a trapdoor and a ladder.

Ronin moved to her side and placed a finger over his mouth. She nodded and started for the ladder, intent on helping Jenna and Colleen, but Ronin didn't follow her. *"What are we waiting for?"*

"Hold up until we see what we face."

She turned reluctantly. *"I know what's up there. Irichna. I can smell them."*

He closed a hand around her upper arm. *"Let me link with Duncan."* Ronin's forehead furrowed and Roz battled burgeoning panic. The noise above them intensified, and she made hurry-up motions with her hands. Waiting was killing her, but she knew better than to disturb his concentration.

At last he nodded sharply. *"I've put out a telepathic distress call. Duncan did too. Help will arrive soon."*

"How soon? I need to move now. Jenna and Colleen need me." Impatience—and fear—chewed a hole in her guts.

"Shield your speech," Ronin cautioned.

"Forget telepathy. No one up there can hear us."

The air two feet ahead of her took on a numinous quality, and two tall figures—one male, one female—stepped through a gateway. The woman's black hair was shot with silver and drawn back into a long braid. Her dark eyes glittered dangerously. A form-fitting black gown covered her from shoulder to mid-calf. Lace-up black boots disappeared beneath its hemline.

Ronin bowed so low his hair swept the basement's dirt floor. "Thank you for heeding my call."

"Thank us when this is over," the man said. Dressed in black trousers and pants, his blond hair was close cropped, and his blue eyes flashed a challenge. "Let's go get those bastards."

Roz wanted to ask who they were, but there was scarcely time for introductions. It was enough they were here and willing to fight on their side. If she lived through the next couple of hours, she could ask all the questions she wanted.

CHAPTER 12

*R*onin led the way across the basement to the ladder and trap door. He'd expected help to arrive—it always did. What he hadn't expected was Gwydion and Ceridwen, powerful Celtic gods. He'd made a rule of never second-guessing outcomes, but he let himself hope they just might win this round. An ear-splitting roar sounded from upstairs.

"Humph," Gwydion grunted. "We've been discovered."

"I don't know as I've ever heard a more appealing call to arms." Ceridwen smirked.

Roz straightened her spine. "I don't care what the rest of you do. You can stay here all day chatting, but I'm leaving." She pushed past everyone and lunged for the ladder.

Ceridwen dropped a hand on her shoulder that stopped her dead. "Brave witch, but let us go first." Roz no sooner shook her off than the Celts levitated, oozing through the low ceiling scattered with heating ducts.

Roz covered the remaining distance to the ladder and climbed. "Who are they?" she shot over a shoulder.

"Gwydion and Ceridwen," Ronin answered. "We got lucky."

"You're fucking kidding me." Roz pushed against the trapdoor.

"I'd hold off on that *lucky* assessment until we see who's still alive up there. Damn!"

"What?" Ronin crowded behind her.

"I can't budge the trapdoor. Something must be on it."

"Climb down."

"No! While we're at it, stop ordering me around."

"Roz. You're not thinking. We can blast it open with magic, but I can't with you right in front of it. Or we could skip the whole thing and teleport upstairs."

The set of her shoulders stiffened. "Damn straight, I'm not thinking. I can funnel magic too. After what happened to Naomi, I don't trust teleporting right about now."

Before he could tell her to be careful because she'd be giving away their position, magic flared bright enough to blind him, and the trap door blew upward. Roz scrambled through the hole with Ronin on her heels. Thick smoke practically obliterated his vision until he fine-tuned his magic to see through it. His eyes teared and his lungs burned from the thick, unnatural air. Screams and shrieks, punctuated by crashes battered his hearing, but they came from the upper floors. He tried to force Roz behind him, but she had other ideas and bolted into the main room.

Ronin's nose twitched. He smelled death, but it was impossible to determine who or how many. He linked to Duncan, figuring he'd be with Colleen. *"Where are you?"*

"Third floor."

Ronin plunged through the murk, following Roz's energy, and grabbed her arm. "They're upstairs."

Roz whirled to face him, her dark eyes ablaze with fury. "I know what I'm doing, sweetie," she hissed. "I also don't need you to find Colleen and Jenna. They're all right. I just linked with them. Your Celt buddies are upstairs kicking some serious ass. Naomi and her witches are here, and they need me."

An Irichna morphed out of the near-impenetrable gloom. Roz loosed a blood-curdling howl and sent magic hurtling into it.

When her first blast didn't stop it, she kept lobbing bolts of death its way. The demon curved its red claws menacingly and side-stepped the worst of Roz's attack, while coming ever closer.

Without hesitating, Ronin opened himself and pulled power from the arcane well he'd used in Seattle. Maybe because he'd done it before, the magic flowed immediately. He focused it at the Irichna and the demon exploded, showering them with stinking bits of burning flesh.

"Thanks." Roz flashed him a feral expression that might have passed for a smile. "I'm going to open the door so some of this crap can leave. Diverting magic so I can see isn't working for me."

She's a warrior flashed through Ronin's mind, followed by momentary confusion. He wasn't sure how to treat her. Clearly, she didn't expect him to protect her, but if something happened to her because he didn't place himself and his magic between her and danger, he didn't know if he'd be able to live with himself.

"Ronin." Roz's hoarse cry cut into his thoughts, and he hastened across the big room by feel. Roz was on the floor, bent over the inert form of a witch he recognized from Seattle. The pair were squarely in front of the door, which was open. A chill breeze wafted in, but at least the thick smoke that stung his eyes and nose was dissipating.

"Aw, shit!" Roz raised her hollow-eyed gaze to meet his. "It's one of Naomi's witches. Damn!" She pounded a fist into the floor. "It's not right for them to die defending us."

Ronin tried out several conciliatory phrases and discarded all of them. Finally, he asked, "What do you need me to do?"

Tears sheened her eyes and she got to her feet. "Let's see who else we can find." She narrowed her eyes. "If the demons aren't already gone, they're at least leaving."

Ronin cast his magic wide. "You're right."

Roz rolled her eyes. "Of course I am," she snapped. "I'm linked to the goddamned things." She shook her head. "Sorry I'm so short-tempered. Or maybe I'm not sorry. I don't work for you."

"No, you don't, but that doesn't mean—"

A weak groan cut off his words and sent him sprinting for the kitchen side of the room. Ronin nearly tripped over Naomi before he fell to his knees by her side and placed a hand on her forehead. His magic augured through her, and he breathed a sigh of relief when he realized he could save her.

"Is she all right?" Roz scuttled next to him and took one of Naomi's hands.

"No, but she will be once I heal her."

Naomi's bloodied mouth moved. The witch's face was a collection of bruises and a long, jagged rent cut through her forearm. "Find Therese, Maggie, and Lou," she gasped.

"I'm on it." Roz sprang upright and disappeared through the smoke. Ronin stared after her. While the muck was thinning, it was still hard to see farther than five feet.

Ronin wanted to call after her and tell her to be careful, but he restrained himself and concentrated his magic on Naomi, whose color had improved. In another few moments, she shook him off. "It's enough," she said hoarsely. "You can do a better job later." She rolled to her side and tried to stand.

"Here." Ronin offered a hand. "Let me help you."

"Found the other two," Roz cried. "They're still alive! Thank the goddess!"

"Christ!" Naomi swore and set her mouth in a severe line. "Does that mean someone didn't make it?"

Ronin just nodded and helped her to her feet. "What happened to the druids and mages who were supposed to help you?"

"Cowardly bastards!" Naomi screwed her face up as if she'd tasted something bitter. "They never actually came out and admitted they were scared shitless, but the minute I said the word *Irichna*, they were chockfull of excuses."

So much for solidarity among magic-wielders.

Ronin swore he'd figure out who'd walked away from Naomi's request and make them sorry they'd ever been born. Several pairs of heavy footsteps sounded on the stairs. He shoved Naomi behind him and raised his hands to call magic.

"Hey, mate!" Duncan strode toward him. "Stand down. We're good."

Colleen and Jenna materialized on either side of Duncan. "Are we ever," Jenna said. "Whoever the hell those two newcomers were, I'd like to have them on our side permanently."

"No shit!" Colleen's smudged face broke into a grin. "The Irichna took one look at them and hightailed it out of here. Not that I wouldn't rather have had them dead—"

"You can talk about that later," Roz yelled. "Get over here. I need help."

"I want to see my witches." Naomi lurched toward the sound of Roz's voice and nearly toppled over.

Ronin wrapped an arm around her. "Lean on me."

"Thanks." Naomi stifled a grunt as she weighted her left foot, and Ronin understood she needed a lot more in the way of healing than he'd provided.

They made their way to where Roz sat between two witches. The air shimmered where she pulled healing magic. "I've got this one under control," she said, her hands on either side of a red-haired witch's shoulders. "The other one wasn't so bad off, but she still needs someone to work on her."

Colleen and Jenna exchanged glances. "I'll take a shot at it," Colleen said, "but Roz is the one with healing talent."

"Just leave me in this chair," Naomi told Ronin and patted a nearby padded lounger. "Help Lou."

Ronin settled her as gently as he could and joined Roz on the floor. The witch she was working on stirred and her eyes fluttered open. "Hush," Roz told her. "You'll be fine. Too much demon stench and a broken arm is all."

"Are they gone?" The woman's head thrashed from side to side as she tried to see. Roz nodded and the witch's hazel eyes flooded with tears. "Sorry," she wheezed between sobs. "But first we got trapped in the traveling ether, and then we got dumped out here in the middle of half a dozen demons."

"It's all right, Maggie," Naomi said. "Pull yourself together. I have a feeling we're a long way from the end of this nightmare."

Roz nudged Ronin and pointed to the comatose witch. He nodded his understanding, laid his hands on her head, and poured healing magic into her. In moments, she made sputtering noises and her eyes opened. Lou's gaze tracked from one of them to the other and she narrowed her eyes. "Where's Therese?"

"She didn't make it," Naomi said and coughed. "By the goddess, I'm amazed any of us did. I thought for sure we were goners when we couldn't escape our teleport spell."

Roz turned to her. "I heard you calling for help."

Naomi furled her dark brows. "So our rescue wasn't accidental. I thought as much. I want to hear about it, but not just now." She twisted her head and looked at Colleen. "Is there a bedroom where the three of us can lie down?"

"Of course." Colleen smiled gently. "It's upstairs, but we'll help you."

"Not until I have a few more minutes with her." Ronin spoke brusquely. "Lou and Maggie are in better shape than Naomi. She needs more healing time." He stood, walked to where the witch sat, and settled next to her so he could infuse more restorative magic into her broken body.

Lou pushed to a sitting position and raked her hands through her short blonde hair. Her blue eyes held a hard edge. "I honestly didn't think we were going to come out the other side of that one," she muttered. "Six Irichna were here when we showed up." She squeezed her eyes shut. "Damn if it didn't seem like they were waiting for us."

"No," Jenna said. "It was us they wanted. You were just collateral damage—"

"Hold up," Colleen cut in. "When's the last time any of you saw Bubba?"

"Who?" Lou looked confused.

"Her familiar," Naomi said and drew her brows together into a thin, worried line. She patted Ronin's hand. "It's enough. I want to be part of the discussion, not zoned out by mage craft."

"One more minute," Ronin murmured and sent a last jolt of treatment to her injured ankle before withdrawing his hands.

"Bubba followed us upstairs," Duncan said.

Colleen nodded slowly. "Yes, and he fought next to me. Then those two strangers showed up, and I don't remember seeing him after that." She worried her lower lip between her teeth and exchanged glances with Duncan. "Who were they?"

"Celtic gods. Gwydion, master enchanter and warrior magician, and Ceridwen—"

"Enchantress, shape-shifter, and mother goddess of the world," Colleen finished for him. "But that doesn't explain what happened to Bubba."

"Did the Celts leave?" Ronin asked, thinking maybe the changeling had gone with them.

Duncan inclined his head. "Yes. Right after it was clear the Irichna were on their way out, Ceridwen and Gywdion left too."

ROZ SCRUBBED the heels of her hands down her face. She hurled magic outward, searching, but couldn't sense Bubba's energy anywhere. "Do you suppose he went with the Celts?" she asked.

"Why would he do a thing like that?" Colleen demanded.

Roz blew out a tired breath. "Just because he's stuck to us like glue for forty years doesn't mean he isn't a free agent. He can come and go. Like when he went off to celebrate with his Scottish kin a couple of weeks back."

"How do I know an Irichna didn't snap him up?" Colleen wailed, hysteria treading just beneath the surface of her voice.

"Because he would've squawked like mad if they nabbed him," Jenna said. "He's done it before."

"Maybe they knocked him out or something," Colleen persisted and wrapped her arms around herself.

"If you want to try to track him, we can do that," Duncan offered.

Colleen nodded mutely. Duncan threaded an arm around her and magic thickened about them.

"Hang on," Ronin said. "We need to think this through a little better before we dilute our forces. Maybe see if we can't raise Gwydion or Ceridwen. They might know something."

"I'd love to help with this, but I'm dead on my feet," Naomi spoke up. "I don't have enough magic left to light a candle, let alone scry where your familiar might be."

"We can make it upstairs," Lou got her feet under her. "Just tell us which bedroom, and we'll get out of the way for a few hours."

"Second floor, first door on the left," Roz said.

"Thank God the smoke's clearing—" Maggie stood too "—but it's colder than a well-digger's ass in here."

"I'll get the door." Jenna loped toward it.

"And we'll see that Therese is laid out," Roz added. "When you get up, we'll have whatever ceremony you want to lay her to rest."

"Thanks." Naomi clutched Maggie's extended hand, and the three witches left the room.

Roz narrowed her eyes and tried to focus her mind on the Bubba disappearance problem. It wasn't like the changeling to take off without saying anything. She got up, walked to the antique cabinet where they kept liquor, and picked a bottle at random. Once she had it in hand, she unscrewed the cap, lifted it to her mouth, and drank. The liquor burned like a mad thing down her throat to her stomach, but it helped clear her head too. Something Naomi had said bounced front and center. She took another swallow of what turned out to be bourbon and surveyed the wrecked room and the small group of them.

"Can any of you scry the past?"

"I can," Ronin said. "Duncan too."

Colleen turned and raced for the stairs. "Come on," she shouted. "One of you come up here and see if you can figure out what happened."

Duncan and Ronin exchanged glances. "I'll go," Duncan said.

"Are you certain?" Ronin asked. "My gift is stronger, and I just teleported with the changeling so I know the feel of his energy."

"Oh, for Christ's sake—" Colleen, who'd disappeared up the stairs, came back into the living room "—would one of you just hurry? I'm worried sick about him."

Roz glanced from Duncan to Ronin. They were communicating. Magic crackled between them, but she had no idea what they said, and it didn't sit well. Despite Duncan being married to Colleen and her own blossoming relationship with Ronin, the Sidhe-witch divide still mocked her.

Ronin tromped across the room to where Colleen stood. "Stay here with Duncan," he said brusquely. "You're upset and that kind of energy muddies things." Without waiting for her assent, he pushed past her and started up the stairs.

Roz took another slug of booze before Jenna wrested the bottle out of her hand and drank deeply. The other witch scrunched her nose at Roz. "Let's get moving on clearing up the worst of this mess. We still have to live here."

"I don't like this," Colleen muttered, still staring up the stairs where Ronin had disappeared.

"Ronin's very good at this sort of thing," Duncan said, obviously trying to support both his wife and his leader.

Roz turned away and began picking up pieces of broken furniture. For the first time since she let Ronin into her life, he'd dropped into his Sidhe leadership role, and he'd done it as easily as most people slide on a well-worn pair of slippers. He didn't discuss things with Colleen. He just made a decision and presented it as a *fait accompli.*

He'd done the same thing with her before leaving for the dream guardian's realm: made a decision and set the wheels in motion without consulting anyone else. As it turned out, she hadn't had much of a role to play beyond being scared shitless on the Dreamers' Paths, and it probably would have been better if she'd stayed in Fairbanks. If she had, maybe Therese would still be alive...

Do I really want to live my life like this, where he pulls rank when he wants and just expects me to go along with whatever he's laid out?

Of course not. He's dynamite in bed, but I'll be damned if I'll sell my soul for the best sex I've ever had.

Roz was tired and cranky and out of sorts, but she didn't like her answer because it meant she should cut her losses and run for the nearest exit before she got in any deeper.

CHAPTER 13

*R*onin made his way to the third floor. Once there, he identified a power point, kicked his way through a mess of broken knickknacks and furniture, and stood dead center. While he lacked a pool, a chalice, or a cauldron, he had his mind. Images wouldn't be as vibrant, but it was the best he could do on short notice. He sucked in a steadying breath, and then another to clear his thoughts. Roz had seemed terribly out of sorts. She was angry with him, and they needed to talk.

He clamped his jaws together. Thinking about Roz was not a good idea. It would ruin the concentration he needed. Looking into the past was harder than reading the future, but a hell of a lot more accurate. He began a chant that would funnel magic through him and take him back an hour or two. The trick would be sifting through images, while not inadvertently inviting a demon into the house. He tightened his warding and felt his gut twist with determination. No way would he do anything to make their current problems worse.

For long moments nothing happened. He upped the ante and poured more juice into his casting. Finally, the deep, still pool in his imagination began to swirl. An Irichna flung magic wrapped in a bolt of black lightning, the image so lifelike, Ronin nearly ducked. Five more demons surged after the first one, and the scene in Ronin's mind came alive with Duncan, Jenna, and Colleen trading jolts of power with the Irichna. Duncan tried to stay between his wife and the demons, but she and Jenna obviously had their own agenda. Worry carved deep lines into Duncan's face as he did his damnedest to protect both witches.

Ronin could relate since attempts on his part to defend Roz had met with the same result. It wasn't so much that the demon assassin witches had a death wish, but they'd worked together for a long time and didn't take kindly to direction from anyone else. He almost lost control of his scrying spell as the reality of that sank in.

No wonder Roz was so surly.

Ronin sharpened his gaze, firing it with an infusion of deeper magic. He was almost certain he'd just seen the changeling in his snake form, slithering around behind the group of demons. Yes! There he was. While Ronin watched the past unfold, Bubba pushed his body upward, cobralike, and lunged at one of the demon's backs. Colleen shrieked at him to let go, but the changeling coiled his odd reptilian arms around the Irichna and sank his fangs into its neck.

Brilliant light flared. Ronin squeezed his eyes shut before he realized he wasn't seeing with *those* eyes. Feeling like a fool, he shifted his attention inward. Sure enough, Ceridwen and Gwydion had jumped into the fray. Ceridwen plucked Bubba from the Irichna, and he wound his snake form around the goddess. The demons hissed, snapped, and snarled, foaming black around their mouths. Gwydion laughed uproariously, made a chopping motion with one ham-sized hand, and the Irichna faded. Moments later, they were gone.

Colleen and Jenna raced toward the Celts, shouting questions. Duncan made a grab for Colleen, but she evaded his reach. Gwydion and Ceridwen exchanged pointed glances just before a spell boiled between them. Once it dispersed, they'd disappeared, taking the changeling with them.

Ronin was panting from the effort of holding the vision. He forced himself to inhale, blow out the breath, and then do it again until his heartbeat slowed. He understood what had happened, though. Not wanting to explain themselves to mere humans, the Celts had cast a spell to temporarily cloud their memories and left, changeling in tow.

"Bubba must have wanted to go," Ronin muttered. He hadn't sensed the Celts forcing the changeling. Who knew? Maybe Niall had met the gods somewhere before. Changelings lived for hundreds of years, and Bubba was one of the older ones. Feeling like he had good news to share, Ronin started for the stairs and stopped dead. It wouldn't be easy telling the witches the Celts had blown them off. They were prickly about their status on the magical totem pole as it was.

He ran alternative explanations through his mind, things he could add a dash of coercion to so they'd believe him…

"Don't." Roz's voice broke into his concentration.

Her footsteps thumped up the last few risers, and she strode into the third floor hallway. Flustered, he felt his face heat. "Don't what? Why couldn't I hear you before just now?"

Her dark eyes glinted a challenge, and she bent to pick up a few pieces of debris, tossing them in a nearby waste can. "Don't sugarcoat whatever you saw in your vision like you were about to do. You didn't hear me because I masked my movements with magic." She crossed her arms beneath her breasts. "Is Bubba all right?"

Ronin met her gaze. "From what I can tell, he went with Ceridwen."

"Mmph. I'll let Colleen know." Her gaze took on an unfocused quality, and he knew she was communicating telepathically.

Ronin opened his arms, but Roz shook her head and held up a hand for him to wait. Once she lowered it, he walked toward her, skirting what looked like the remains of a bookcase, but she shook her head again. "Hold it right there, bud."

Shocked, he ground to a halt. "What's wrong? I know you're angry, but…"

Her forehead stitched into concerned lines. "I want to be fair about this, but you're used to issuing orders and having everybody jump to your tune." She blew out a tense breath. "I can't do that. I should've stayed here, not gone with you to the dream guardian. When we finally got back, I wanted to go upstairs immediately." She lowered her gaze. "With Irichna, sometimes a minute or two makes the difference between life and death. To have you hold me in the basement until you deemed it safe…" She met his gaze again, anguish—and fury—stamped into her features. "That doesn't work for me."

Ronin swallowed, but his throat was dry. "Roz. I'm sorry. It will take time—"

"That would be great if we had some," she cut in. "My gut tells me things are going to do nothing but escalate." She dropped her arms and balled her hands into fists. "You will never stand between me and Jenna and Colleen again. Do you understand?"

"I do, but—"

"No buts. Maybe this thing between us was a mistake. I got carried away watching Colleen and Duncan. Just because they found common ground that works for them doesn't mean—"

"Stop it!" Ronin thundered. "It doesn't work any better for them than it does for you and me. In my vision, I just watched Duncan try to protect Colleen while she jetted sidelong past him."

"Don't yell at me." She opened one fist and pounded the other one into her open palm.

"I'll do whatever I have to if it gets your attention." He strode to within two feet of her, crunching through broken glass. "There's a very good reason you're alone."

"Oh really?" Sarcasm dripped from her words. "I suppose you're going to tell me whether I want you to or not."

"Yes. I am. You're just like me. Scared to the marrow of your bones about making a commitment. Ready to bolt at the first sign things aren't perfect, so you won't run the risk of being vulnerable, of being hurt."

She narrowed her eyes, and he saw her throat working. "Maybe part of that's true, but it still doesn't mean we're good for each other. No one's ordered me around since I left home."

"If it sounds like I'm issuing orders—" he began.

"It doesn't just sound like it. You are." She drew herself up tall. "Furthermore, you've been in charge of the Sidhe for so long, I don't think you recognize what you're doing. You've run this well-oiled machine for centuries, hell, maybe even longer than that, and the Sidhe scurry to do your bidding."

Ronin couldn't help himself. He burst out laughing, hooting, and snorting.

"What's so fucking funny?" she asked, her tone as sharp and jagged as the glass shards beneath their feet.

"Hardly any of them *do my bidding*. They're as likely to tell me to bugger off as they are to… What was your other phrase? Oh yes, *dance to my tune*."

"If that's true, why do your people even have a leader?"

"Because the buck has to stop somewhere." He took another step toward her, relieved when she didn't tell him to stay put. "This isn't about the Sidhe, Roz. It's about you and me. I care about you. If I were honest, it's more than that. I'm falling in love with you. The last thing I want is for you to think I don't respect you. I'm trying, goddammit, but I've been alone for a long time too."

Her eyes had widened somewhere around the time he'd said *love,* and Ronin allowed himself to hope she wouldn't shut him out completely. She unclenched her fists and flexed her fingers, her expressive features alive with conflicting emotions. He wanted to close the remaining few inches between them and fold her into his arms, but he waited, giving her space until she asked for his affection. He'd just said he respected her, and if he pushed his own agenda, it would refute his words.

The furrow between her dark brows deepened, but at least she met his gaze head on, taking his measure. Ronin stood straighter. He couldn't remember when he'd been so desperate for another person to think well of him. She bent her elbows and clasped her hands together beneath her chin. "Thank you."

"For what?" Ronin was almost sure he knew, but things were unsettled enough he wanted to make certain.

"Showing consideration for my limits." She pressed her chin against her steepled fingers. "Look. We're both tired and stressed, at least I know I am. Maybe we can talk some more about all this once we've plowed through the rest of the wreckage here and on the first floor and taken care of Therese's body."

Ronin extended his arms again and held his breath. Would she come to him? He ached to feel her against him. Not a sexual ache, though of course he wanted her. More of a soul ache. Roz filled a void deep inside him, one he'd lived with since Lorelei's death. He didn't say anything, but he hoped his heart's need shone through his eyes.

The harsh planes of her face softened, and she dropped her arms to her sides. "When you look at me like that, I can't turn away, but you must know that." She took a step toward him, and then another; something crunched as she stepped on it. Two more steps and he closed his arms around her and cradled her against him, crooning to her in Gaelic.

"I didn't say a word until just now," he murmured against her hair. "And I didn't use magic, either."

"Maybe that's why it felt safe to come to you." Her words were muffled against his neck where she'd tucked her head. "We have a lot to figure out. Sex is great, but we have to get along out of bed too."

He stroked her braids where they fell down her back. "I agree.

I can be a heavy-handed bastard. You just need to let me know when I've stepped over one of your lines."

Roz tilted her head so she looked at him. "If I do that, will you back off?"

A corner of his mouth twitched. "The truth?" When she nodded, he went on. "I'll try, but you're my woman." At the look on her face, he laid a finger over her lips. "Let me finish. I don't know if I could stand by and watch you throw your life away. I'd probably do something to at least try to save you."

"And pick up the pieces of my pissed off ego later?" Wry humor sparkled beneath her words, and something coiled tight in Ronin started to relax.

He cocked his head to one side. "Not very much later. I'd want to attend to each little sector of your *pissed off ego* immediately." He trailed his fingertips down the side of her face. "It's a fine line. Sometimes I'm bound to fuck up."

"Fine line between?"

"Not getting in your way and satisfying the warrior inside me that he's done everything possible to ensure your safety."

"What was that part about being your woman?" She caught her full lower lip between her teeth. "Not that I don't like the words, but they feel premature."

"Scrying is one of my gifts."

Roz eyed him. "What? You looked into the future and saw me?"

"Yes and no."

She rolled her eyes. "Look, Mr. Inscrutable, you'll need to say more than that."

He nodded and tightened his arms around her. Damn but she felt good, like she'd been born to be there. "I stopped looking into my future a long time ago. It's a gray area, and you're not supposed to scry your own future." He paused for a beat. "But once I met you in the U.K., I was so smitten, I broke one of my cardinal rules and peeked."

"And?"

"Peering into the future isn't as precise as looking into the past, but I did see at least the possibility that you and I would come together."

A corner of her mouth turned downward. "What if I wouldn't have wanted to?"

Ronin felt taken aback. He understood she might still be angry with him, but the possibility she wouldn't want him at all, would end their relationship before it had a chance to deepen and grow, had never entered his mind. "Uh, well, of course, I'd never force you—" He stumbled over the words.

She touched his mouth with her fingertips. "That's okay. You can stop. Mostly I was curious what you'd say." Her face set itself in solemn lines. "Even if this works out, I'm not immortal like you."

"I know that. But I want to be with you when you die from old age, not because some demon ripped you stem to stern, or worse, dragged you to one of their borderworlds and used you for a broodmare to further their line."

Roz drew back, the shock on her face genuine. "Abbadon plucks new demons from the ranks of the dead."

Ronin nodded. "That he does, but he's been known to breed with living women too. Where do you think his princes come from?"

She blew out an anxious breath and drew her brows together. "Christ on a crutch! I had no idea Abbadon even had princes. All the Irichna look about the same to me."

Ronin considered his next words carefully. It was bad enough they'd forced the witches into taking over as demon assassins. Apparently, none of the Sidhe had cared enough to educate them about the Irichna. He tried to think who he'd assigned to do that, but it didn't matter since two hundred years had passed.

"I'm starting to know that look." Roz pressed her lips together. "It means you're weighing your words. What else about the Irichna don't we know?"

"I'm guessing Duncan hasn't said anything about them, either," Ronin hedged.

"When would he have had a chance?" Roz asked indignantly. "He's been up to his ass in Irichna alligators ever since he stormed into our shop that day, intent on finding Colleen."

"How about this?" Ronin touched his lips to her forehead. He wanted to crush his mouth down on hers, but they had more urgent matters to attend to just now. Her body melted against him, and she tilted her face to make it easier to kiss her. "I'd love to, darling, but let's clear up this mess and go help the others first."

"Of course." An uncomfortable expression flitted across her features and she moved out of the circle of his arms. "I don't know what it is about you, but when you're this close, I can't think about anything except getting naked."

He tamped down the satisfied grin that wanted out. "Thank the goddess for small favors." He drew her off to one side of the long hall and began an incantation.

"What are you doing?"

"Add your magic to mine, and we'll have this space cleared out in a jiffy."

Roz scanned the hall. "Where are you going to put all of it?"

"I was going to move it wherever we're constructing a funeral pyre for Therese."

"But not everything will burn." She eyed him sharply. "How did you know we burn our dead?"

"I didn't, but the ground's frozen, so burying her is out of the question." Ronin shrugged. "If we get the fire hot enough—and we can do that with magic—everything here should incinerate."

He loosed the spell he'd been creating while they talked, pleased when she wove her power in with his. A small whirlwind whooshed everything together. Roz jerked a thumb toward the north, and he pushed the mess that way, careful to shroud everything once it ended up outside the house.

Roz looked up and down the empty hall. "Guess we can skip

spring cleaning this year, but there were a few things in that bookshelf I'll miss."

"Like what?" Ronin raised a curious eyebrow.

"Mostly magical source books. We kept the ones we all used out here so they'd be easy to access."

"There's a fairly comprehensive library at my home. When we're there next, feel free to browse through it. I'll bet you can find whatever you're missing."

She smiled. "Somehow I don't doubt it."

"There's even a set of scrolls about the Irichnas that you'll probably want to read."

"I'm fairly sure we have our own, but I've never spent much time studying them." Roz stopped, looking uncomfortable.

"If you have them, why haven't you read them?" Ronin felt relieved his kin had at least made certain the witches had access to information about the demons, even if they weren't using it. He gazed at her, trying to understand what made her tick.

"My Gaelic isn't that sharp, and—" She shook her head sharply. "The truth is I didn't want to know any more about them. When we got breaks from fighting them, the last thing I wanted in my head was Irichnas. Some of the older witches—the dead ones— spent hours studying those scrolls. Didn't seem to help them stay alive."

Guilt twisted like a knife, plunging deep. "I'm sorry—"

Roz made a chopping motion with the flat of her hand. "Never mind. Let's change the subject."

"I can do that." Ronin took her arm and guided her toward the stairs. "What you said about getting naked made me feel ten feet tall. I'd be terribly disappointed if you were tired of me already."

She leaned into him. "I don't know about ten feet tall, but you are special. We still need to hammer some things out, though." She started down the stairs.

"I agree."

Roz stopped on the second floor landing and turned to face

him. "We need to hammer them out before we have sex again." She shot a meaningful look at the belled out front of his trousers.

Ronin moved his hard on to a more comfortable position. "Not that I'm arguing the point, but why?"

She inhaled sharply and skewered him with her dark-eyed gaze. "Because I'm almost in so deep I won't be able to walk away."

"What? You think one more climax will make you my prisoner?"

She mock-slugged his arm. "You're making fun of me. I may look tough, but I have a tender core."

He placed his hands on her shoulders. "I know that, Roxanne Lantry. Part of caring about someone is seeing all of them and accepting each idiosyncrasy and foible."

She snorted, tossed her head back, and laughed. When she could talk again, she sputtered, "At least now I have a way to categorize your overbearing mannerisms. They're foibles."

"Indeed," Ronin murmured, feeling like he was drowning in the wonder of her eyes.

Her mouth was parted, the lower lip glistening slightly. Ronin tried to hold back, but need and the erection that hadn't retreated drove him, and he slashed his mouth over hers. Roz threaded her arms around him, clinging to him as if he were life itself, and his heart cracked open with joy.

They were still kissing, tongues tangled together, when Duncan's mind voice intruded. *"Say there, mate. We could use a bit of help down here."*

CHAPTER 14

Hours later, Roz stood over Therese's corpse with power thrumming around her. She pulled her winter parka closer and snugged the hood under her chin against blowing wind and snow. Duncan and Ronin had hogged a generous pit behind their house right next to the pile of burnable debris. They'd dug through snow until they hit earth, but as Ronin had predicted, it was frozen solid.

Because most of the work on the first floor involved sorting and straightening, it had taken much longer than what they'd done upstairs. Somewhere in between, Jenna had ginned up sandwich makings, and everyone grabbed something. Roz was so tired, she barely tasted her food. It could've been cardboard for all she cared. But she needed to eat something. Either that or fall on her face.

Fragrant smoke from traditional death herbs rose skyward. Sidhe magic masked it from the rest of the world. She cast a sidelong glance at Ronin. He stood off to one side with Duncan manipulating the spell that hid their ritual from prying eyes. Not that any were likely since another blizzard had blown in. She focused her mind, which was spinning in a hundred directions. Part of her was ashamed at how easily Ronin had lured her back into his arms, and it embarrassed her how much she craved the hard planes of his body.

Do I just give up being me? Who the hell am I, if I strip away killing demons?

The second question made her wince at its absurdity. When you got right down to bedrock, who was anybody when you took away their livelihood?

She did a mental eye roll, recognizing her tendency to over-dramatize things. Some of what Ronin had said was spot on. Both of them were used to running independent ships. It would take time, and a whole lot of compromises, for them to find a way not to tear each other's throats out.

Is he who I really want? Can I spend the rest of my life with him?

No matter how badly she wanted to answer yes and have done with things, she couldn't. Ronin was an amazing man. He tugged at her heartstrings and made her feel things she hadn't believed were possible...

So what was wrong? Because something definitely was. She mouthed the words to the witches' funeral dirge as she dug deep, desperate for answers. She was scared of being hurt again, but beyond that, she was worried. The demon confrontations were escalating. Could she live with herself if Ronin did something heroic and ended up locked in the *Dreaming* forever because he stood between her and a demon? She squeezed her eyes shut for a moment, and her head swam dizzily.

Since Roz felt like she was chasing her tail, she fixed her attention on Naomi and her deep, husky voice. Looking more-or-less revived, the Witches' Northwest Coven leader conducted the simple ceremony using dried herbs from one of the upstairs bedrooms to help the witch's spirit on its trip beyond the veil. Lou and Maggie recounted memories of their friend and companion.

Quite soon, the ritual would be over and they'd scatter the remains with magic.

It was faint, but Roz sensed something beyond their warding and her head snapped up. Apparently Colleen felt it too because she scanned the group and whispered something to Duncan. Naomi chanted the final words and gestured to Ronin and Duncan. The Sidhe refocused their spell, and Therese's still-smoldering body shimmered and dispersed in a volley of multi-hued motes.

"Thank you." Naomi inclined her head toward the two Sidhe. She narrowed her eyes. "What do I sense?"

"Whatever it is, they're cloaking their presence." Colleen shook her parka-shrouded head. When she glanced up, her mouth was set in a tense line.

"Back in the house," Roz said, shivering from more than the minus twenty temperature.

Ronin caught her up in the back hall off the living room. "The energy feels a lot like Titania and Oberon to me."

Roz felt the swift bite of annoyance and spun to face him. "Why didn't you say something outside? Everyone's worried."

"Because I wasn't certain. And I'm still not." He looked hard at her. "Come on, Roz. I thought we were past you being peeved with me."

"I'm pissed at myself," she snapped, opened her mouth to say more, and then shut it so hard her teeth clacked together.

"Do you want to talk about it?"

"No. I need to sit somewhere and not think about anything for a while."

He moved so his body blocked the entrance to the rest of the house. He didn't say anything, just laid his hands on her shoulders and pushed her hood back so it fell on her shoulders. The others made their way around them and someone shut both doors, the one leading to the living room, and the one that went into the backyard.

"Let me go." She pushed against him, but he may as well have been a concrete statue.

"I will, but first you need to hear me out."

"We already did this upstairs."

"Apparently, we didn't do quite enough." He moved a hand and tilted her head so their gazes met. "I've made my position and my feelings clear, but I will not pursue you if I'm not wanted. I can't fight with you and keep a clear head so the demons don't annihilate us. After we walk out of this room, I won't approach you again unless you ask me. There are a lot of bedrooms in this house. I'll move my things into one of them."

Shock stabbed her, sharp as any knife, and she blinked back tears before a shell formed around her heart. At least this was familiar territory. She'd been here before—lots of times.

"Go on. Go. I figured none of this was real, anyway." She wrenched her chin from his grip.

"It could be, if you'd only let it." Something sad and forlorn hovered in the depths of his eyes. He kissed her forehead gently, let go of her, and opened the door leading into the living room. Before she could figure out what she wanted to say, he was gone.

Because she couldn't face anyone, she pulled her hood back over her head and went outside. It was getting dark, the brief Alaskan day shading to the perpetual gloom of winter, but at least the gray matched her mood. She post-holed through knee-deep snow to the front of the house and the plowed street. Once there, she looked at her car, realized she didn't have the keys or her driver's license, and turned her face into the wind. Walking was probably better than driving. The cold would clear her head.

She hadn't gotten a quarter mile when the snow-filled air just ahead of her brightened. Her gut twisted into a knot, and she raised her gloved hands to summon magic. Whatever wanted her was close, too close for her to make a run for the house.

"Show yourself," Roz snarled, ready for a fight to the death. At least anger made a dent in her bleak mood.

Titania shimmered out of a fine mist dressed in her usual gossamer finery. Roz clapped a hand to her chest. "Christ! You scared the crap out of me. Aren't you cold?"

"I would be without magic. What are you doing out here by yourself?" The queen narrowed her blue eyes, and Roz felt her trolling through her mind. "Oh, I see. A lover's spat."

"If you're just going to help yourself to my thoughts, why bother to ask me anything?" Roz heard the surly undertone in her words and muttered, "Sorry."

"No matter what passed between you and Ronin, it is far from safe for you to be here where demons might attack. What did he do to upset you?"

"Why not just pluck it out of my head?"

"Because I'm attempting to show you respect." Titania's sharp tone matched her own, but the queen's next words were softer. "Maybe I can help, child."

"I don't see how. You're one of *them*, which means you'd take his side."

"A few years ago, hell, maybe even last week, I might have. Oberon talked sense into me." Titania spread milky-white hands in front of her, the skin so translucent, Roz saw blood pumping through the veins. "I'm not exactly viewing the Sidhe as a superior race at the moment."

The queen's unguarded posture loosened something inside Roz, and the wall she'd taken refuge behind crumbled. "I'm not sure what happened."

"You need to say more than that, dear."

"Ronin didn't do anything, except be himself. I guess, if I were truthful, maybe it's me. I might not be able to let anyone in far enough to do more than bed them."

The queen's long hair fluttered in the wind. "Aye, bedding is the easy part. It's the living with them that's a challenge."

Roz never knew where her next words came from, but they fled the safety of her throat before she was able to stop them. "Can you help me?" She clapped a hand over her mouth, but it was too late.

"Maybe." Titania leveled an appraising glance her way. "What does your heart want?"

"Ronin."

"Then you two will find a way. Don't lose yourself in *what-ifs*. Most of them never come true anyway." She crooked a finger. "Walk with me. So long as I'm here, I must speak with all of you."

A million questions cascaded through Roz's mind. Were the dark fae in place and waiting for the next demon attack? She quested about for a subtle way to ask, but Titania shook her head. "Wait until I can tell everyone."

RONIN'S HEART ACHED. It took all his self-discipline, but he forced himself to walk away from Roz. He sensed her conflicts and understood she had to come to terms with her ambivalence, not about him, but about being in love with anyone. He'd lived long enough to realize you gave up part of yourself to bond with another. She had to come to that willingness on her own. He couldn't push her. He'd tried that when they stood in the upstairs hall. While she'd capitulated, seduced by the magic their bodies spun, once she had time alone to think, everything unraveled.

Duncan caught his eye when he walked into the living room and raised a quizzical brow, but Ronin shook his head, turned hard right, and continued up to the second floor. The sooner he eradicated all evidence of his presence from Roz's room, the better. He didn't want to be gathering his few items with her looking on.

It didn't take him long to resettle himself one floor up. He chose a room obviously dedicated to drying herbs and flowers. A pallet beneath a window would make an adequate bed. He'd slept on far worse in the field during many interminable wars the Sidhe had waged over time. The room smelled of summer and promise, the scents homey and soothing. He tossed his armful of clothing and his travel sack on a chair and forced a calm center. Nothing would be gained by giving in to the grief washing through him. Roz's room was full of her scent, it clung to his things and made him yearn for her.

"Ronin!" Titania's summons yanked him from his funk. So he'd been right about the queen being close.

"Yes, my liege."

"Never mind that. Get downstairs now."

Two more steadying breaths and he left the sanctuary of the herb room and did everything he could to prepare himself for being in the same room with Roz, except not with her.

We're allies, he reminded himself. *Never mind I want far more than that, but at least we can fight our common enemy. Even if she doesn't want me as her lover, there's nothing that says we can't be friends.*

"Yeah, right," he muttered as he took the steps two at a time. "Comrades in arms and all that hogwash." He strode into the living room, nodded pleasantly at Titania, and detoured to the liquor cabinet where he dug out a bottle of single malt Scotch and a glass. Roz's energy pulsed from a corner of the room. He didn't have to look to know where she stood, flanked by Colleen and Jenna.

Ronin leaned against a nearby wall, glass in hand, and focused his next words for Titania. "I hear and obey, my liege. What news do you bring?"

"My," she smirked. "How formal." When Ronin didn't dignify her comment with a response, she went on. "Oberon and I are… close enough to watch over things. Unfortunately, we didn't get here in time to be of any help for the last demon attack, but I understand the Celts filled in nicely."

"They were amazing," Jenna cut in. "Is there anything we can do so they'll be more available?"

"Probably not," Duncan answered.

"No kidding." Ronin found his voice. "Shocked the hell out of me they showed up when we called."

Titania clapped her hands smartly together. "There are too many of us to go off on conversational side streets. What you need to know is this: dark fae are near enough to help as well."

"Forget about the druids and mages." Naomi spoke up. "Now that I've had some time to process how they dodged my request for help, I'm furious."

"I'd like to hear more about that," Titania said, "but not right now."

"You and me both," Ronin mumbled.

Colleen broke from Duncan's side, walked to Titania, and half-bowed. "Do you have any idea where my changeling is? Ronin did some sort of scrying spell, and he believes Bubba left with Ceridwen."

"Curious." Titania drew her finely arched brows together and eyed Colleen. "You do know he's not exactly *yours*, don't you? The bond confers loyalty, not possession."

Colleen nodded sharply. "Poor choice of words, but I'm worried about him."

"You know," Roz said, "I just thought of something. We'd asked him to come up with a couple more changelings. He was having trouble locating any, so maybe he asked the goddess to help him."

"It makes sense." A thoughtful look formed on Colleen's face.

Roz trotted to her side and wrapped an arm around her. "Waiting is hard."

"Not so much waiting," Colleen said. "It's waiting and not knowing. Not for sure."

"Ronin's scrying skills are impeccable." Titania shot a look his way. "If that's what he saw, it's what happened."

"Thanks for the vote of confidence." Ronin raised his glass in her direction before moving it to his mouth and drinking deeply. The liquor burned on its way down, but at least it turned his focus away from Roz for a moment. Dear goddess but she looked lovely. Clumps of her dark hair had come loose from its braids, and strands framed her face, softening its stark bone structure.

"Anytime." Titania winked. "Now, listen up. At the first whiff of demon, one of you needs to let Oberon and me know. Any sort of telepathic sending will do."

"What happens then?" Roz leveled her frank gaze at the queen.

"Why, we all show up and kick some demon ass."

After looking shocked, Roz grinned. "For a moment there, it was easy to forget you've been around since the world began."

"Oh, not quite that long, my dear. Just remember—" Titania waggled a finger at Roz and Colleen "—the key to living a long time is flexibility and fitting in." The air around her took on a glistening quality and the queen vanished.

"So you just happened to find her outside in the snowstorm?" Colleen looked hard at Roz.

"Yup. That's about the size of it."

"What were you doing out there?" Jenna joined them. "Last place I saw you was—"

Roz made a hacking motion with one hand. "I needed some time to think. Didn't have my car keys, so I took a walk."

"That was really stupid." Colleen shook her head, clearly exasperated.

"It didn't feel like it at the time." A muscle twitched in Roz's jaw, and Ronin knew she was at least trying to hang onto her temper. "I've taken lots of walks in this neighborhood."

"Not in the dead of winter and not when you had no fucking idea when the next demon would show up," Jenna sputtered.

"Fine." Roz tossed her hands skyward. "I'm going to get something going for dinner." She stalked toward the kitchen, leaving Colleen and Jenna staring after her.

"What the hell got into her?" Jenna asked.

Colleen twisted until she was looking right at Ronin. "I'll bet you know the answer to that one."

He shrugged. "Haven't the foggiest." Before they could question him further—or worse, delve into his mind—he hurried toward the stairs, drink in hand, intent on carving out some private time before dinner. Maybe by then he'd be able to slick some sort of veneer over the tender places inside himself.

Footsteps followed him. Duncan's. The other Sidhe caught up to him on the second floor landing. "Lover's quarrel?"

Ronin didn't bother to turn around. "Go away."

"Are you certain about that?"

Maybe because Ronin had known him for a long time, something in Duncan's tone burrowed through his foul mood. "No."

"It goes without saying—" Duncan clapped a hand on his shoulder "—whatever you say remains between us. Really. I don't tell Colleen everything."

Because Ronin needed to talk with someone, he grunted, "Follow me. I want to go somewhere we won't be overheard."

"That would be nowhere unless you ward our conversation."

"Exactly. I moved up another floor. Are you coming?"

"Sure you want me to?"

"Oh for Christ's sake, I invited you, didn't I?" Ronin clumped heavily up the stairs, relieved when he heard the other Sidhe right behind him.

"This isn't totally altruistic on my part."

Ronin cleared the stairs and trudged to his new room, pushing the door open. He gestured Duncan inside. "Really, what's your ulterior motive?"

"Once you get to the bottom of whatever's bothering you, we need a better battle plan than what we have. We got damned lucky this last time, with only one casualty."

Ronin nodded solemnly. "Maybe we should do that first."

Duncan shook his head. "No. You need a clearer head. Come on, mate. Spit it out, and we'll take it from there."

Sinking onto the low pallet, Ronin laced his fingers together. "I don't know what to do. Every time I turn around, Roz is tied up in knots over something I said or did…"

159

*R*oz banged pots down from their hanging rack and chopped vegetables with a vengeance. It felt good to do something other than stand in the living room smiling vapidly while Ronin stood across from her, studiously not looking her way. Fatigue and fury weren't a good combination, and she nicked a finger with the knife. Blood spurted.

"Goddammit all to hell."

She pivoted until she was bent over the sink and let cool tap water run over her cut before wrapping it in a paper towel. Even though a Band-Aid would have been faster, she sent healing magic to her wound, glad to have something to focus on besides Ronin.

The kitchen door slammed against its stops, and Colleen and Jenna marched in. "What's this?" Jenna eyed the bloody scrap of towel. "Some new dinner spell where we get your blood along with the chicken and vegetables?"

"Shut up," Roz growled. "Just shut up."

"Would you like some help?" Colleen asked, her voice carefully neutral.

"Depends what time you want to eat. I need to finish healing this before I can do anything else."

"Humph." Jenna pushed past her and picked up the knife. "What were we having, exactly?"

"You have eyes." Roz turned away, chagrined by her sarcasm. "Aw, crap! I'm sorry. I thought I'd chuck everything into the roaster and pop it into the oven with a bunch of potatoes."

"We could mash them for a change," Colleen suggested.

"Sure, but if we do that, maybe we ought to boil them." Jenna bent to pull a large saucepot from a lower cupboard. "It'd be faster."

Roz looked from Jenna to Colleen. "You're taking over my dinner project."

"We are," they said in unison.

"But I need something to do," Roz protested. "This isn't one of those times I want oodles of time to stew in my own juice."

Colleen trotted to the pantry and returned with a ten-pound bag of spuds. "What happened, hon?"

Roz already had magic brewing for her hand, so she diverted some to ward the kitchen from prying ears. She hooked one booted foot into the rungs of a kitchen chair and spun it around to sit in. "I'm not sure."

"You have to say more than that." Jenna transferred food into the roasting pan and set to work chopping onions.

"Ronin just takes things for granted. Damn near everything, actually."

"Like that you'll do exactly what he wants?" Colleen shot a knowing glance her way. When Roz nodded, she went on. "Duncan's exactly the same way. I ignore him when he tries to shove his weight around."

"How?" Roz heard anguish in the single word. "I want to please Ronin, and then I hate myself for capitulating. Worse, I want to strangle him for setting me up where it feels like I can't win."

Colleen scrubbed potatoes at the sink, dropping them into the pot as she finished them. "Maybe because Duncan made a bunch of mistakes, like almost letting an Irichna seduce him, it's fairly easy to budge him when he adopts a *moral high ground* attitude."

"Mmph. Too bad I don't have any leverage like that with Ronin."

"Sure you do," Colleen said. "There's that trip he dragged you on to the dream guardian. Even at the time, it seemed to me that he didn't really need you with him. He just wanted you there."

"But he couldn't have known—" Roz started, and then choked back a laugh because she was defending him. "Regardless. I'm not sure it matters because he just walked away from me. Told me I needed to sort things out and that he was moving his stuff out of my bedroom."

"Let's switch how we're approaching this." Jenna clapped a lid on the roaster and slid it into the oven. "How do you want him to be? Surely you don't want a lap dog that fawns over you and never has an opinion of his own."

A bitter laugh bubbled past Roz's lips, and she cast an appraising look at Jenna. "Considering you've never hooked up with anyone for long, you're amazingly smart."

Jenna furled her brows. "Hah! At last, you're coming to appreciate me." She grabbed a chair and sat opposite Roz. "Did it ever occur to you I haven't exactly had men standing in line to date me? I'm hella tall. Most guys don't want a woman who outweighs them by fifty pounds, either."

"But you're beautiful," Roz cut in.

"That's only because you know me, sweetie. Hey, back to you. You never answered my question."

Colleen plunked the potato pan on the stove, lit the gas under it, and joined her friends. She turned a third chair around so they were arranged in a circle. "How about wine or something? We can pass the bottle around just like the old days when we weren't old enough to drink."

"Great idea!" Jenna crowed. "If there's anything left, we can spike the stew."

"There won't be," Roz said, already feeling a little better. "How about something red?"

"I'm on it." Colleen walked back to the pantry, returning with a bottle and a corkscrew. "We're waiting," she said as she opened the wine.

Roz rolled her eyes. "It's not as if I've spent years building lists of what my ideal man looks like."

"But if you had," Jenna persisted, holding out a hand for the wine, "what would be on it?"

"You'll laugh at me."

"No, we won't," Colleen said. "Promise."

Roz sucked in a breath. "Okay. Here goes nothing." She ticked, "Strong, courageous, confident," off on three fingers, took the wine, and drank. "He'd also have to have magic and be tolerant of mine. Um, let's see, what else? Bright, well-read, creative." Roz found herself warming to the task and winked lewdly. "It wouldn't hurt if he was red-hot in the sack and handsome. Plus he needs to be tall. I hate looking down on men."

"Gosh." Jenna used magic to force Roz to look at her. "That sounds a lot like someone we know."

"Sure does," Colleen agreed blandly and grabbed the bottle from Roz.

"Awk! You two are impossible." The corners of Roz's mouth twitched. "I will say it shocked me when he just dumped the ball in my court and walked away."

"I'm not trying to be crass," Colleen said, "but you've got to decide which horse you're going to ride. And damn quick. Either you suck up your reservations and let your attraction for Ronin play itself out, or you decide it's too risky and shut that door permanently."

Roz bit her lower lip hard enough to hurt. "Right, huh? Not the time to wallow in my own shit here."

"No. It's not," Colleen said matter of factly. "We have other problems. Lots of them. Irichna. Dark fae. Our fellow witches.

And even if Ronin believes Bubba is with the Celts, I'm still worried sick about him."

"Never mind we need to be better organized before the Irichna show up again," Jenna muttered. "I feel guilty as sin we lost one of Naomi's witches, but things went to hell really fast after you and Ronin left to visit the dream guardian."

"Did the demons show up before Naomi and her witches?" Roz asked.

Colleen nodded. "It was like they were waiting in some sort of psychic ether. You hadn't been gone two minutes before those fucking fiery gateways they use formed."

"We made a run for the upper floors because they're more defensible," Jenna said.

"Turns out we should've stayed down here because when Naomi and her witches showed up, they were disoriented. I'm surprised the Irichna didn't kill all of them." Colleen shook her head, tipped the wine bottle back, and drained it. "Should I get another?" Roz and Jenna nodded, and Colleen got to her feet.

"I think the demons would have killed the other three," Jenna said slowly, "but by then you and Ronin were probably back."

"But we were in the basement," Roz protested.

"So?" Colleen picked up the corkscrew and stripped foil off a fresh wine bottle. "You think Irichna can't sense us if there's a layer of wood in between?"

"Okay, so it was a dumb thing to say." Roz exhaled wearily. "I'm tired."

"We all are, but we're not done. Let's circle back to Ronin." Jenna belted more wine and handed the bottle to Roz. "He fits your dream dude to a *T*, so what's wrong?"

"Maybe I'm scared he'll get tired of me and break my heart. Gawk!" Roz dropped the bottle into Colleen's hands. "What's in there? Truth serum?"

"Your heart's already broken," Colleen murmured.

"Yeah, but it could be worse," Roz countered.

"Oh, for Christ's sake." Jenna rolled her eyes. "Grow up. You put your life on the line every time we face demons, but you want to build a wall around your heart."

"When you put it like that, I feel like an idiot." Roz pinched the bridge of her nose between her thumb and forefinger. "The decision isn't about Ronin, but about me and if I've got the courage to give it my best shot."

"Well said." Colleen raised the bottle her way. "Do you?"

"You've bitched about being alone forever," Jenna cut in.

"She also bitched about both husbands and every single boyfriend," Colleen added snidely. "They were weak sucks." She leveled her gaze at Roz. "That's a direct quote."

"That's the problem with friends," Roz muttered. "Long memories."

"Interesting." Jenna narrowed her eyes. "Your complaint about Ronin is he's too far the other way."

"Some middle ground would be nice." Roz shot her a pained look.

"Sweetie." Colleen laid a hand on her knee. "You haven't spent enough time with the man to find middle ground. Hell, Duncan and I are still figuring out what it looks like."

"Okay. Enough of this." Roz got up and poked the potatoes. "These are done. Who wants to mash them?"

"You can't just change the subject like that." Jenna stomped over to where Roz stood in front of the stove.

"Of course I can." She drained the potatoes into a colander.

"We want to know what you're going to do," Colleen said.

Roz turned and grinned at her. "The sisterhood did its job. Once dinner's in better shape, I'm going to find Ronin and lay my heart at his feet."

"Woot!" Jenna fist-pumped the air and caught Roz up in a huge hug. Before she let go, Colleen had joined them.

"I'll mash," Colleen said. "Let's try to figure out a better plan for the Irichna before we lose Roz in Ronin's bed."

The kitchen door rattled. Roz twirled to face it, and raised her hands to summon power. Her heart thudded from a rush of adrenaline on top of all the wine she'd drunk.

"Who locked the goddamned door?" Bubba's voice sounded from the other side.

"Thank fucking God." Colleen sprinted for the door, drew back the deadbolt, and flung it open. Bubba skittered through, flanked by two more just like him. When Roz looked closely, she realized one of the changelings was female.

Colleen snapped Bubba into a tight hug, murmuring about how worried she'd been. The other two marched to the stove and pulled the oven door open.

"Hey!" Jenna protested. "What do you think you're doing?"

"We're hungry," one of the changelings said.

"So are we," Roz countered, "but dinner's not done yet. What are your names?"

RONIN WISHED he'd brought the bottle of Scotch upstairs. His glass was long since empty, and the alcohol hadn't quite conferred the fuzzed out mental place he'd hoped for.

"...so," he continued, "no matter what I do, she finds fault." He shrugged. "I could spend more time reading her mind, but that feels like cheating. Plus, she'd know I was there. Maybe not all the time, but a lot of it."

"Did you ever truly say good-bye to Lorelei?"

Ronin drew his brows together. "Where'd that come from?"

"Well, did you?" Duncan persisted.

"Yes, at least I think so. What does she have to do with Roz?"

Duncan turned the force of his green gaze on Ronin. "Do you really have to ask?"

"Yes, apparently I do, since I'm not seeing a connection. They're two different women from very different times."

"Exactly." Duncan nodded sagely. "I remember Lorelei. There were a lot of times you hurt her, and a lot of things you did that she didn't like, but she never said a word because women didn't then."

Ronin drew back. "She talked with you?"

"Uh-huh."

Curiosity and a desperate need to know Lorelei's secrets clawed at Ronin, making his guts burn, but he shook his head. "It's best if the dead remain so."

A corner of Duncan's mouth turned down. "I wouldn't have spilled her secrets any more than I'd divulge yours." He paused a beat. "My only point was that relationship wasn't perfect, either, but you were spared knowing it because Lorelei always put on her game face for you."

Ronin sputtered in annoyance. The application of modern terms to his sixteenth century love grated. Duncan quirked a brow. "We can switch to Gaelic if you'd prefer."

"You can ditch the sarcasm."

"Very well. You need to decide if you can let go of a relationship you've enshrined, never mind your memories aren't the truth of how things were, and take a chance on something new."

"You think I'm trying to resurrect my relationship with Lorelei?"

"Or something very close to it."

"But she and Roz aren't anything alike," Ronin protested.

"Uh-huh." Duncan nodded. "Precisely."

Understanding flooded Ronin, and he stumbled to his feet and paced in a tight circle. "I have more apologizing to do."

"Maybe not so much." Duncan stood too. "I've made a bunch of mistakes with Colleen too. Telling her *I'm sorry* doesn't count nearly as much as making certain I include her in my decision-making the next time around."

Ronin stopped moving and faced the other Sidhe. "When I

scryed the past, I watched her and Jenna ignore you and tackle the Irichna their own way."

Duncan's jaw tightened. "Which is why we need to have a war council. We have to be on the same page before the next attack. If that page is you and me and whatever other magic wielders we can raise supporting the three witches, so be it, but we can't have competing agendas. If we do, the demons may well succeed killing the witches."

A sharp rap sounded on the door. Ronin exchanged looks with Duncan and sent a thread of magic snaking through his ward to see who'd bothered them. Joy slammed his heart into overdrive, and he said, "It's Roz." Before the words were out, he was moving toward the door, but she flung it open before he got there.

"Bubba's back," she announced, "with two more changelings." She tilted her chin up defiantly. "And we need to talk."

"Colleen must be ecstatic," Duncan said. "I'm anxious to meet the other changelings. Knowing them, I'm surprised they didn't show up at our door ahead of you."

"They'd be running amok through the house—" Roz's full mouth curved in half a grin "—but Jenna and Colleen told them if they didn't stay in the kitchen, they wouldn't get any supper."

Duncan slipped past Roz. "We'll take care of that war council over dinner," he said as he disappeared down the hall.

Ronin's throat thickened with emotion. He closed the distance between them and wrapped Roz in his arms. After the briefest hesitation, she wove her arms around him and pressed her body against his. His cock hardened instantly and his breath quickened. He caressed her back and ran a hand down so it cupped her shapely ass, drawing her against him.

She tilted her head and flicked her tongue over his lower lip. "This is wonderful," she said, sounding as breathless as he felt. "You're wonderful. I'm falling in love with you. There. I said it." She grinned sheepishly. "It wasn't as hard as I thought."

Ronin grinned back. "You expected the words to stick in your craw and choke you?"

"Something like that."

"What changed your mind?"

"Nothing." She must have read confusion on his face, because she forged ahead. "My feelings for you haven't changed, except maybe they're growing stronger. The girls and I had a heart-to-heart. It clarified a lot of things for me."

"Sort of like Duncan and I just did. Here's to friends, eh?"

"I'd drink to that, but there's probably not a bottle up here."

"No bottle, just us." He tightened his hold on her butt. "How long before the meal I smell is ready?"

"Why would you want to know that?" she inquired roguishly and wriggled her hips against his erect cock.

"You know exactly why, you little vixen."

"Ummm, I just love it when men talk dirty to me. How fast do you think we could get down to business?"

"Pretty damned fast."

"I was hoping you'd say that." She toed off her house slippers. "Traded my boots for these before I came up here to save time."

CHAPTER 16

$\mathcal{R}$oz twirled away from him, shucking clothing as she went. By the time she made it to the pallet beneath the window, she was naked. She grabbed a quilt off a nearby chair, tossed it over the pallet's cotton batting, and then sat cross-legged and watched him.

He grinned and said, "An audience. Why do I feel like I should prance about like those American male strippers?"

"Prance away. I'll start without you." She reached between her legs and cupped a breast with her other hand. Her pussy was slick with desire, and her clit throbbed where she ran a lazy finger over its swollen head. Her nipple was already peaked, and she rolled it between her fingers.

Ronin groaned, the sound ripe with yearning, and tugged his sweater over his head, followed by his wool long underwear top. He bent and unlaced his outdoor Pac boots and hung onto a table to work his feet out of them.

"If I'd known," he panted, "I would've divested myself of these clodhoppers a long time ago. Goddess's tits, but you're lovely. Do you know your skin glows when you're aroused?" He unfastened his trousers, and they pooled around his feet where he stepped out of them. His cock curved in front of him, standing proud from its tangle of black curls.

Roz stared as his body emerged, unable to tear her gaze away. She'd never seen such a perfect man, and the reality of all of him rendered her breathless. Muscles rippled beneath his golden skin. Dark hair fell past his shoulders, framing his strong, square jaw and sculpted cheekbones. Roz rubbed herself faster. Just looking at him was all the stimulation she needed.

"What, no long john bottoms?" she teased, but she was breathing hard, and it was tough to get the words out. "While we're at it, what happened to your regular underwear?"

"It must've gotten misplaced last time we fucked."

He fell to his knees in front of her and covered her mouth with his, tumbling them back onto the quilt. She stopped touching herself, wrapped her arms and legs around him, and felt his cockhead demanding entrance to her body. His shaft slid into her, and his tongue flicked inside her mouth. She wriggled beneath his weight, letting herself stretch as he plumbed her. Heat flooded her pussy as he buried his length deep inside. His skin was electric against hers, every point of contact urging her higher.

She tore her mouth from his. "Do that thing where I feel you too," she demanded.

"Oh you liked that, did you?" He slashed his mouth back over hers, and she felt his urgency and his need in the way he touched her. It set her soul on fire, and she gave herself up to sensation spilling through her.

Her perspective shifted. She felt the heat of her body urging him on and the hardness of his pushing her higher. The dual viewpoint heightened everything until she almost couldn't stand it. She thrust upward hard and felt him drive into her with a desperation borne of having almost lost her. A climax boiled upward from the roots of her being, followed almost immediately by a second even stronger one. She shrieked and clawed at his back, feeling him holding back but wanting the intensity of his orgasm to flood her senses.

His gaze locked onto hers, and she let him draw her in. "We'll do this together," he rasped. "Feel me, join me, let me all the way inside your mind."

Roz pushed her last doubts away and something shifted. Desire, powerful and relentless, radiated through every nerve ending. Her nipples were hard little points. So were his. His cock swelled inside her, bigger, harder, right along with her clit.

"Yes," she shrieked. "Now." And was carried away on the tide of their combined lust. Her whole body orgasmed from the tip of her head to her toes. Release ripped through her just as she felt him pulse inside her.

Ronin held her gaze. Once his orgasm spun itself out, he twitched his cock deep within her. Once. Again. And again. His gorgeous face was rosy with sexual heat and his eyes on fire with wanting her. "Do you want more?"

She smiled lazily, feeling indulgent and sated. "I always want more of you, but we should join the others."

He folded his arms and lay atop her. "I suppose so, darling. My darling. Much as I'd love to shut out the rest of the world, we have things to work out with everyone." He kissed her gently, pulled himself from her body, and stood.

"Thank you."

Ronin shook his head. "We shouldn't have to thank one another. I'm sorry I—"

"Uh-uh, no *I'm sorries*, either." She rolled to a sit and glanced around the room. "I've always loved this space, maybe because of all the dried flowers and herbs. Winters are so pervasive here, I often spend time in this room to remind myself spring will show up sometime."

"Perhaps that's why I picked it, because I recognized at a

subliminal level it was special for you." He leveled his gaze at her. "Even though I walked away, I hadn't given up." He plucked a small towel off a craft table and tossed it her way.

"I'm glad you didn't go away, even though I was bitchy as all get-out."

"Oh, I'm much harder to get rid of than that." He winked roguishly. "Tell me about Bubba's buddies."

"Do not call him Bubba anymore. He was most clear on that. When Jenna slipped up, the other two rolled around on the floor laughing, and then chastised him for allowing such an informality in the first place."

"I see." Ronin started to dress. "Before I ask more about them, you said we needed to talk."

Roz grinned, got to her feet, and collected her own clothing. "I didn't say we had to use words. Sometimes they muddy the waters."

"You're right. What just passed between us runs far deeper than words." He smiled crookedly. "I knew there was a reason I was drawn to you."

"Beyond my raw, witchy sensuality?" She blotted her pussy and stepped into her insulated winter pants.

"That's quite a draw as well." He patted his still hard cock before pulling his pants over it. "I never get enough of you."

"Music to my ears. See if you can't hold that pose until later tonight."

He laughed. "I'll do my best. Now tell me more about the changelings. If Danu is smiling on me, I won't know any of them."

Roz sent a sympathetic glance his way and wriggled into the rest of her clothes. Witches hadn't been the only ones to suffer at Sidhe hands. They'd stripped the Scottish changelings of most of their power, only recently righting that old wrong. Ronin had been smack in the middle of that, just as he'd been a lynchpin in the decision to snooker witches into taking over as Irichna hunters.

"What exactly did the changelings do to piss you off?" she asked, curious.

"It wasn't me, but I probably should have dug deeper before I allowed such a Draconian action."

"Yes, but what did they do?" she persisted.

Ronin winced. "It's been so long, I don't remember exactly. I think some of the Sidhe were concerned the changelings were throwing their power about and had gotten too big for themselves."

"It does seem like a bit of an overreaction. Ready to face the world?"

"Sure." He hugged her and she leaned into him, inhaling his wonderful scent. Sandalwood tickled her nose like an exotic herb, and amber added just the right undernote. "You need to tell me just a little about Bubba, er Niall's, buddies."

"I didn't get quite all of the story because I wanted time with you before dinner was ready, but it seems Ceridwen rustled up the others and dropped all three off on our doorstep."

"Good she saw them safely home."

"Mmph. I suppose that's true."

"What do they look like?"

Roz shrugged. "The male looks a lot like Bubba. Damn! Niall. Erk. Hope I don't fuck up in front of him. Anyway, the other male is dark and about his size. The female has flame-red hair and the greenest eyes I've ever seen. Greener than Duncan's." She was looking right at Ronin, so she saw him grimace. "What?"

"I know her."

"You can't possibly be sure about that."

"Oh yes I can. Very few of them have red hair, and almost none have green eyes. She's very strong magically, one of the elders of their race."

"Great!" Roz clapped her hands together. "She'll be an asset."

Ronin nodded. "Yes, I'm certain it's why Ceridwen summoned

her." He held out a hand and Roz clasped it. "Guess I'd best face the music. This seems to be my day to eat humble pie."

"Gosh, I haven't heard that expression in a long time. Granny used to say it."

"I'm much older than she was."

"Really? I'd never have guessed." She hip-butted him and they walked into the hall.

RONIN FELT at peace with Roz by his side. At least he'd gotten them back on an even keel. *No,* he corrected himself, *we did that together.* He sifted through memories trying to come up with the female changeling's name. Just before they reached the main floor, he snapped his fingers and said, "Krae."

"That's one of their names," Roz confirmed. "You could've asked me. The other one is Llyr."

"Humph. I might know him too."

"Well, if it isn't Ronin," a piercing, high-pitched voice rasped. "I thought I sensed your wretched presence." The female changeling moved through the front room like a small cyclone and planted herself right in front of him, elbows akimbo. Her eyes burned like mossy coals as she skewered him with her gaze.

"Krae." Ronin inclined his head. "We meet again."

She screwed her face into a disgusted moue. "Indeed. Bad apples have a way of rising to the top."

Ronin let go of Roz and hunkered so he was at eye level with the changeling. "You have every right to be unhappy with me. I apologize for what my people did to yours, but there is nothing I can do to return lost years to you." He paused for a beat, but Krae remained silent. "We face a deadly enemy," he went on. "If you don't feel you can fight by my side, I will see you safely returned to your people."

"Niall told me you'd changed, but I didn't believe him."

Ronin raised a curious brow. "Do you now?"

"I set a truth spell between us. You didn't lie to me."

Ronin extended a hand. After a long pause, Krae took it.

Niall and Llyr closed behind her. "Satisfied?" Niall asked.

"For now." Krae tossed her hair over a shoulder and glared at Ronin. "You're not in the clear yet, Sidhe-man. I plan to keep a very close eye on you."

"I wouldn't expect any less of you." Ronin released her hand and straightened.

"The other witches are all in the kitchen," Llyr said. "Dinner's ready."

"Why didn't you say so?" Krae spun and dashed back across the room.

"I hope there's enough food," Roz murmured. "When I started cooking, I didn't plan on three changelings. If they all eat like Bubba— Crap!" She slammed her forehead with her palm. "I've been calling him by one name for forty years. It just sort of slides off my tongue."

"I get the picture." Ronin draped an arm around her shoulders. "If they all eat like him, we should get in there while there's still something left."

"We can always order pizza. That's one thing they always deliver, even in Alaska in the middle of winter." Roz led the way into the kitchen.

Ronin glanced at the table; it was already crowded. He pitched his voice to be heard over the general hum of conversation. "Not that I'm trying to ruin anyone's appetite, but we need to discuss strategy. I'd thought we could do it over dinner, but—"

"We still can." Colleen stood. "I'll grab a couple of chairs, and you two can squeeze in at this end of things."

Ronin waited until he'd worked his way through a plate of the chicken vegetable mixture atop a mound of mashed potatoes. He was famished, and no wonder. He couldn't recall eating anything beyond half a sandwich sometime earlier in the day. From time to time, he glanced around the table. Naomi, Lou, and Maggie sat at the far end, chatting companionably among themselves. The three changelings were across from them with Niall in the middle holding court. Ronin knew enough about their race to understand how rare it was for one to leave the Old Country for very long. Jenna, Colleen, and Duncan were at his end of the table, along with Roz.

He'd been running battle strategies through his mind while he ate, responding to conversational gambits from time to time, but not attending to them. He clinked his knife on a glass and talk died. Many sets of eyes focused on him. "Let's open a discussion on who will do what when the next attack comes."

"We need another Sidhe," Duncan said. "There are multiples of three for witches and changelings, but only two of us."

"It might give us an edge," Ronin agreed. "Did you ask Titania to send someone our way?" Duncan nodded.

"They're going to be targeting Colleen, Jenna, and me." Roz looked up from her plate. "It seems unlikely they'd know the Sidhe agreed to share demon assassination duties with us."

"Don't underestimate them," Jenna muttered.

"They have spies everywhere," Colleen added.

"True." Roz made a disgusted face and set her fork down. "Nothing like talking about Irichna to kill my appetite. There's no way for us to figure out what they know."

"Any idea when they'll strike again?" Krae asked.

"No," Roz said. "It might be in five minutes, or they'll lie low for so long we'll abandon our plan to lure them here."

"That last doesn't seem likely to me," Ronin cut in. "They'll want to finish things off. They rose to the bait damned fast last time they showed up. I don't see them fading back to some hell-spawned hole for years."

"I had some time after we paid our last respects to Therese," Naomi said, "so I cast a few Tarot spreads."

"I almost hate to ask," Roz said, "but what'd you find out?"

Naomi cocked her head to one side and frowned. "It's all a matter of interpretation, but I tend to agree with Ronin. Darkness surrounds us, and I couldn't see the end of it."

CHAPTER 17

*R*oz shivered at the finality in Naomi's words. She wanted to ask for particulars, for how the cards had actually formed patterns, but held herself back. The spreads held truth in the moment they were cast, for the practitioner casting them, and the other witch's interpretation was good enough for her.

The meal she'd just eaten curdled in her stomach, and she muttered, "So, we wait."

"No," Ronin said. "We do more than that. We need to set a trap and do enough harm to those bastards they think twice before coming back."

"I suppose there's no way we can kill all of them," Niall spoke up.

"Even if all of them showed up, which won't happen, it's unlikely they'd just hang around and wait for us to annihilate them," Colleen agreed and pushed her chair back.

"Where are you going?" Duncan asked, smiling fondly at his wife.

"To the basement to bring more wine up here." She gestured at the empty bottles littering the table. "I've run out of red in the pantry, and I prefer it to white."

"Do you need help?" Jenna asked. "I probably drank more than my share."

"Nope. I'm good." Colleen moved to the corner of the kitchen that held the trap door, pulled it back, and faced in to work her way down the ladder. Roz's scalp prickled unpleasantly. She bolted from her chair and made a beeline for the opening in the kitchen floor, yelling Colleen's name.

"I'm fine, silly," floated back to her, but Roz didn't feel any better about things.

"What?" Jenna must've been alarmed by Roz's abrupt movement because she shoved out of her chair and joined her. Both of them stared into the basement's dark maw.

"Something doesn't feel right to me." Roz turned to navigate the ladder, but Ronin shoved between her and Jenna.

"I agree. You stay here," he barked. "I'll go."

Roz shook her head and called Colleen's name again. When the other witch didn't answer, Roz swore, "Goddammit all to hell," and disappeared into the hole. She heard Jenna and Ronin arguing, but Jenna must've won because she slithered down the ladder and landed on the dirt floor with a solid *thunk*.

"Colleen!" Jenna's voice rang out. "Aw crap! I smell Irichna."

Roz did too. She gripped Jenna's hand. "It could be from their last visit."

"Guess again, witch," a breathy voice rasped from the darkness.

"What have you done with our friend?" Roz demanded with a bravado she was far from feeling. Behind her, the ladder shook and she figured the Sidhe were climbing down it.

Demonic laughter chilled her blood. "Not much point waiting for the cavalry to show up," the demon snarled.

Fiery light flashed, and the basement disappeared so fast Roz's head spun.

She fought a sensation of falling while waves of nausea roiled through her. She had enough presence of mind to draw magic to soften her landing, assuming she came out of freefall sometime. Narrowing her eyes, she peered through inky shadows but couldn't see a thing. Panic narrowed her throat, and she forced herself to breathe before she blacked out. If she lost consciousness, she was a dead woman.

What had Ronin said about demons mating with humans? The Irichna had just kidnapped all of them. Why not kill them outright and be done with things? Demons were more than capable of that.

I'm still alive, and their prisoner. Shit, but this does not bode well.

"Roz?" Jenna said into her mind.

"Still here."

"I am too," Colleen said.

"The good news is we're all alive," Roz said.

"Let's make sure we stay that way," Colleen muttered. *"Ooph. Watch it. I just pitched up against something."*

The unremitting black around her lightened to a sickly gray. Roz funneled magic into the protective cushion around her. Good thing because she still landed hard. Colleen limped out of the murk. "Wish I'd have wound more magic around myself."

"Are you hurt?"

"My foot. It's not bad, just twisted a little."

Jenna plummeted past and crumpled into a twisted heap. Roz crawled to her, but by the time she placed her hands on the other witch, Jenna shook her off and pushed to an unsteady sit. "I'm all right. Where the fuck are we?"

"My guess is a borderworld," Roz said. "This doesn't feel much like Earth."

"My magic seems intact. How about if we teleport out of here?" The air around Colleen brightened.

Hopeful, Roz tested hers, dismayed to feel half of it slip through her fingers. "It may have been intact when we got here," she said, "but something about this world mutes it."

Jenna got to her feet and shook herself like a dog might. "We've always said the Irichna aren't stupid. Why would they go to all the trouble to move us here and then leave us the means to exit stage right?"

"I suppose you have a point." Roz stood too. "Ick. The air smells putrid."

"It smells like *them*," Colleen said. "Makes sense if this is one of their worlds."

"Do you think anyone will be able to find us?" Jenna asked. A muscle twitched in her jaw. "If we can't get ourselves out of here, we need help."

"The thing I don't get—" Roz raised her hands over her head and stretched her torso from side to side "—is why they didn't do this a long time ago."

"Yeah," Colleen muttered. "If we were that easy to nab, why bother trifling with us when it meant them losing demons?"

"Rather than trying to delve into their psychology," Jenna said dryly, "let's concentrate on seeing if there's a way out of here."

Roz turned in a full circle and scanned their surroundings. A flat, cracked dirt plain stretched ahead. Behind them, jagged piles of rocks got progressively higher, eventually forming a mountain range that didn't look too far away. Dirty snow glistened on the tops of some of the peaks. There wasn't a tree or bush in sight. When she deployed what was left of her magic, she didn't sense anything else alive.

"I think we should go that way." Roz pointed toward the mountains.

"Why?" Jenna looked at her feet. "Guess it's a good thing I'm wearing Pac boots and not my usual high heels."

"We'll need water. At least there's snow up there. Hopefully whatever fell out of the sky and froze is safe to drink."

"Beats staying here." Colleen drew her sweater closer around her. "Crap! If I'd known we were going to take a trip, I'd have brought a jacket."

"You and me both." Roz zipped her wool turtleneck up as far as it would go. Magic zinged through the air, foul power that set her teeth on edge. She turned to face whatever it was.

"So sorry to interrupt your plans," an amorphous voice grated. "You three are coming with me."

"Show yourself," Roz growled.

"I don't answer to you."

"What if we'd rather stay here?" Jenna drew herself tall.

"Not one of your choices. Come nicely, or I'm authorized to use force." The voice tittered unpleasantly. "Either way, the outcome will be the same."

Jenna made a derisive grunting sound, turned a one-eighty and marched the other direction. She made it about six steps before she shrieked and twirled, cradling one arm against her body. "You fucking bastard," she ground out. "What did you do to me?"

Colleen hurried to Jenna's side. "Straighten your arm. Let me see."

Jenna shook her head. "Nothing to look at. That thing shocked me. It felt like a cattle prod slammed into my elbow." She extended her arm and flexed her fingers. "I'm okay."

Roz dropped back until she stood next to the other two witches and bit her lip so hard she tasted blood. "Fine." She projected her voice. "Have it your way, for now. Since we can't see you, how will we—?"

"Follow my voice," the thing interrupted, obviously anticipating her question.

"What are you planning to do?" Colleen sniped. "Sing a little marching ditty?"

"The way will become clear very soon. If you stray from the path, you'll plunge to your deaths."

"This doesn't make sense," Colleen sent. *"If the path is that precarious, how could that thing force us? Besides, it's starting to look as if they want us alive."*

"I can hear you," the thing—demon or minion—mocked.

"Then answer her question," Jenna said.

"Not required. Coming, witches?"

"It doesn't appear we have much choice," Roz said and reached for Colleen and Jenna. They followed the voice three abreast until the path narrowed and they had to drop into single file. It wasn't as bad as the Dreamers' Paths, though there was a subtle similarity in its silvery surface. As Roz walked the narrow road, an idea formed. Hadn't Ronin said the dream guardian held some sort of ownership or responsibility for all psychic pathways? If that was true, maybe she could reach him through his link to what they walked on.

Roz wrestled with her truncated power. It was like snipping through thick, sticky spider webs with a toothpick. Careful to shield her mind, she snaked a bit of a spell outward, binding it to the medium beneath her feet.

"Noooooo!" Ronin shrieked as his feet hit the basement floor and he was blinded by a demonic flash.

"Quick!" Duncan pulled magic as if his life depended on it. "After them."

"We have no idea where they went." Ronin added a string of Gaelic curses that made Duncan raise his eyebrows.

"The magic is fresh. We can follow it," Duncan insisted.

"I've done that before," Ronin spat. "All it did was lose me in the ether."

The three changelings swarmed down the ladder. "They got Colleen, didn't they?" Niall demanded.

"I'm afraid so." Duncan blew out a bitter-sounding breath.

"What are we waiting for?" Krae shouted. "We have to leave now while the magic is fresh."

"Duncan is of that opinion too. Have you ever gone into the traveling portals without a destination in mind?" Ronin asked her.

"Of course. Look, Sidhe-man," she reached up and jabbed his chest with her long index finger, "we're wasting time."

"Do you need us?" Naomi called from the trapdoor.

Ronin exchanged glances with Duncan. There were almost too many of them with the three changelings, but talking Niall into remaining here wouldn't go well. The changeling spirit was intensely loyal to Colleen and would probably go after her—no matter what he and Duncan did.

"Since we have no bloody idea what we're doing, probably not," Ronin told Naomi. "I'll raise Titania and Oberon and ask them to send reinforcements."

"Already done," Duncan said, his tone terse. "Let's get moving. It's my wife out there in Irichna clutches."

"You think I'm not aware of that?" Ronin bit off the words. "Roz is snared in the same trap. I'm just as frantic as you, but if we make a mistake—like losing ourselves between worlds—it might mean both their deaths. Jenna's too."

Krae gestured to Llyr and Niall. Magic boiled among them, strong earth magic that startled Ronin with its ferocity. "If you're coming—" Krae balanced power that looked like small lightning bolts between her hands "—bind your magic to ours. We shouldn't get separated."

Ronin hated running headlong into the unknown. He was a planner, a tactician. Plunging into demon-land unprepared went against the grain. "One moment." He leaned toward Duncan. "Did Titania say who she's sending to help Naomi and her witches?"

An uncomfortable look flitted across Duncan's expressive features. "Dark fae."

Breath whistled from between Ronin's clenched teeth. While he didn't dislike the Unseelie as much as Titania, still he didn't trust the mirror image of his race. "What? None of us were willing to volunteer?"

"I don't think that was it," Duncan muttered. "It's the same Unseelie couple I worked with before. They gleaned what was going on and offered to help."

"Indeed we did." A woman's voice trilled from a darkened corner of the basement.

"If we'd stayed around to engage in endless Seelie debates about the best way to do something—" a man mocked as he strode forward "—we'd lose the witches' trail for sure."

"Humph. Same thing I told him. What a stiff-necked race they are," Krae muttered in a voice loud enough to carry.

"Now just wait a minute." Ronin straightened his spine and faced the Unseelie pair. "You're here to help the witches upstairs."

"Ye only think we are," the man retorted. "We don't answer to you." He sidestepped Ronin, stopped near Duncan, and grinned. "Seems we're destined to cross each other's paths." When he inclined his head, his dark hair shimmied around him, falling to chest level. Eyes the color of gray smoke held an otherworldly aspect. Like all fae, he was beautiful, with a gamin's face and a perpetually youthful look. Black robes sashed with red swirled around his tall, lithe form.

"Look." Krae ground out the word. "I'm getting tired of holding power in abeyance. Let's get moving."

"A most excellent idea, dear." The Unseelie female trotted forward. Shoulder-length black hair bobbed as she shook her head, and lines formed around the corners of her green eyes. As tall as her male partner, she wore a skintight black jumpsuit that fit her like a second skin, and her feet were bare.

"We should go," Duncan nudged Ronin. "We can sort out the fine points later."

Like where we're going and what the fuck we'll do once we get there?

Ronin almost choked on his ambivalence, muttered, "Fine," and wove a binding spell to hold them in tandem with the changelings. The Unseelie did the same.

"Finally. Goddess preserve me from both halves of the Faerie court." Krae loosed her spell. The basement walls glistened wetly and winked out of existence.

Ronin tallied up their hunting party. Three changelings and four fae. He had no idea how his magic would blend with the Unseelie workings, and little enough experience with changelings. None of that mattered, though. The only thing that did was finding the three witches. Things had happened so fast, he hadn't had time to absorb what it would mean to lose Roz.

I'm not going to lose her. I can't.

What if she's already dead?

She's not. If she were, I'd know it.

Ashamed he hadn't thought of it sooner, he spun magic outward, searching, but came up dry.

"I already tried that," Duncan said. *"We have to be closer. At least on the same world."*

"Once we find the women, we're going to annihilate every single one of those Irichna bastards—and blow their sorry excuse for a world to kingdom come."

"Know how you feel," Duncan said, *"but we have to get the women to safety first."*

"They won't take that well. They'll want to fight."

"Too bad." A defiant bitterness rang in Duncan's mind voice. *"If I'd done things my way, Colleen would be safe in my manor house in the U.K."*

"You can't lock her up like that." Niall's unmistakable Irish burr intruded into their conversation.

"Aye," another voice, maybe Llyr's, weighed in. *"Didn't you learn anything from what you did to us?"*

"If I'd wanted public input, I'd have asked for it," Duncan snarled.

"Quiet everyone," Krae said. *"Mute your magic and your chatter, we're almost there."*

Ronin sucked in a tense breath and prayed *there* was where they'd find the witches. Time was critical and being wrong wasn't an option. The unremitting black of the traveling ether lightened, and he landed hard on dried out dirt. Krae had said to mute his magic, but he had to know if Roz was here, so he sent a tracking thread zinging outward.

"Thank fucking Christ," he mumbled. "Not just here, but still alive."

"Colleen too," Duncan said, his voice pitched low.

"You two are impossible." Krae tossed her hands skyward and twisted her mouth in annoyance.

"We need a plan." The Unseelie male walked toward the group from where he'd emerged a few feet away, flanked by the woman.

"For once, we agree," Ronin said. He eyed the dark fae. "What are your names?"

"I am Sperrin. My mate is Moire. Depending which border-world we ended up on, our magic may dwindle the longer we're here, but it should be fully operable for at least the next hour or two, perhaps longer. This is how I believe we should proceed..."

Because he was used to the mantle of command, Ronin recognized a fellow leader in Sperrin and bent close to catch the Unseelie's words.

CHAPTER 18

The path before Roz gleamed in the gray light of the borderworld, the only thing alive in an otherwise dead landscape. She might've imagined it, but she thought she felt a slight jolt through her feet. Had the dream guardian heard her?

God, I hope so.

With startling abruptness, the silvery trail ended and she was back on hard-packed dirt. Jenna and Colleen moved to either side of her. Because her friends should know the worst, and she didn't care what their ghostly guide thought, she said, "Ronin told me something I didn't know about the demons. Brace yourselves, it's not good."

"Spit it out," Jenna snapped. "Since we're not dead yet, I figured something worse might be in the offing."

"Crap!" Colleen leaned into Roz. "I'm not sure I want to hear it, but knowledge is power, so shoot."

"Watch what you say, witch." The disembodied voice was back. "Show respect."

Roz gathered what saliva she could from her dry mouth and spat on the ground. "Never. The day I respect an abomination is the day—" Searing pain shot through her right temple, and she clutched her head and moaned.

Colleen pried Roz's hands away and sent weak, soothing magic into her. Jenna faced the direction of the voice. "Show yourself, goddammit. Come out here and fight like a man."

"Oh, but I'm not. Unlike some of the others here, I never was."

"Fine. Take whatever twisted, fucked-up form is native for you."

"I'm going to ignore that. Help the other one, we're behind schedule."

"Hear that?" Roz straightened and shook herself. "The Irichna have schedules. Do you suppose they calendared the last attack in Outlook?"

"March!" The voice commanded. "We are on a road. Follow it."

When Roz glanced down, she saw a faint track carving through the dirt. She'd scarcely call it a road, but wasn't anxious for another shot to the head, so she kept her mouth shut. Jenna hooked a hand under one elbow, Colleen the other, and they moved forward. The sky developed a purplish hue, and twin moons crested the far horizon.

She missed Ronin fiercely, ached for him, but wishing for the impossible might divert her enough to get herself killed. No. She had to be on top of her game, not mooning over the only man she'd ever truly cared about.

I've got to escape or I'll never see him again.

Her stomach twisted sourly. She wanted to fight back, not follow meekly behind something she couldn't even see.

"What were you going to tell us?" Colleen asked.

Roz aimed for a neutral tone. "Apparently Irichna breed with human women to create their royalty."

"Son of a bitch." Jenna stopped dead.

"You've got to be kidding." Colleen ground to a halt too.

"I wish I was," Roz said.

"Have we ever run across Irichna royalty?" Jenna asked.

Roz shrugged. "How would I know? I didn't even know they existed until a day or so ago. Apparently all that information is in those scrolls moldering away in our downstairs cabinet."

"Do your kings and queens dirty their hands with war?" the voice inquired archly, and then added, "I did not give you permission to stop."

"We don't have kings or queens," Roz said. "They went out with the seventeen hundreds."

"The Sidhe do." The voice developed a sly undernote.

"Fine. Maybe you should ask them," Jenna growled.

"Such a thing might be possible since several just arrived. This is so exciting," the voice trilled, edging higher. "A rescue party. They're doing exactly what master said they would."

"What exactly are you?" Colleen asked.

"Scratch that," Roz cut in. "Who's your master?"

"Oh I doubt you'd recognize his name. Hurry now, witches. Not much farther."

Nice of him to let us know.

Roz culled through her brain for strategies while they walked as slowly as they dared. Once they were delivered to whoever *master* was, escape would become much harder.

"Ooph." She folded her ankle sideways and slid to the ground. "Damn it!" she groaned, hoping to do a credible job faking pain. "Ouch! God but that hurts. I should watch where I'm walking."

Picking up on her cue, Jenna and Colleen dropped to the dirt on either side of her. "Here." Jenna laid a hand on either side of Roz's ankle. "Let me see what I can do."

"Your magic doesn't work very well here," Colleen warned, while Roz kept up a low, tortured whimper.

"Can't the two of you help her?" the voice cut in.

"I don't see how," Jenna murmured, still running her hands over the outside of Roz's boot. "Here, I need to take your boot off. What's left of my magic isn't burly enough to reach through it." She plucked at the laces.

Roz shrieked when Jenna levered her boot off, and the voice dissolved into a language she'd never heard.

"Don't touch me," Roz cried and slapped at Jenna's hands. "Let my foot rest for a minute."

"I will reinstate your magic so you can fix her." The voice held an uncertain note, as if the creature were crawling onto a rickety limb.

"Healing would go faster if both of us worked on her," Colleen said blandly.

Roz's pulse rate gathered momentum. If two of them were even temporarily restored, Colleen could jump them out of here. She thought about what the creature had said about Sidhe—presumably Ronin and Duncan—being close and wondered if it was telling the truth. If it was, leaving was out of the question. They couldn't abandon their mates.

"We're all in this together..." Roz kept her mind voice shuttered, just in case the thing could glean her thoughts.

"Very well," the voice said. "But I will be watching closely. You've seen what I can do. At the first hint of disobedience, I will strike first and ask questions later."

A revelation brought Roz to full attention. It wasn't the world muting their magic but some machination on the part of their captor. All they'd have to do would be to immobilize whatever held them prisoner and... She clamped down on her thoughts and exchanged glances with Colleen, who nodded almost imperceptibly.

"I'm good," Colleen told Jenna. "I'll help you get her boot back on. Now that we have enough magic to reach through the leather, the lacing should help stabilize her foot and ankle to heal them."

"Awk! Do you have to?" Roz bent forward and cradled her ankle.

"'Fraid so, sweetie." Jenna worked the laces farther open, and she and Colleen jockeyed the boot on with Roz moaning and cursing.

"Buck up." Colleen shot her an annoyed look.

"She always was a baby." Jenna rolled her eyes and directed her next words at Colleen. "Ready whenever you are."

Roz girded herself. She wouldn't be able to help much, but every little bit of magic would be critical. Power built around her, making the air sizzle. The voice let out a banshee howl, followed by incomprehensible words. Its last shot to her head was nothing compared with pain that lanced through her now. It felt like someone had driven a spear in through her eye and into her brain, but Colleen had them encased in a portal. Escape was all that mattered. She could live with pain.

"Where to?" Her mind voice vibrated with tension.

"If Duncan and Ronin are here, we can't leave," Colleen answered.

"Why not?" Jenna asked. *"Anywhere we land on this godforsaken world, that thing will find us again."*

"We have to locate the Sidhe first," Roz said. *"While we were on that path, I asked the dream guardian for help. If we get really lucky—"*

"Like that's going to happen," Jenna cut in. *"He's a surly son of a bitch, at least according to one of my aunts. Why would he help us?"*

"I'm taking us back to where we started," Colleen broke in. *"It's almost the only place I know here, and I have to visualize something. How's your head, Roz?"*

"I'll live. There's something wrong with the vision in my right eye, though."

"How can you tell anything in here?" Jenna demanded. *"It's pitch black."*

"Because my sight went to hell before Colleen finished her spell."

"Maybe it's temporary." Colleen was at least trying to sound hopeful. *"Hang on. I'm bringing us down."*

Roz tucked her body into a roll and landed smoothly. She bolted to her feet and waited for Jenna and Colleen to join her. "I still think we should've left while we could," Jenna muttered darkly.

"I sure hope you're not right." Roz shot a crooked grin her way.

"I can't see anything out of my right eye, but other than that I'm more-or-less okay, and my magic is back online."

"Do you want me to see if I can fix your eye?" Colleen asked.

"No. We need to find the others, unless that creature was lying to us and they're not really here."

"Whatever it was didn't seem disingenuous enough to lie," Jenna said.

"No, it didn't, and it was hella easy to fake it out," Roz agreed and projected her mind voice. *"Ronin!"*

Seconds later his voice rang in her head, pulsing with relief. *"Stay put. We'll follow your energy."*

Three Irichna swept through a fiery portal that formed out of nowhere. One moment the air was empty—and then it wasn't. "Best of luck to him," one demon said.

"Indeed," another chortled, "since it would appear we found you first."

"Tsk, tsk," the third chimed. "We sent such a nice messenger to greet you and assure you of our good intentions. Tricking him was a huge mistake."

"They're setting a trap. Spread out," Roz cried, but she was too late. The air fizzed and hissed around them. Something she couldn't see settled with an audible clunk. She reached for it, felt an electric charge sizzle, and yanked her hand back before she fried herself.

"Ronin! Irichna found us," she sent, frantic he and Duncan would teleport into a trap. She waited, but Ronin didn't answer.

"My magic still works," Colleen said, sticking with telepathy.

"Fat lot of good it will do us inside this pen," Jenna mumbled.

Roz watched the Irichna. They didn't seem to be paying attention to the witches' telepathic communication.

They're arrogant. They figure they've got us trapped, so they're just waiting to destroy whomever shows up to rescue us.

She held out her hands to her closest friends, encouraged by their touch. *"We will not go down without a hell of a contest. Wait until*

Ronin and Duncan show up. While the demons' attention is caught up in fighting them, let's blast our way out of here."

"Oh my God," Colleen cried, *"we need to warn the men."*

"I already did," Roz said.

"Great. Let's harness what magic we can while we're waiting," Jenna said and started a low chant.

∾

RONIN OPENED himself to as much power as he could hold. The air around him bubbled with energy. "Come on!" he called to the others. "I've found their trail."

"Ye got that telepathic message from Roz, but it could be a con," Sperrin cautioned.

"And I just got another that the women are surrounded by demons," Ronin retorted. "I'm not thinking that's a trap."

"Doesn't matter." Niall leapt forward with Llyr and Krae right behind him. "Colleen needs us."

"This whole place reeks of Irichna," Krae complained.

"Of course it does." Niall shot her a patronizing look. "They live here."

"Forty years with humans hasn't improved you at all." The female changeling stretched her long fingers and peered through a curtain of flame-colored hair. "Let's get this over with."

"I agree," Llyr said. "I love borrowing demon energy."

"Sucking them dry you mean," Krae chortled.

"That too." Llyr's dark eyes shone with anticipation.

Ronin tossed a spell over all of them, but their teleport was over so soon walls barely had a chance to form. He tumbled onto a dried-out plain, indistinguishable from every other place on this goddess-forsaken world. Power held in abeyance crackled between his hands.

Three Irichna leered at him, their vacant, smoke-colored eyes rimmed in fiery tones. Long, gray hair swirled around them.

"Nice of you to drop in, Sidhe," one screeched. Black robes masked his true form.

"Saves us the trouble of hunting you down," another in blue robes cut in.

"And clears the decks," the third, also garbed in black, noted with satisfaction. "No one else will search for these three." He gestured toward the witches who stood together, obviously trapped behind an invisible barrier powered by demon magic. Roz gave Ronin a thumbs-up sign, and Colleen blew Duncan a kiss.

Duncan, Sperrin, Moire, and the changelings formed a ragged line with Ronin at its center. "Counting your chickens a wee bit early, eh?" Moire quirked a brow.

"You forget," the first Irichna said, "this is our world. Home court advantage and all that rot."

"Since you've picked up modern idioms, you've spent entirely too much time in our world," Duncan growled.

"What's it to you, Sidhe?"

"You're garbage. I prefer cleaner air in my nest."

"Interesting, Sidhe scum. We feel the same way. Remember, you came to us." A jagged hole yawned in front of them sucking dirt and pebbles into its maw, and Ronin stepped back a pace. He opened himself to the arcane power source, wondering if he could tap into it from this world. Dirt crumbled around his boots as the cavity in the ground deepened and he scrambled backward. He pushed his spell harder but couldn't latch onto the power that was sure to mow through the demons like a sharp scythe.

"I can't coax it to life, either," Duncan panted.

"I didn't come to talk. I came to fight." Niall jumped across the opening and launched himself at one of the demons. He shape-shifted in the air and sank reptilian fangs into an Irichna neck, but the demon shook him off.

"No," Llyr said. "Like this. Borrow power from your target first." The air around the changeling boiled red and he shifted into a dragon, opened his mouth, and shot fire at one of the demons. To Ronin's intense surprise, the Irichna shrieked in pain and lunged for Llyr, who flew out of reach, trumpeting his success in the dead air of the borderworld.

It was as if the changelings had issued a call to arms. Irichna poured out of the ether, columns of them. More demons than Ronin imagined existed. He heard Krae curse and understood they had to create a defensible perimeter or they'd all be lost.

"Wards," he cried. "Project your magic. Do it now."

"Ye think?" Sperrin muttered dryly.

"Do you have a better idea?" Ronin pulled magic like a madman and glanced at the dark fae.

"Nope. Same thing I'd have done. The two changelings will be on the wrong side, but there's not much we can do about it."

Ronin tested the strength of their hastily created barrier. It wasn't bad, but it wouldn't hold forever, not at the rate Irichna were flinging jolts of power their way. The air filled with dirty smoke and reeked of ozone and sulfur mixed with demon stench. At least the witches seemed safe behind whatever the demons had erected around them. They'd joined hands and their heads were bent together. Ronin bet they were up to something but didn't want to risk drawing the Irichnas' attention by using telepathic speech.

He yearned for Roz, needed to feel her next to him and breathe her in. Duncan had said they'd nab the women and hightail it out of here. Too bad it wasn't that easy. One thing was certain. He and Roz would marry just as soon as he could find someone to officiate.

Whoa. First, I have to ask her.

And then she has to say yes.

"What now?" Duncan asked, breaking into Ronin's train of thought.

"We keep firing back. Maybe we'll get lucky," Sperrin said, his mouth set in a hard line.

"Lucky how?" Ronin asked.

"I don't think all of them are real. If we hit the nexus powering their illusion, things could improve fast."

Ronin ducked and wove, patching the ward when it weakened and sending as much power as he could to different locations in an attempt to find the demons' weak spot, if they had one. In a corner of his mind, he thought maybe if he and Duncan joined forces, they could find the mother lode again, but there wasn't time for anything beyond evasive maneuvers.

Niall and Llyr shifted form so many times, Ronin lost track. At least their plasticity conferred some level of protection. Whenever a demon cornered one, they slithered out of the trap and emerged as something different. Maybe they were able to siphon off enough Irichna energy to weaken at least a few.

Ronin sucked in a breath and winced at how awful the demons smelled. Road kill ripened in the sun mixed with rotten eggs would just about describe it. A ripping, tearing noise raked across his ears, and then the witches pelted across the open ground between them. Heedless it would leave him defenseless, Ronin ripped a hole in the warding, stood dead center, and gestured them his way. His heart jumped into double time, and he switched to defensive magic, doing his level best to drape it around the witches as they ran.

Magic crackled around him, uncomfortably close. Sperrin, Moire, Duncan, and Krae had joined forces and staved off a barrage of dark magic that would have sent him to the *Dreaming* forever and been the end of the witches. Llyr and Niall jumped into the fray from the other side. Time stopped for Ronin as he watched Roz feint and dodge. He threw everything he had into protective magic and tamped down jubilation as she got progressively closer. Finally, one mighty leap, and she tumbled against him. He wanted to crush her to him, but he thrust her to the side where the warding was intact and waited until Colleen stumbled through with Jenna at her heels.

Before he could resurrect the ward, its weave formed before his eyes, and he realized Sperrin and Moire had taken care of it.

"Jesus fucking Christ," Jenna blurted. "That was hideous. Their magic hurt like hell when we blasted through it. My skin still feels like it's on fire."

"Mine too," Colleen said. Duncan made a beeline for her, but she shook her head. "I love you too, but we've got to keep fighting."

It was risky to take his eyes off the demons even for a second, but Ronin had to know if Roz was hurt. A quick glance was far from reassuring. One side of her face was bruised and swollen, and blood trickled from one eye. After a brief nod his way, she'd joined their scruffy line, helping their counterattack along with Jenna and Colleen.

Ronin made his way to Roz's side. "You're hurt."

"I'll live." She tried to wink, but her swollen face distorted in a way that looked painful. "Thanks for caring."

"It's more than that." He jumped a blast that came through a hole in their ward and bent his attention to repairing it.

"I'm happy to see you too," Roz said, lethal energy blazing from her outstretched hands.

Ronin knew it was a mistake before the words were out, but he couldn't help himself. "You could teleport to safety. To where Naomi or Titania could take care of your wounds. I'll join you once we've cleared things up here."

"If I wasn't so busy, I'd slap you," she hissed and shot a glance of pure fury his way. "What part of not separating me, Jenna, and Colleen didn't you get?"

"Sorry. I'm sorry." He pivoted to avoid being hit and knit the wards together—again.

"Look," her voice was softer, "I know you were probably frantic and feeling helpless after the demons nabbed us. None of this sits well with me, either, but we have to see this through to the end. There's no choice, not really."

Admiration swelled for the woman before him. "God, but I love you. You remind me of the Valkyrie warriors."

"I'll take that as a high compliment. Think of some way to outsmart those bastards. If it's just a show of sheer power, ours against theirs, we'll lose eventually."

Ronin clenched his jaws in determination and said, "I'll work on it."

"We have to get Bubba back." Colleen stared at the changeling.

"He seems to be holding his own." Duncan flung power at a particularly loathsome demon, and it brayed laughter, seemingly uninjured by a direct hit.

"If the changelings were on this side of the ward, we could teleport out of here," Jenna said.

"It'll never happen." Colleen jerked her chin upward. "There's oodles of real estate, and at least fifty Irichna, between us and them."

Ronin eyed Krae. Of all of them, she seemed to be having a wonderful time with a broad, unwavering grin on her face. She lured power and it flowed from the earth through her body, sparking from her extended fingers. He trotted to her side and said, "Can we get them back here?"

"What do you think, Sidhe-man? Niall's been trying to get back to us ever since the witches made a break for it. The demons cut him off every time."

Breath whistled through Ronin's teeth. "If they can't get to us," he muttered, "we need to come up with a plan to rescue them."

"My assessment too," Krae said, sounding fierce. "We're not leaving without them. Ideas? You Sidhe are usually good for things like that."

Ronin suspected if they didn't cut their losses and leave, none of them would survive, but he just nodded, still choking on his anxiety to gather Roz against him and go. She was hurt, needed medical attention of some sort...

He checked himself. A good commander didn't prioritize one

soldier over another, even if he loved her to distraction, and not being able to move her to safety was killing him.

Marshaling his fading wits, Ronin made his way to where Duncan fought on the other side of Colleen. Maybe if they worked together, they could tap into enough power to weaken the Irichna long enough to collect the two changelings and get the hell out of there.

CHAPTER 19

Time dribbled past. Roz had no idea how much, but she was nearing the end of her energy. Her magic was sluggish and slow to respond. Not being able to see very well didn't help. She flung as big a bolt of magic as she could manage, and it barely made it through the warding. Taking a steadying breath and following it with another, she shored up her flagging strength. If there was ever a time to not crap out, this was it.

Why do I feel so bad? Like I'm swimming upstream in concrete.

"Master told me to stay away, but we have a score to settle, witch. Or was that bitch?"

Roz whipped her head around. The sudden shot of adrenaline was welcome as was knowing the minion must have been draining her energy. "Shit! Go away!" she shrieked.

"Who are you talking to?" Colleen grabbed her arm.

"It's the fucking voice again."

"The one from earlier?" Colleen raked her other hand through her hair. "I didn't hear a thing."

"Maybe that's because you're not the one who duped him," Roz growled. "I'm so wiped out my head's spinning and I can't think."

"What's going on?" Ronin yelled.

"A minion. It was the original greeting party and we pissed it off," Colleen yelled back.

Ronin twisted his head from side to side. "Where the hell is it?"

"That's just it," Roz answered. "It's invisible."

"Fucking great. Is there only one?" Ronin edged toward them.

"My sentiments exactly," Colleen muttered. "And yeah, there's only one."

"We think there's only one," Jenna answered. "There might be more. Hard to tell when you can't see the fuckers." She pivoted and sent power toward a group of Irichna that were chivvying Niall and Llyr.

Roz felt her consciousness slipping. She swayed from foot to foot to hold herself upright. Had she reached the end of her reserves, or was the minion shoving her toward a mental abyss? Pain sprayed across the injured side of her face, and she screamed and clasped her head.

"Nooooo!" Ronin cried. "You cannot have her."

Magic surged around Roz, the heat from the mix of Sidhe and demonic power felt as if it were flaying the skin from her bones. She made an enormous effort to clear her fuzzed-out head.

"Fight back, goddammit," Jenna shouted so close to Roz's ear, it set her teeth on edge, but she welcomed the pain because it helped her focus. Colleen and Jenna dove into her mind, shoring her up, giving her strength. She tapped their gifts shamelessly and hoped to hell she wasn't draining them. The world stopped whirling and she managed to croak. "I'm okay now. Save your magic."

"You sure?" Colleen asked from inside her head.

"Yes. Go." Roz fought a temporary disorientation as the other witches retreated, but her mind was much clearer than it had been once they withdrew.

"Where's the minion?" Ronin demanded. "Is it still there?"

Roz reached for it, but all she found was emptiness. She licked her dry lips. "I can't sense it anymore. Maybe it took a hike once it realized it was outnumbered. I was fading back there, probably because of something it did, and I suppose the thing sensed it and closed in for its version of retribution. It wasn't banking on having to fight three of us."

"Four." Ronin corrected her, sounding fiercely protective. Roz wanted to hug him and never let go.

She gazed at the smoke and the jagged hole in the earth not two feet from their warding. "We've got to leave here. They'll wear us down one by one. Shit! They nearly had me, and I'm still nowhere close to a hundred percent."

"I'll watch out for her," Jenna closed a protective arm around Roz. She exchanged a pointed glance with Ronin. "Do something to get us out of here."

~

"DUNCAN," Ronin bellowed.

"Right here." The other Sidhe trotted over. Soot streaked his face and darkened his hair.

Sperrin closed from the other side. "Before ye start issuing orders," he told Ronin, "we already command the means to get out of this mess, but we'll have to work together."

"Talk fast," Ronin said.

"We've never actually done this," Moire cautioned, "mostly because we've never had a Sidhe who was willing."

"I didn't say anything before because I was hoping there'd be another way," Sperrin cut in.

"You're talking in circles," Duncan muttered, followed by, "Damn it!" as he leapt to avoid a blast of Irichna magic that powered through their wards. Snarling in frustration, he streamed magic to repair the warding and cried, "Keep talking. I can listen while I take care of this."

"Between us we control the dark and light halves of Faerie,"

Sperrin said. "Like with most magic, it's a gestalt, stronger than either part individually."

"How do we blend our power?" Ronin asked. "Beyond fighting side by side, since we're already doing that."

"There are spells so old they've fallen out of memory," Sperrin murmured. "Once long ago, I knew them, but I'm not certain—"

"Give me free rein in your mind." Moire sounded determined, and her green eyes flashed fire. "I'll find them."

"Yes, but can you locate them fast enough?" Duncan asked. "Mind sifting is labor intensive. I'm not certain we can do without your magic for the amount of time it will take you to unearth what we need to know."

"It's a bad idea," Ronin said flatly. "Too uncertain. Let's move on."

"Ye're afraid," Sperrin jeered.

"Of what?" Ronin's tone was derisive. "We don't have time for this."

Colleen, who'd been trading blows with Irichna, loosed a blood-curdling cry. "Fuck! Bubba's cornered and he can't shape-shift out of it." She ripped a hole in the warding and bolted through.

"Colleen! No!" Duncan hurtled through behind her.

"I can't let him die," she called over a shoulder.

Ronin opened his mouth to order both of them back behind the wards but knew it wouldn't do any good. Colleen wasn't bound to obey him, and Duncan wouldn't leave his wife unguarded. He snapped his jaws shut hard enough to hurt.

"I've got the spell," Sperrin bit off the words. "I remembered. Ronin. Are you with me?"

Ronin stared into the dark fae's smoke gray eyes and asked, "Is there a downside?"

"Ye might turn into one of us," Moire smirked.

"It's better than being locked in the *Dreaming* for the next ten millennia. Tell me what to do."

"Your trust will go far toward repairing the divide between our people." Sperrin shot him a triumphant look. "The first step is this…"

White-hot power flared through Ronin. In many ways, it reminded him of the deep well he'd tapped into at Duncan's wedding. Slippery, razor sharp, and almost stronger than he was.

"Wait," Sperrin cautioned. "Let it build. We won't have a second go at this. I told ye earlier, this world saps our ability."

Grim-faced, Moire seemed to be having her own struggles. Krae stomped to her side and touched her. Shock rampaged across the dark fae's face. "Whatever ye did helped."

"Of course it did. I strengthened your bonding to earth magic."

"Ready." Sperrin's voice was strained. "On my count of three, but watch your aim. We don't want to hit our own."

"You scarcely needed to remind me," Ronin muttered. "Focus on the three who spoke to us. At least we know they're real."

Roz shook Jenna off and made her way to his side. "You shouldn't be here," he rasped.

"This will either work or it won't," Roz said. "If it doesn't, we're all dead, and I'd like to spend my last moments near you. Besides—" a flicker of her dry humor resurrected itself "—my magical well's not totally dry. Maybe I can help."

He tossed half a crooked grin her way and loosed the magic burning a path through him. Irichna shrieked imprecations, but they folded in on themselves and scattered to nothingness. Sometimes the air simply sizzled, and he understood the demon he'd targeted had been illusion. For the first time, he let himself hope they might see the other side of this. Victory felt close, and it lightened the burden that had been crushing him.

"Excellent call," he told Sperrin. "We'll have to insist our armies learn this maneuver."

"That would mean working together," Sperrin panted, targeted another Irichna, and let magic fly. The demon scattered into hundreds of fiery motes.

"If we can do it, the rest of our people can too."

Roaring filled his ears like a deafening tide, and Ronin shook his head from side to side. The air took on a glittering aspect in the midst of the remaining Irichna. "What the hell is that?"

"I have no bloody idea," Sperrin answered. "Let's kill it before it's fully corporeal."

"Bully idea." Ronin found himself liking the dark fae, and even more than that, respecting him. He pivoted and took careful aim.

"Stop," Krae cried and jumped in front of him. "It's the dream guardian."

"That seems incredibly unlikely." Ronin pulled air like a bellows with the effort of holding his magic back.

"You'll just have to trust me on this one, Sidhe-man. Besides, you wouldn't hurt him. All you'd do is piss him off." Krae whirled and bowed deeply in the direction of the rapidly brightening patch of air. Once she straightened she said, "We must be truly blessed as he rarely leaves the Dreamers' Paths."

"Son of a bitch." Moire narrowed her eyes and shuttered her power. "I do believe the changeling is right."

"OH MY GOD, I'd almost forgotten about him." Roz stared hard at the luminous air out of her good eye. "When the minion forced us to follow it, we walked along something that was a lot like the Dreamers' Paths, so I guessed maybe it might be a way to link to the guardian and ask him for help."

A sense of profound wonder moved through her, and all her hurt places eased just a little.

The air brightened still more, and the guardian took shape. He looked exactly as he had the night Roz had seen him, his brown robes sashed with moonbeams and a circlet of them holding his silvery hair at bay. His blue eyes reflected the wisdom of ages in an ever-shifting collage of imagery.

Three new Irichna emerged from the smoke and faced the guardian. Their dark robes were sashed in crimson, and each wore a heavy gold necklace set with onyx. "What are you doing in our world?" one asked.

The guardian's eyes glittered dangerously. "You used my pathways to abduct the innocent. It is not permitted."

"Those *innocents* have been trying to kill us," the middle Irichna said sweetly. "We merely acted in self-defense."

"Lies. You have always struck first." The guardian held up a hand. "I am not here to trade philosophies. I have no purview over your kind, but I will sever your ability to use any of my traveling pathways on this world and others. Between worlds as well."

An Irichna stepped forward. "You wouldn't."

"I already have. I am opening a way for the witches, Sidhe, and changelings. We shall depart and leave you to your own company."

"We need to talk about this," two Irichna said so close together they sounded like an echo.

"We already have." The dream guardian lifted his arms. "To me."

Power flashed from the middle Irichna. It bounced off the guardian, who turned the full force of his unsettling gaze on the trio. "You would raise magic against me? My power is rooted in the original making. Try it again at your peril."

The guardian swept his gaze over the rest of them. When it landed on Roz, she felt as if she'd found redemption, and then dunned herself for being a fool. The only redemption was that she was still alive and could fight another day.

"Come on, Jenna." Roz crooked two fingers her way, and then she leaned on Ronin as they skirted the fissure in front of their warding and moved to the guardian's side. Bubba was in his snake form. Colleen scooped him into her arms and joined them, with Duncan next to her. Llyr, Krae, and the two dark fae trotted close.

"That was great sport." Llyr grinned so broadly even his back teeth showed. "At least until Niall got himself trapped."

The changeling writhed in Colleen's arms. Roz knew he wanted to stage a snappy comeback but couldn't talk in his reptile form.

"That may be true, but it is time to leave now." The guardian eyed Llyr, and the changeling looked down.

Krae bowed so low her forehead swept the ground. "That you have come to our aid is a deep honor," she said as she straightened.

"The honor is all mine, creature of the earth." The guardian extended his hand and Krae clasped it, her green eyes shining with pleasure.

"We shall reconvene at my altar in the Dreamers' Paths." The guardian swept his hands to the side and upward, and Roz felt his teleport spell snap her up. She sagged against Ronin, who kept an arm closed tight about her.

"When we get home," she said, "I'm going to sleep for a week."

"First we'll see about healing you," Ronin's voice buzzed against her ear. "You look like hell."

"Just the sort of thing to warm a girl's heart."

"Ssht. Rest while you have a few moments. I have a feeling the guardian wants to talk with us, or he'd have sent us to our respective homes."

The black of the traveling ether shifted to gray much sooner than Roz anticipated, but when she thought about it, it made sense. If the guardian controlled all pathways, no wonder they could scoot through them in record time since he'd summoned the traveling spell. Ronin scooped her into his arms and cushioned her landing.

"Put me down." She wriggled against him, but not too hard, thinking how good it felt to be held.

The verdant clearing and ancient trees surrounding the guardian's altar took form, a welcome counterpoint to the lifelessness of the borderworld. Ronin ignored her request and continued to clasp her close. "I love you, Roz," he whispered.

"Bring the witch to my altar," the guardian instructed, and Ronin started forward.

"How do you know he meant me?" Roz asked.

"His magic called to mine." Ronin turned his attention to the guardian. "My mate is injured."

"Yes. Let me help. I am not certain I can save her sight, but if Danu is merciful, she will work through me."

Ronin's hands tightened around Roz. "Oberon's balls! You can't see? You should have said something."

"It's just my right eye."

"Damn it! If I'd known—"

"Enough, Sidhe." The guardian's voice held a harsh edge. "You can indulge in all the recriminations you want to later. Put her down so she can walk to me."

Roz stumbled at first, but the guardian extended his arms. Power pulsed from his hands, and it drew her like a lodestone. He placed a hand over her eyes and chanted in Gaelic so ancient she couldn't pick out one word in ten. Pain as fresh as when the minion had attacked flared, and she stifled a cry.

Ronin must have started forward because she heard him say, "Let go of me."

"There are demon bits lodged within her," Sperrin said in his rumbling, musical voice. "Let the guardian work undisturbed. There are worse things than blindness."

No wonder I felt so shitty.

Roz sent up a prayer—and she wasn't the praying type—that the dream guardian would cleanse her of every last bit of taint. The hum of voices rose and fell around her. After a while, they blended into a soothing mélange, and all she heard was the dream guardian. Though he still spoke Gaelic, something shifted in her mind so she understood every word. Roz soaked in his secrets, his healing, and his compassion like a woman dying of thirst who'd unexpectedly been offered cool water.

"It is done," the guardian said in English and let go of her.

Roz realized her eyes had been closed. When she opened them, her vision was intact, but more than that, her bruised places didn't hurt anymore. Tears spilled over and she bowed low. "Thank you," she murmured before straightening and meeting the medley of images in his eyes.

"You are most welcome." He snapped his fingers and the others drew near. "I am encouraged the two halves of Faerie have found common ground. You will leave here and do whatever you must to ensure the animosity between you stops now."

A murmur of assent swept through the group. Ronin moved to Roz's side and placed an arm around her shoulders. "Are the Irichna trapped on their borderworld for good?" he asked the guardian.

"And they call me a dreamer!" The guardian blew out a disgusted breath. "If it were that simple, I'd have done away with them eons ago. They'll find a way past my sanctions. Beyond that, they are far from the only Irichna demons in existence."

"Oh." Jenna glanced up from where she stood between Colleen and Niall, who looked like a gnome again. "I guess I'd hoped—"

"—your job was over?" The dream guardian cut it. "No. Our destinies are what shape us. Never forget that, witch. There is much yet that must be done, but making Faerie whole is a necessary first step. A second is the Daoine Sidhe working with you witches to rid the Earth of Irichna. If all the foot soldiers on our side stand together, we will win eventually."

"I'm not being disrespectful—" Krae stood straighter "—but how can you be sure?"

"Some things must be taken on faith, little daughter. You and I are overdue for a long conversation, but it will not happen today. Now off with all of you. You've overstayed your welcome as it is."

Ronin had barely begun to make plans to meet up with Sperrin and Moire when the world twisted into blackness.

Before she could blink twice, Roz thumped onto her living room floor and into the midst of a very surprised group of witches and the queen and king of Faerie. Ronin still clung to her hand. She pried her fingers out of his and scrambled to her feet before he could help her.

"Thank fucking God," she said, gazing around the familiar space. "I honestly never thought I'd see this place again." Relief flooded her, the taste indescribably sweet.

"It's about time," Titania said from a choice spot next to the woodstove.

Roz glanced out a window. It was dark, but that didn't mean much. "What time is it?" she asked.

"Closing on eight at night," the queen replied. "You've been gone for better than twenty-four hours."

"Yes, we were this close—" Naomi held her thumb and forefinger next to one another "—to going after you."

Colleen, Duncan, Jenna, and the changelings materialized on the far side of the room. Once they untangled arms and legs, they stood and dusted themselves off. Duncan swept Colleen into a tight embrace, oblivious to everyone else. Roz looked away to give them a bit of privacy for what was clearly an intimate moment.

"Tell us what happened," Oberon urged. "If you ended up on the Irichnas' borderworld, clearly they didn't totally sap your ability." He stood and reached a hand to help Titania to her feet.

Jenna blew out an audible snort. "Maybe before this is over, someone could give us a quickie tutorial on just what happens to our magic on that world. We figured out some of it, but far from all."

"It would be my pleasure." Titania locked gazes with Jenna, favoring her with a rare smile.

Ronin inclined his head toward his king and queen. "Let's

move the party into the kitchen. I'm starving and I'm sure everyone else is too. We can talk over food."

"Hey there, sister." Jenna caught Roz up and hugged her. "Jesus but I'm glad you're okay."

"That makes two of us," Ronin said. "None of you mentioned how badly she was hurt. Why not?"

"Hold it," Oberon said. "I want to hear this in chronological order. If the bunch of you would sit, we'll feed you and all you'll have to do is talk."

"We'll be along in just a moment." Ronin threaded his arm around Roz's waist and drew her off to one side. He turned her to face him and covered her mouth with his.

Roz kissed him back with a desperation that swept the breath from her lungs. She loved the man in her arms, adored him beyond wisdom or reason. Her blood heated as he explored her mouth with his tongue, and she hooked her arms beneath his and drew him as close as she could. He cupped her ass and snugged her against an obvious erection. Knowing he wanted her with the same ferocity that made her want to take him right here and right now fanned the flames of her lust. The world dissolved until the only reality was Ronin with his arms around her and his mouth pressed on hers.

"Roxanne Lantry!" Someone yanked on her arm, but she ignored them. They just tugged harder.

Roz pulled her mouth away from Ronin's, opened her eyes, and looked into Titania's pale blue gaze. The queen of Faerie shook a finger at her. "Not now. You have duties, obligations. Your love life will have to wait."

Roz started to protest that she wasn't duty-bound to Faerie, but Ronin blew out a frustrated-sounding breath. "Yes, my liege. I'm the one you should be addressing yourself to. We'll come along like good subjects and answer all your questions, but there's something I want you to do for me."

Titania arched an inquisitive brow. "I can imagine, but tell me."

Ronin pinned Roz with his untamed gaze, sexual, protective, and demanding all at once. "If you'll marry us, I'll make certain the ceremony happens very soon."

Roz's eyes widened, but her soul took flight. Still, she had to make certain it wasn't because he'd nearly just lost her. "Don't you, um, want to wait? You know, get to know each other better. It's a big step."

"I know what I want." He ran a hand down the side of her face.

A corner of her mouth twitched. "How about just one more night as a fallen woman before I sell my soul into connubial bliss?"

"Och." Titania tossed her head. "You're one of them who finds illicit sex more exciting."

Roz couldn't help herself, she laughed until tears came.

"I fail to see what's so funny," Titania huffed.

"I'm sorry," Roz said when she could talk again. "I wasn't trying to be obnoxious, but it's not the sixteenth century anymore. It's gotten so married sex is probably in the minority. There's sex everywhere you look. TV, the Internet, magazines, newspapers. Boy-boy sex, girl-girl sex, group sex… It's gotten so the plain old boy-girl stuff is hard to find."

Ronin tipped her chin so she had to look at him. "Does that mean you'll marry me tomorrow, providing I satisfy your every perverse whim tonight, my little vixen, who's now an expert on twenty-first century sexual practices?"

"Done!" She grinned. "I just love it when you talk dirty to me. You'd get your way all the time if you did more of that. I guess you know vixen was the original name for female demons who screwed the life right out of you."

"Of course I know that. It was what we used to call the succubi."

Titania rolled her eyes and made shooing motions with both hands. "Get moving, both of you." When Roz walked toward the kitchen, she heard the queen muttering about how she'd never understand the modern generation. Never.

CHAPTER 20

It was well past four a.m. when Ronin excused them and shepherded Roz toward their second floor rooms. Despite their fragile détente with Sperrin and Moire, Titania had not taken the dream guardian's edict about working hand-in-glove with the Unseelie Court well. Come to think of it, Oberon hadn't been particularly enthusiastic, either. Between Duncan and himself, it had taken a lot of persuasion to secure royal consent to move forward. Ronin knew he was in for many repeat performances with the other Sidhe once they returned to the U.K, and the whole sorry mess made him tired. When he'd suggested Titania and Oberon might help, they told him they'd made him the Sidhe leader for a reason.

Roz blew out a weary-sounding breath. "Sheesh. I thought we'd never get out of there. I would have said something hours ago, but they're your king and queen and I didn't want to be rude."

Ronin snorted. "Krae was abrasive enough for a small army."

Roz giggled. "You're not kidding. At one point there, I was certain Titania was going to turn her into a toad."

He pushed the door to her bedroom open and gestured her inside. "If I read what the guardian said correctly, working with the

Unseelie isn't really a choice anymore, which was why I kept talking. I was nearly as distrustful of them as Titania until this last go-round."

"I imagine Sperrin and Moire will have the same mini-insurrection on their hands."

"Probably." Ronin closed his arms around her from behind. "Let's leave all that on the far side of our bedchamber door. We could continue to talk it to death, but I'd rather be your lover for what's left of tonight."

"Are we still getting married tomorrow? Or actually, it would be later on today since its grown so late." She leaned back against him and snaked a hand between their bodies to curl around his cock, which was already hard. Just walking up the stairs next to her had that effect on him.

"If Titania gets over her snit."

"Even if she doesn't," Roz rubbed his erection through the fabric of his trousers, "Naomi can do the honors."

Ronin nuzzled her neck, breathing in the pine and jasmine scent that was hers and hers alone. "You seem to be warming to the idea of long-term commitment." He kicked the door shut.

"Only because it feels risky and tickles my *live dangerously* gene."

"I see." He ran his tongue down her neck, pleased when she shivered slightly and rubbed him harder. "I love you, Roz. Not following my heart and snatching you out of harm's way on the Irichna borderworld was one of the hardest things I've ever done."

She turned in his arms. "I wouldn't have left Jenna and Colleen."

He gazed deep into her dark eyes. "I know, and your loyalty and courage are things I love about you."

"Thank you."

"For what?" He ran his hands slowly down her back, savoring the clean lines of her body.

"Letting me be who I am."

"It's not always easy. I have to remind myself your independence is one of the things I fell in love with. Let me take your hair down."

"We should bathe. We're both filthy. If I breathe deep, I still smell demons."

He brushed his thumb over her lower lip. "I'll start a bath. I really appreciate all the oversized claw-foot tubs in this house. Reminds me of Europe."

"Don't forget the hundred gallon water heater. The gals and I can help things along with magic, but there were a bunch of fights before we replaced the smaller one."

"I'll just bet." He kissed her gently and walked to the adjoining bathroom to draw water for them. Along the way, he grabbed a couple of candles, lit them with magic, and set them on the window ledge. When Roz joined him, the tub was half-full and she was naked.

Ronin whistled appreciatively. "Didn't lose any time, I see. The view is great, but I dearly love undressing you."

She shrugged, her expressive eyes twinkling like stars. "It's my practical side." He reached for her, but she batted his hands away. "You have too many clothes on, Mr. Redstone, or is that Count or Earl or Lord?" She pulled his sweater over his head and followed it with his long underwear top, dumping both in a heap on the floor.

"Technically, it's Earl, but I never use that title anymore. It was replaced by Duke in the Middle Ages."

Roz busied herself with the fastenings to his trousers. "So what would that make me, an Earlette or something? Once we're married, that is." His pants pooled over his boot tops. She knelt and unlaced them, her mouth microns from his erect cock tenting his underwear. She was careful not to touch him, but her hot breath was more erotic than her tongue would have been. He worked his way out of his boots while she helped.

"Duchess," he managed through a throat thick with desire. "You'll be Duchess Redstone."

"Ooh." She tugged his shorts out of the way and ran her index finger up the length of his ridged flesh. "I rather like that."

"The title or me?" He lifted her to her feet and untangled himself from his pants and underwear, kicking them aside.

"Mostly you." Her gaze skittered down his body and her breath hitched. "God, but you're gorgeous."

"So are you. I think the water's deep enough." He scooped her into his arms, stepped over the tub's edge, and settled them in wonderfully warm water. She turned off the taps and leaned back against him while steam rose around them. He worked pins and rubber bands from her hair and smoothed his fingers through it once it was loose. The ends floated in the water like exotic sea anemones.

"Mmmm, that feels heavenly." She grabbed the soap, but he took it from her, reached around her body, and laved her breasts and belly. Once she was covered in suds and her nipples were stiff peaks, he dipped his hand between her legs and she squirmed against him. "No fair."

"It's all fair, darling."

"You can touch me, but the tub's too narrow for me to turn around. Or maybe it isn't." She dipped low in the water to clear the soap off her, lifted her legs, and pivoted on her butt until she faced him. Grinning like a reincarnation of Aphrodite, she wrapped her legs behind him. "Much better." She curved a hand around his shaft. Strands of dark hair trailed down her body, and her skin glowed bronze in the muted light from the candles he'd lit.

She plucked the soap from the tub's edge and rubbed it over his chest and stomach. When she was done, she splashed water his way to rinse him. Ronin laughed and wiped water off his face. "Don't you have bathing cloths here?"

"Probably." She captured her lower lip between her teeth. "I have an idea."

"So long as it includes getting inside you, I'm game." He flicked his hard-on with a finger. "I've been this way for so long, I'm starting to hurt."

She tightened her legs around his back. "If you lift me up just a little bit…"

Ronin slid his hands beneath her butt and she did the rest, gripping him with one hand and lowering herself over him. The heat of her bloomed around him and nearly blew the top of his head off with its intensity. He dug his fingers into her ass, and she rocked against him.

"Perfect," he breathed. "I get to watch your face when you come."

"What makes you so certain I will?" She writhed against his pubic bone and moaned softly.

Instead of answering with words, he settled his hands on her hips and drove himself into her. She clutched his shoulders and gave in to the rhythm he set. After the first few strokes, the world could've dissolved around them and he wouldn't have stopped. Her body fit him as if it had been made just for his cock. True to his words, he gazed at the woman in his arms. Her head was thrown back on her slender stalk of a neck. Her nipples were hard little nubbins. He wanted to touch them, tweak them to greater sensation, but his hands were busy.

Magic bubbled between them. He commanded it to do what he couldn't and saw pleasure heighten the color of her already dark skin.

"Two can play that game," she panted, and he felt something press against his anus, delicate, probing, teasing the sensitive tissue just past the opening.

She tightened her pussy around him and gripped his shoulders as if her life depended on it. He sensed her orgasm just beneath the surface and gave it a good boost with magic, delighted when he felt the spasms of her release. Her dark eyes fluttered open. She focused a dreamy, otherworldly look his way, and her magic moved from his anus to just behind his balls. Without warning a bone-jarring climax roared out of him. All he could do was hang on and let it happen.

"I wish you could see yourself," she murmured once his body quieted. "I swear you look like something profanely beautiful when you come. Any illusions I have about you being human like me take a hike when that happens."

He caught her face between his hands. "You're not exactly human, either. So is the death of these illusions of yours good or bad?"

"Neither. Not good. Not bad. I love you, Ronin. There, I said it."

"And it was even better than when you told me you were falling in love." Tenderness swamped him, and a deep protective-ness surged. "I'll make you the happiest woman alive."

"No." She shook her head. "We'll make each other happy." She clenched her pussy around his still-hard cock. "Ready to move from here to the bed? There are better prospects there."

"What could possibly be better than being inside you?"

"Want to find out?" She winked lewdly, placed her hands on the sides of the tub, and lifted herself off him. Once she was on her feet, she stepped from the tub and wrapped herself in a towel. "I'll wash my hair tomorrow."

Ronin opened the drain and followed her out of the tub. She held out a towel and began to dry him, but he grabbed it. "You do not have to wait on me."

"Give that back. I love touching you. Look at it as foreplay."

He smiled. "Isn't that what you do before?"

"And in-between and after. God, but I hope you never get tired of me."

"Not much chance of that, darling. I'm dry enough. Let's go to bed."

~

Roz pushed the quilts aside, stretched out on her back, and watched him cross the room to join her. His body was a study in perfection, lithe as a panther, beautiful as any of the Greek gods. He lay on his side next to her and took her into his arms. When he kissed her, she opened herself to him, loving the taste of him as he teased her lips and tongue with his own. She stroked his back and felt electric sensation flow from his body into her fingertips and straight to her pussy. Already wet, she dissolved in a flood of heat.

Slowly, taking his time, he moved from her mouth to her neck and down her chest to her breasts. He suckled them one at a time, trading back and forth. She arched her back, nearly overcome with sensation, drowning in wanting him. He moved lower still, licking and kissing down her rib cage and stomach until his mouth was poised over her sex, but he didn't touch her, not quite. He breathed heat into her, teasing her with magic or his warm breath, she couldn't tell which, and it didn't matter. She thrust her hips upward, desperate for contact with his mouth, but he kept himself just out of reach.

An orgasm hovered, spooled in the bottom of her belly wanting out. It wouldn't take much, just the tiniest contact. Half out of her mind with needing release, she reached for her clit but didn't get far. The hand above her head was bound with magic. She didn't bother trying the other one.

"What are you doing?" she gasped. "Psychic BDSM?"

He lifted his face from her crotch, his blue eyes glittering with lust. "I can't keep track of all the American acronyms. I want you to come so hard you'll carve my name in every tree we walk past. Every bedpost too." Ronin bent his head again. This time he had to be using magic because what felt like small streamers swirled around her clit, while others twisted inside her, teasing, pushing, hitting every nerve she had. Somehow, he kept her just at the edge, backing off when one more stroke would send her over.

She clawed the sheets beneath her hands, and her hips bucked uncontrollably. "Please," she shrieked. "Now. I have to come now."

The magic scattered, replaced by the fire of his mouth and tongue and his fingers pressed inside her. When she reached for him to plunge her hands into his hair, she discovered she was free. The climax that shook her was so wicked, she couldn't absorb the sensation streaming through her. When she opened her eyes, the air around them pulsed in a multi-hued vortex, and she understood it was her own power that had escaped its bounds.

He moved up her body and cradled her against him. His cock jutted into her belly, rigid with need. "Tell me how to pleasure you," she murmured.

"You should know better than to issue open invitations." He snaked his tongue into her ear, and shivers ran down her body. "Up on your hands and knees, wench. I rather liked that day I had you over your desk. It's become a favorite image."

She wriggled out of his embrace and flipped herself over with her ass in the air. A muted growl told her the sight of her sex presented like that stirred him. He rubbed her labia with his fingers, spreading her juices, and then seated his cockhead at the entrance to her body.

"This won't be as elegant as I'd like," he said. "That last episode almost made me come right along with you. The magic spills over, and it's not as easy to control when all I can think about is the wonder of your body."

"Sweet words." She waggled her butt. "How about some of that sweet cock? We can talk later."

"A woman after my own heart." Ronin held onto her ass cheeks and pressed inside until he hit bottom.

He felt so good inside her, reaching places no one else had ever gotten close to. Before she could get too used to him filling her, he withdrew in little spiraling twists that intensified everything. A couple more strokes like the first, and he gave up and drove his incredible cock into her.

Ronin brought a hand around and cradled her pussy. Caught between his penis inside her and his fingers urging her clit to go higher still, an orgasm ricocheted through her, followed by another. Before the spasms from the second had quieted, she felt him judder hard within her. He groaned as his climax shook him, and she tightened her muscles to give him just as much pleasure as she could.

He let his body down atop hers and rolled them onto their sides with him still buried in her. Settling a hand over one of her breasts, he murmured in Gaelic.

"English, please. It's funny. When the dream guardian spoke into my mind, I understood him, even though it was Gaelic, and an ancient form at that. Why can't I understand you?"

"You understood because it was his will. There are phrases in Gaelic, meanings for which there's no English translation. Sleep, my love. I'll keep you safe."

Roz's eyelids felt heavy, but she asked, "What happens next?"

"You mean after tomorrow?"

"Uh-huh."

"We'll have to return to the U.K. All of us. For one thing, I don't suppose the demons have done anything but raise more hell. For another, I'll have to make the Sidhe see reason and accept our Unseelie kin."

"Yeah." A flash of annoyance broke into her sleepy reverie. "I really didn't like how Titania dumped that one back in your lap."

"Don't waste energy on it. She and Oberon will probably end up helping, once they see which way the wind is blowing. After all, the Unseelie will be their subjects too."

"I need to revisit what I know about both halves of Faerie." Roz stirred against him. "Jenna and Colleen too. We don't have any choice. Neither do Oberon and Titania. Not that they don't know their own history, but they'll have to make peace with the dark fae."

Ronin stroked hair back from her face. "I'm sure Titania and

Oberon will come around and get past the snit they threw. If they weren't absorbing and planning for this new development, they'd have sent Duncan and me packing long before you and I finally left."

"If they, um, sort of set an example, will it be easier to convince the rest of your people?"

"Not necessarily. Most of the Sidhe ignore their royalty, which is how I ended up leader. Enough, darling. I can almost feel the wheels turning in your head. Sleep. We can figure everything out later. The important thing is we're together, now and always."

"Yes, love. Now and always. I like that." Darkness closed almost before the words were out. Roz suspected Ronin had cast a spell, but she didn't fight it. Her last thought before sleep claimed her was she loved him all the more for taking care of her.

CHAPTER 21

"Holy shit, this feels like déjà vu." Roz twisted this way and that, trying to get a sense of how her hair looked streaming down her back with tiny, fragrant dried flowers woven into it. She wore a long cream-colored silk skirt and an emerald green tunic set off with Navaho turquoise and silver jewelry.

"How?" Colleen asked sweetly. Her pale blue silk dress fit like a glove, with a provocative slit up one side. The color matched her eyes, and her red hair hung loose to her waist.

Roz rolled her eyes. "You should know. You had a fucking meltdown before you married Duncan."

"I don't recall."

"Oh, brother." Jenna glanced from Roz to Colleen and back. "I'm beginning to feel pretty damned lonely here."

Roz started to tell her nothing would change but bit back the words. They weren't true, and her longtime friend would know it. Instead, she said, "We're headed for the U.K. tomorrow. I'm sure Tristan will be waiting."

"Like I'm the only thing he has to think about," Jenna scoffed.

"I know next to nothing about him. For all I know, he has a string of women from Inverness to London."

"That's a pretty long reach," Colleen cut in.

"Well, they'd have to be spread out—unless he's into the group scene." Jenna flapped her hands in front of her and smoothed a mid-calf, smoke-gray sheath over her curves. Golden hoops graced her ears, and an emerald choker set off her blonde hair and hazel eyes. "I'm resigned to being a maiden auntie. Just hurry up and produce some kids for me to spoil, okay?"

"Let's get the Irichna problem taken care of first, ducks." Roz gave up on seeing all of her back, walked to Jenna, and wrapped an arm around her. "We're all needed front and center until they're out of the picture."

Jenna narrowed her eyes. "You sound like the dream guardian."

Roz wasn't surprised. The ancient mage was in her thoughts frequently, but his presence was soothing, and she welcomed the sense that he was close. When she'd talked with Ronin about it earlier in the day, he'd told her he was surprised the guardian healed her because he rarely interacted with any of them: human, Sidhe, Unseelie, changeling, or any other manner of being. That he'd spent so much time with Roz, taken an interest in her, meant he saw her as special.

"It's a lot to live up to," she'd told Ronin, but he'd just hugged her and told her she was more than capable of fulfilling the guardian's expectations, whatever they might be. Roz wasn't so sure about that, but she'd kept her reservations to herself.

"Are we ready?" Colleen pointed at the grandfather clock just coming up on six o'clock.

"Ready as I'll ever be." Roz grinned. "Funny I'm not more nervous."

"Bride's jitters hit everyone differently," Colleen remarked sagely, and Roz turned away to hide a smile.

"Yes, well, if I turn tail and try to run out of the house, drop a magic net over me and make me stay."

"Somehow, I think Ronin would beat us to it." Jenna walked to the door on perilously high heels and pulled it open. "Let's go. I still have to check on my cake. The changelings were decorating it."

"Awk!" Colleen's hand flew to her chest. "They probably ate it down to the plate."

"They promised they wouldn't," Jenna said with a bright smile.

"It doesn't matter." Roz rotated her shoulders to loosen them. "I never cared much for sweets."

"The rest of us do." Jenna stalked out the door. "Let's do this thing. I'll meet you in the living room. You've got me worried about my cake, so I'm going to detour through the kitchen first."

Roz made her way downstairs, her bare feet quiet on the carpeted risers. "What are you thinking?" Colleen asked from behind her.

Roz stopped moving until her friend stood next to her. "Lots of things, but mostly about how fast our lives have changed."

"They couldn't have stayed the same. The Irichna would have killed us."

"I know. I guess I've been thinking of everyone who won't be at my wedding—and who wasn't at yours. Witches who didn't make it because Irichna slaughtered them. They would have been overjoyed to see us married."

"We'll just have to build new families, starting with now," Colleen said fiercely. "We've always had each other, but that was short-sighted on our part."

"Not so much short-sighted as practical." Roz closed her teeth over her lower lip. "There wasn't anything we could've done to stop the demons from mowing through our relatives."

Sadness pinched the corners of Colleen's blue eyes, and Roz felt bad for reminding her. "It's hard to hear it point blank like that," Colleen murmured and gripped Roz's hand.

"I'm sorry." Roz hugged her.

"Not your fault. Let's not think about that. It's your wedding night, and we shouldn't be glum."

Roz snorted. "Glum is where I live most of the time. Back to your earlier idea about families. Do you really think enough Sidhe will accept us for that to happen?"

"I do." Colleen spoke slowly. "It will be harder for them to get their minds around forgiving the Unseelie than accepting us."

Roz nodded thoughtfully, and then she and Colleen walked into the living room. Someone had decked it with dozens of lit candles and sprays of evergreens from the upstairs drying rooms. The effect was truly lovely, but the best part was Ronin. He stood at the makeshift altar with Titania and Naomi behind him. When he extended an arm toward her, her heart took flight, and something warm and tender rooted itself in her soul. She strode to his side and took his hand.

Colleen made her way to Duncan, who kissed her cheek and said, "You look lovely as always, my heart."

"You too, you handsome devil. Come on, we're supposed to be on this side of the bridal pair."

"Where's the other one?" Titania asked, her jeweled gown rustling about her.

Roz quirked a brow. "She has a name. It's Jenna."

"Yes, yes, dear. Details. Where is *Jenna*?" The queen emphasized her last word.

"I'm right here." The witch in question scurried out of the kitchen with the changelings at her heels. All three had colored frosting on their faces and fingers, but at least they were dressed, the men in dark trousers and jackets with white shirts, and Krae in an embroidered teal robe that was truly lovely.

Oberon frowned from where he stood a few feet away and disappeared into the hall bathroom. As usual, he wore a black silk robe, sashed with crimson. When he emerged, he held a damp cloth and set to cleaning the changelings' mouths and cheeks.

"There." He looked up. "A bit more presentable." He eyed Niall sharply. "Do you still have the ring?"

"Of course." The changeling drew himself up.

"Shall we begin?" Naomi swept the room with her gaze. Roz turned for a moment and did the same. In contrast to the hundreds of guests at Colleen and Duncan's wedding, there were just them and Lou and Maggie from the Witches' Northwest Coven. The smaller group was actually more to her liking. Something caught her eye near the front door, an almost imperceptible thickening in the air. Roz twirled to face the disturbance, hands raised to summon destruction on whoever dared violate her wedding.

"It's all right." Ronin clasped one of her hands midair.

"Someone's trying to get in here," she protested.

"Yes, I know. It's Sperrin and Moire. I invited them."

"Actually, I did because you were busy," Duncan spoke up.

"Details." Ronin sounded a lot like Titania when he drew Roz's hand downward.

"You might've told me," Roz murmured.

"It's not as if we've had scads of time," he said. "Would you have preferred they didn't come?"

"No, it's not that. It's good they're here. Maybe Titania and Oberon can—"

Ronin cut her off with a look and said, *"It's best to let these things unfold as they will,"* into her mind. The air near the door glimmered, a portal formed, and the two Unseelie stepped through.

Sperrin barked a word to close their gateway and turned to face Ronin and Roz. "Many thanks for inviting us. Blessings on your union."

"Aye, 'tis truly a pleasure to be here." Moire dropped half a curtsy. "Where would ye like us?"

"Come stand by me," Oberon invited.

"'Twould be an honor. I remember you from years gone by," Sperrin said.

"And I you." Oberon held out a hand. "From the days when our people were still undivided." Sperrin drew close and clasped Oberon's extended hand. When he let go, Moire gripped it, and the King of Faerie bent low over her hand and kissed it.

Maybe this will turn out better than Ronin thinks.

Roz faced Titania and Naomi. "I do believe we're ready."

"So are we." Naomi grinned. She'd borrowed a simple black dress from Colleen, and its tiny jet beads sparkled in the candlelight. "Titania and I are getting quite good at this."

"Hear that?" Colleen said to Jenna. "They should have it down perfectly by the time your turn comes."

"My dear, we have it perfect now," Titania said. "Stop talking and pay attention."

The ritual passed in a blur, from the traditional witch joining to the Sidhe one. Roz was surprised when Titania took one of her hands, laid it atop Ronin's, and said, "I pronounce you wed. May the luck of the goddess bless your union." She plucked the ring from Niall, who'd been bouncing up and down with excitement, and handed it to Ronin. "You may place this on your wife's finger."

Cheers and clapping sounded from around the room. Ronin slid the ring onto her finger, drew her into his arms, and kissed her solemnly. When he moved his lips from hers, he whispered in her ear, "You've made me a very happy man today. Thank you for taking a chance on us."

Leaning close, she whispered back, "You haven't seen my temper in full bloom. I should be the one kissing your feet."

"Och aye, and now the lass tells me," he teased in an exaggerated brogue.

"We want to eat." Niall trotted close and tugged on her arm. "Can we start dinner while you play kissy-face with your groom?"

"We're all going to eat," Ronin informed him.

"Aw, does that mean kissy-face will have to wait till later?" Roz tried for a sad expression, but couldn't quite pull it off.

"I'll make it up to you. After all, we'll have our whole lives." Ronin looked like he was struggling to keep a straight face.

"Stop hogging the bride." Oberon jammed his body between them and bent to kiss Roz. "This is the best part." The King of Faerie grinned. "I get to kiss young, beautiful brides, and Titania can't give me grief over it."

"I heard that." Titania strode forward.

"Of course you did, dear." Oberon winked at her. "You were only about five feet away." He extended his arm and she took it.

Ronin wove an arm around Roz's waist. "Let's mosey into the kitchen. I am hungry."

She walked by his side. "Me too, now I let myself think about it. We can get our plates, settle somewhere, and let everyone stop by and wish us well."

"Excellent plan. I have a surprise for you."

She clapped her hands together and then felt foolish. "What?"

"I booked the honeymoon suite at the Regency Hotel and already checked us in. Once we've finished dinner, we can teleport right into it."

"Really? It's the fanciest hotel in Fairbanks."

"I know. I asked Colleen and Jenna to recommend someplace. Both of them told me you'd always wanted to stay there. I reserved one of the older rooms with all the antiques."

"I—" Her throat thickened with emotion cutting off her words, so she tried again. "I don't know quite what to say."

"You don't have to say anything, love. I wanted our first night as a married couple to be something very special." He spun her to face him and closed his mouth over hers. Roz lost herself in the wonder of his arms and mouth. It was easy to do since his nearness obliterated everything. When they finally stopped kissing, they were alone, and she assumed everyone else was already in the kitchen.

"Do you suppose they saved us anything to eat?" she asked.

"Let's find out. If they didn't, I'm sure the hotel has room service."

"Spoken like a true twenty-first century male."

"Aw hell, Roz. We had room service in the fourteen hundreds. It wasn't quite as user-friendly, though."

"Yeah sure, you probably got the serving wench along with her tray."

He cocked his head to one side. "You certain you weren't around then?"

Roz elbowed him. "Quite certain, but I've read a lot of history. Let's go. We can trade historical barbs later."

"After you, darling." He pushed the swinging door to the kitchen wide and held it while she walked through. Roz was almost past him when he closed a hand over her ass and squeezed.

"What was that for?" She leaned into his grip on her.

"To make sure you remember our date for kissy-face later."

"As if I could forget."

"Gawk!" Niall screeched around a mouthful of something Roz didn't want to examine too closely. "They're at it again."

"No, we're not." Roz strolled into the kitchen, so overcome with happiness she expected to see it oozing out of her. Someone had set up card tables, and there was enough seating space for everyone.

"I made them save you some food," Colleen informed her with a stern glance Niall's way.

"Excellent." Ronin picked up a plate. "Let me serve you, sweetheart. What would you like?"

"Two of everything, that way we can share a plate."

He quirked a brow and set to work. "As you Americans say, I'm on it."

"We've been waiting to open this fine, old bottle of mead to toast you." Oberon waggled an amber bottle with an ancient looking wax seal in front of him.

"Start pouring," Roz said. "I'll collect a couple of glasses and—"

"Oh my goodness no, dear." Titania motioned her forward. "The bridal cup is already up here. Duncan and Colleen's wedding went to hell before we got to this part, so you'd have no way of knowing about it."

Ronin set their plate down between two empty seats and joined her. Oberon poured fragrant amber liquid into a shiny, intricately embossed metal cup with two spouts. "Hook elbows with me," Ronin said, "and then we'll drink together. It symbolizes the joining of our lives."

As the honey wine poured into her mouth and down her throat, Roz felt at peace. They'd face challenges, maybe even lethal ones. And so soon she didn't want to think about it. But being joined to Ronin added a new dimension. Surely, working with other witches, the Sidhe, the Unseelie, the dream guardian, and whoever else was willing to lend their magic, there'd be a way to corral the Irichna once and for all.

They set the cup down and she looked closely at it. "The workmanship is beautiful. The cup looks very old. Is it Norse?"

Titania nodded. "You have sharp eyes. Most of our Celtic rituals have Norse roots. Actually, it's a chalice not a cup."

"Of course," Roz murmured. "Silly me."

Ronin took her arm. "Our food's probably getting cold, and our hotel room's waiting."

"What?" Oberon nailed them with his amber gaze. "What hotel room? You mean we don't get to stand outside the bridal chamber and holler suggestions?"

Roz burst out laughing and told Ronin, "Now I understand why you ponied up five hundred bucks for the Regency."

"Actually it was closer to a thousand, but I could be off by a hundred dollars either way since the pound-dollar conversion gets me every time."

"Waited until after the wedding to admit you don't like math, huh?" She followed him to their table and sat.

"Just wait till you hear the catalogue of my other faults." He picked up a fork and dug in.

"Be sure to run whatever he tells you by me." Duncan grinned from the other side of the table. "I'll let you know what he missed."

Colleen leaned toward her. "You look radiant, sweetie."

"Thanks," Roz murmured. "It's because I've never been happier."

Colleen raised her wine glass. "Here's to a less eventful wedding night than I had."

"Thanks." Roz grinned. "You didn't exactly get a wedding night."

"Touché." Colleen grinned back.

"You'll have to forgive my bride," Duncan said. "She's mildly prone to sarcasm. We may not have gotten the wedding night of her dreams, but—"

Ribald laughter drowned him out and everyone clinked glasses. As Roz gazed fondly at the people seated in her comfortable kitchen, she sent up a prayer to Danu to keep them all safe from harm before turning her attention back to her brand new husband.

THIS IS the end of *Witch's Bane*. The story continues in *Witches Rule*, Jenna and Tristan's story. Oh yes, it's Kiernan's tale as well. Read on for a sample.

ABOUT THE AUTHOR

Ann Gimpel is a national bestselling author. A lifelong aficionado of the unusual, she began writing speculative fiction a few years ago. Since then her short fiction has appeared in a number of webzines and anthologies. Her longer books run the gamut from urban fantasy to paranormal romance. Once upon a time, she nurtured clients, now she nurtures dark, gritty fantasy stories that push hard against reality. When she's not writing, she's in the backcountry getting down and dirty with her camera. She's published over fifty books to date, with several more planned for 2018 and beyond. A husband, grown children, grandchildren, and wolf hybrids round out her family.

Keep up with her at www.anngimpel.com or http://anngimpel.blogspot.com

If you enjoyed what you read, get in line for special offers and pre-release special reads. Sign up for Ann's newsletter on her website or her blog.

DEMON ASSASSINS, BOOK THREE

Jenna Neil sank heavily onto her airplane seat and kicked off her high heels, shoving them beneath the seat in front of her. With a small sigh of relief, she rotated her ankles to take the pressure off her aching arches. She'd always loved high heels and insisted on wearing them, never mind they definitely lacked a comfort factor. Once she'd shot past six feet, she figured it didn't matter if she added a few inches to her already overbearing height.

A flight attendant leaned over to hand her a pillow and blanket, and Jenna tucked the pillow behind her head as she listened to the safety briefing and estimates of their arrival time in London.

She closed her eyes, but it didn't ease how tired and gritty they felt, and smoothed her too-short denim skirt down her thighs. A red wool sweater and matching denim jacket finished off her outfit. She'd been so excited about getting out of Alaska and away from the layers she was forced to wear through the winter, she'd probably underdressed for the current jaunt. Less trendy clothes were tucked in her checked luggage, but they weren't exactly accessible.

The last few days hadn't offered much opportunity for rest.

She, Colleen Kelly, and Roxanne Lantry—Roz to everyone who knew her well—were the last of the assassin witches. Having escaped Irichna demons by a ridiculously narrow margin—again—the three of them were on their way to the U.K. where they could do it all over again.

Jenna grinned ruefully. Demons running amok through the British countryside had thrown witches and the Daoine Sidhe together after two hundred years of enmity. It had also netted impossibly hunky husbands for her sister witches, but that was beside the point. Staying alive was a much more front and center problem.

Because Irichna demons had become so much more aggressive, everyone but her thought it would be best to travel separately. She hadn't agreed, but she'd been the one dissenting vote. As far as Jenna was concerned, there was always strength in numbers, but the others were convinced their current strategy would confuse the demons long enough for everyone to regroup on the eastern side of the Atlantic. Colleen and Roz were teleporting with their husbands. Niall, Colleen's Irish changeling familiar, was making his own way back home along with two Scottish changelings, Llyr and Krae. Jenna had never been much good at teleporting, so she'd opted to fly commercial. It would place her arrival at least twelve hours after everyone else, but she could live with that. At least the first leg of her journey, from Fairbanks to Seattle, and thence to New York, had been uneventful.

Thinking about Irichna made her shiver, so she unfolded her blanket and draped it around her shoulders. Demons didn't get much worse than Irichna. As Abbadon's chosen henchmen, they played for keeps, and Abbadon was the biggest and baddest of Hell's denizens, so nothing was off limits. Demon assassin witches had been a craw in his throat for a long time, and lately he'd upped the ante to get rid of them—permanently.

Them means me, and I'd do well not to forget that.

Jenna blew out a weary breath. One of her not-so-distant

ancestors had been forced into demon containment two hundred years ago by the Sidhe, breaking every rule that bound magic-wielders, but the Sidhe hadn't cared. In the intervening years, demons had managed to kill every single witch with demon-assassin ability—except for her, Roz, and Colleen. The Sidhe were primed to take back some responsibility for ferrying Irichna to the Ninth Circle of Hell where the gatekeeper locked them away, but that hadn't exactly happened yet.

She gritted her teeth and unclenched hands she'd balled into fists around the edge of the thin airline blanket. The aircraft backed out of its slip and headed for one of the many runways at JFK Airport. While it would be lovely to have help with the demons, working with the Sidhe held its own set of problems. For one thing, most of them were insufferably autocratic, which was how Jenna's great-grandmother had ended up being suckered into picking up the demon banner in the first place.

Even though Titania, Queen of Faerie, appeared marginally tolerant of Colleen's and Roz's marriages to Sidhe, she'd given Duncan, a Daoine Sidhe prince, quite a bit of grief over his proposed marriage to Colleen at the front end of things. By the time Ronin, the *de facto* Sidhe leader, made it clear he'd set his sights on Roz, Titania had backed down a few notches, probably because they were beset by Irichna.

Jenna thinned her lips into a hard line. Hundreds of years before, Ronin's human partner had died in childbirth, and the child along with her. Apparently, both the Queen and King of Faerie had made it clear Ronin had sunk himself by choosing to marry someone outside his race. In the face of their indifference, Ronin had carried his grief alone.

It's just like it is with humans. Everybody's got to have somebody to look down on... Jenna tamped back a cynical grin. The Sidhe had made strides accepting other races, but they had a way to go before they moved beyond their intolerant past.

Jenna pictured her friends' husbands and a small sigh escaped.

Like all the Daoine Sidhe, Duncan and Ronin were heartbreakingly stunning. Duncan's blond good looks and green eyes provided a counterpart for Ronin's dark hair and deep blue gaze. When Jenna scratched the surface and did a little soul-searching, she had to admit she'd never expected to find a permanent partner. Girls like her—well-rounded and obscenely tall—weren't exactly in demand. Colleen was beautiful with her waist length auburn hair and pale blue eyes, and Roz was unusual and striking. Her Native American heritage and long, lean frame turned heads whenever she passed by.

Guess I'm the odd witch out these days...

Jenna pressed her lips together. It remained to be seen how her friends' marriages would impact their lives. Some things would have to change because she couldn't quite envision Duncan and Ronin simply moving in to her Fairbanks, Alaska, home along with their new wives. For one thing, all the Sidhe had amazing country homes in the U.K. that resembled castles more than houses.

Jenna reined in her thoughts. There were a lot of unknowns, but the main problem would be surviving the next few weeks. Once they got the Irichna on the run—if that was even possible—then she could figure out more prosaic things, like if she'd be the only one still living in Fairbanks and running their magicians' supply shop. Before the thought even finished forming, she knew that arrangement wouldn't work. She, Roz, and Colleen had to stay together, and if the others insisted on remaining in the U.K., well then she wouldn't have much choice in the matter. If she returned to Alaska by herself, she'd be a sitting duck for Irichna to swoop down and overpower her.

She shivered again and considered asking for a second blanket.

In an attempt to divert herself and maybe unwind, though it seemed unlikely, Jenna started to push her seat back and then remembered she wasn't supposed to quite yet. The plane's engines were revving, but they hadn't left the ground. She heard the captain instruct the flight attendants to prepare the cabin for takeoff and tried to relax in her plush first-class seat. If the goddess was good to her, maybe she'd catch a few hours of sleep before the plane landed.

A flurry of supernatural energy caught the edges of her attention, and Jenna's gut twisted into a sour knot. She sat up straight and craned her neck to scan the cabin, defensive magic at the ready. Her eyes widened in disbelief as Krae's unmistakable form shimmered into being, and the changeling bounded into the empty seat next to Jenna. Her long, bright red hair hung loose, and her eyes shone like emeralds. Krae's stocky body was draped in wide-bottomed green silk pants and an embroidered black tunic. As was usual with changelings, her feet were bare. The creatures drew their power from the earth, and Jenna assumed they didn't want layers of leather or rubber or neoprene between themselves and their magical well. With their three-foot height, broad shoulders, and longish arms, they looked like a missing link between humans and the great apes.

"What are you doing here?" Jenna kept her voice low.

"Don't worry," Krae replied, not exactly answering Jenna's question. "No one can see me except you."

"Where are Niall and Llyr?"

"Niall joined Colleen and Duncan, and Llyr is with Roz and Ronin."

Of course, why didn't I think of that?

Jenna cleared her throat. "Why did you make different plans?"

Krae cocked her head to one side and crinkled her gnome-like face, making her look even more outlandish. "We discussed it and decided you might need help." A corner of her mouth curved into a frown. "Personally, I thought it was a bit over-drawn, but Niall was most insistent about remaining with Colleen."

"Can he join her teleport spell after it's already set in motion?" Jenna was curious, but if Krae could teleport into this aircraft, maybe the other two could tap into a spell she'd always considered sacrosanct.

"Not directly, but he communicated with Colleen telepathically, and she altered her destination to pick him up. Llyr did the same with Roz and Ronin." Krae dusted her palms together and grinned. "Nothing easier." The changeling swept her agate-green gaze around the first-class cabin. "When will they feed us?"

"As soon as we pass through ten thousand feet. Not long since we just took off." Jenna paused for a beat. "If you weren't thrilled about the plans to get to the U.K., why didn't you speak up back in Alaska?"

"We did. No one listened to us. Roz and Ronin were so wrapped up in lust and pawing at each other, all they wanted to do was get to his manor house as fast as they could."

"Well, they did just get married," Jenna pointed out in defense of her friend. "And I don't recall anyone but me voicing concerns about splitting up to travel."

"That's because you weren't paying attention, either. Look, sweetie, if the Irichna win, no one will be tupping anyone." Despite being much shorter than Jenna, the changeling managed to send a withering glance her way.

"Point taken." Jenna shot an equally scathing glance back. "Next time, if you feel strongly about something and no one's paying attention, talk louder."

"Rehashing the past is a waste of time." Krae bounced up and down in her seat. Jenna considered telling her to fasten her seatbelt, but if no one could see her, there wasn't much point. "Be sure to take everything they offer," the changeling instructed. "I'm hungry."

"Shouldn't be a problem since I'm not." Jenna lapsed into silence.

"Why so glum, witchy girl?" Krae trained her ancient eyes, which probably didn't miss a trick, on Jenna.

"Oh, no particular reason." Jenna stifled a snort and rolled her eyes. "I find facing death several times a day downright exhilarating."

A bell sounded, and the fasten seat belt icon winked out. Moments later, the first-class cabin flight attendant leaned close. "Are you all right?"

"Why wouldn't I be?" Jenna snapped and then winced at how surly she sounded.

"I heard you talking and thought maybe you needed something." The flight attendant smiled encouragingly. Airlines had moved past using Barbie clones long since, and this woman was middle-aged with streaks of gray in her dark, shoulder-length hair, the beginnings of wrinkles around her blue eyes, and a kind expression.

"Food," Krae prodded, not bothering with telepathic speech.

"Thanks for being concerned." Jenna managed a genuine smile for the cabin attendant. "I am hungry, so food would be appreciated whenever you get around to serving."

"Of course." The woman smiled back. "I'm Suzanne." She tapped the nametag hanging around her neck. "Just press your call button if you need anything. Other than that, relax and enjoy your flight."

"You could've been a bit more assertive about our dinner," Krae complained.

"I'm guessing they can't hear you, either." Jenna switched to telepathic speech.

"Of course they can't." Krae blew out an annoyed-sounding breath. "Look, witchy-girl, draw a spot of magic and shield your speech. That way no one will bother us, and we can talk."

Feeling like an idiot because she hadn't come up with the idea herself, Jenna drew the requisite spell before she spoke again. "I was actually hoping to sleep."

"You can do that after we eat and talk."

Jenna turned to face the changeling and raised a quizzical brow. "This is starting to sound bigger than you. Whose idea was it really for the three of you to split up, and for you to join me?"

Krae's generous mouth twitched into a grin, and she jabbed a finger in the air between them. "Smart witch."

"You didn't exactly answer me."

"No. I didn't."

Jenna pressed her tongue against her teeth to manage her annoyance. The last thing she needed was a rousing game of twenty questions, so she trained what she hoped was a non-confrontational gaze on Krae and shrugged. "We have seven hours, feel free to take your time."

The changeling's green eyes sparkled with mischief. "You're burning up with curiosity. I can smell it."

Jenna didn't bother to point out she was so trashed from the past few weeks that she doubted she had enough energy to *burn up* with anything. Suzanne handed her a bottle of water and a tray with an assortment of appetizers. The flight attendant had no sooner moved on to the next passenger when Krae bent over the tray and dug in.

The changeling looked up after inhaling half the finger sandwiches and most of the nuts. "Sure you don't want any of this?"

"Help yourself." Jenna adjusted her seat so it tilted backward, twisted the cap off the water, and drank deeply.

"Beer, wine, or a cocktail, miss?" a masculine voice asked.

Jenna glanced up at a cabin attendant she hadn't seen before. He was tall and rangy with very blue eyes, white-blond hair, and a gold band on the third finger of his left hand. She swallowed a smile. With looks like his, he might have begun wearing the ring in self-defense, to slow the tide of women throwing themselves at his feet. He arched a brow and gestured toward the drink cart.

"Um, maybe a cup of coffee with a side of Irish whiskey."

"Excellent choice." He beamed at her, displaying very white, very even teeth. He may have winked, but she wasn't quite certain. "Would you care for cream or sugar?"

"Both."

Once he handed her drink over, she uncapped the small bottle of spirits and dumped a little into her cup. She'd traveled through so many time zones already, it scarcely mattered what time it was, and the liquor might have a salutary effect. The steward's gaze traveled up her body in frank appraisal before he moved to the passenger across the aisle. Jenna felt her face flush.

Krae twisted her head and stared at the man. The air glistened wetly where the changeling deployed magic. She wasn't particularly subtle, and the man's spine stiffened, but he didn't turn around.

"He felt that." Jenna pitched her mind voice just for Krae and shielded it to boot.

"Indeed he did." Krae narrowed her eyes. *"Do you know what he is?"* Jenna shook her head. *"Pity,"* the changeling went on, *"neither do I."*

"I don't think it's a good idea to send more magic his way," Jenna murmured. *"As it is, what you did tipped him off. How did you know something was wrong?"*

"How else?" Krae shrugged. *"I almost missed it, but there was something...odd in the way he looked at you. If he'd been human, his gaze would have held more heat, but there was an...unnatural hunger."* She hesitated. *"More like he was relieved he'd found you rather than wanting sex."*

A shudder iced Jenna's blood. Unlike Roz and Colleen, she couldn't simply teleport off the airplane. Her heartbeat sped up. *"Maybe you should leave,"* she told Krae. *"No point in both of us being trapped."*

"Uh-uh. We hold our ground for now. It's possible his presence has nothing to do with you."

"Not very fucking likely."

Krae picked up another small sandwich and stuffed it into her mouth. Jenna snuck a peek at the steward just in time to see him disappear through the curtain separating first class from the remainder of the aircraft. Because she was desperate for information, she sent a tendril of magic snaking outward and yanked it back as soon as she determined the man wasn't an Irichna disguised as human. Duncan had run up against one masquerading as a priest near the Witches' Northwest Coven headquarters in Seattle. It had lured two female teenagers and would have drained them of life if Duncan hadn't intervened. As it was, he wasn't certain either had survived because he'd left them at a hospital and hadn't hung around long enough to find out.

Jenna ran options through her mind, not liking any of them. She didn't want to end up in a pitched battle inside the aircraft. Hell, they'd probably lock her away as a terrorist the minute the plane landed, and Irichna would pick her off from her cell.

"I was serious," Krae's out loud voice intruded. "There's at least a small possibility he's simply some sort of mage. He might have gotten a magical hit off your aura and was curious."

"What did you want to talk about earlier?" Jenna changed the subject because she could speculate about the mystery steward from now until he made a move against her, and it wouldn't change the outcome, other than making her more aware to watch out for him.

"How much do you know about my race?" Krae countered, answering Jenna by asking a question of her own.

"Mostly what I've gleaned from living with Niall for forty years. Why?"

Krae popped the last sandwich into her mouth, chewed, and swallowed. "We've always known we would have a key role to play in major battles against the Irichna. It's written in our histories, and we've prepared as best we could."

Jenna drew her brows together. "Niall never mentioned it."

"He's one of the younger ones. It's quite possible he didn't know. We've done our damnedest to ensure the knowledge passed to everyone, but Niall was young by our standards when he chose to bond with Colleen."

"So how is any of that relevant?" Jenna rolled her shoulders to offset the iron bar of tension sitting between them. "You sound like a preacher threatening the latter days are nearly upon us."

"They are." Krae's expression turned deadly serious.

"More whiskey, miss?"

Jenna started at the sound of the steward's voice. He'd returned to the cabin so quietly, she hadn't heard him. "Um, no." She resisted the temptation to look at him. It would give her more information, but that was a two-way street.

"As you will, miss." He pushed the drink cart past her. It made quite a bit of noise, which led her to suspect he'd used magic to muffle his presence earlier.

How long had he studied her without her knowing?

Why hadn't Krae sensed him?

Worse, he'd apparently made his way back to the front of the plane, pushed the rattling cart past her, and served other passengers without alerting her to his presence. Not good. Jenna shielded her mind—just in case—and clamped her jaws together when he sashayed into the curtained galley alcove between first class and the cockpit. Her heart thudded against her ribcage, and her throat was dry. It was looking like she'd need to do something, but what would attract the least attention?

Krae uttered a muted expletive in Gaelic, bolted from her seat, and whisked after the steward. Jenna stared after the changeling with her mouth hanging open. She pushed upright, remembered her seatbelt, and fumbled with the clasp. By the time she was free of it, a flash of multicolored light practically blinded her, flaring above, below, and through the curtain. Heedless of the other first class passengers, who couldn't sense expended magic anyway, she threw her power wide open.

Jenna didn't realize she'd been holding her breath until it whistled from between her clenched teeth. She drew her lips back, hissing in satisfaction once she realized the blast of power had come from Krae, not the man. Balancing on the balls of her stocking-clad feet, Jenna strode forward and pushed past the curtain.

The steward was shaking his head back and forth, his face screwed into a mask of pain. Power flashed from the changeling's hands. "No more," he rasped, tottering from foot to foot. "I won't hurt either of you."

Jenna dragged an invisibility spell over all of them, layered a *don't look here* spell over that, and prayed to the goddess no one would enter the small, enclosed space for the next few minutes.

"What are you?" She shoved the question hard into his mind.

"I already figured that out," Krae said sourly. "He's a minor demon sent to keep an eye on you and report back."

"I already told you I hadn't," he whined. "And I won't. You can bind me with magic."

"That's not good enough," Jenna growled. "Demons lie."

"So do changelings and witches." He shot her a venomous look that belied his promises of non-interference.

"We're wasting time," Krae said and settled into a low chant.

A look of horror twisted the steward's handsome face into something unrecognizable. He tried to walk past them but clearly couldn't move. The air thickened, took on a blackish tinge, and stank of ozone just before smoke rose from the creature and he vanished.

Jenna drew back, impressed. Whatever Krae had done was magic well beyond her own abilities. Footsteps sounded on the far side of the curtain. Suzanne. Jenna recognized her energy and ducked into a passenger restroom. If Krae was powerful enough to banish the demon, shielding herself from the flight attendant should prove trivial. Kicking herself for being sloppy, Jenna pulled the magic from her spells to make the cramped galley appear as normal as possible.

"Paul," Suzanne's voice was pitched low, "your drink cart's here. Where are you?"

Jenna flushed the toilet and splashed cold water on her overheated face. She took her time drying off and settled her features into a bland expression before stepping out of the john. With a nod and a smile at Suzanne, she pushed the curtain aside and returned to her seat. Krae was already there, doing her best to mask a self-satisfied grin.

"Okay, I give up." Jenna eyed the changeling. "What did you do?"

"Teleported him outside the plane. Nature took care of the rest."

Jenna thought about it. "While it's good he's gone, how will we know he didn't report in somehow?"

"We won't," Krae said shortly. "Which means we'll have to be very careful not to lead the enemy right to wherever we're staying after we land."